ROYALLY CRUSHED

A Crazy Royal Love, Book 1

MELANIE SUMMERS

Indigo Group

Copyright

Cover by Victoria Cooper.

Edited by Kristi Yanta and Nancy Sway.

Proofread by Melissa Martin, Nevia Brudnicki, Laura Albert, and Kellie Porth-Bagne.

❀ Created with Vellum

Praise For Melanie Summers

"A fun, often humorous, escapist tale that will have readers blushing, laughing and rooting for its characters." ~ *Kirkus Reviews*

A gorgeously funny, romantic and seductive modern fairy tale...

I have never laughed out loud so much in my life. I don't think that I've ever said that about a book before, and yet that doesn't even seem accurate as to just how incredibly funny, witty, romantic, swoony...and other wonderfully charming and deliriously dreamy *The Royal Treatment* was. I was so gutted when this book finished, I still haven't even processed my sadness at having to temporarily say goodbye to my latest favourite Royal couple.

~ *MammieBabbie Book Club*

The Royal Treatment is a quick and easy read with an in depth, well thought out plot. It's perfect for someone that needs a break from this world and wants to delve into a modern-day fairy tale that will keep them laughing and rooting for the main characters throughout the story. *~ ChickLit Café*

I have to HIGHLY HIGHLY HIGHLY RECOMMEND *The Royal Treatment* to EVERYONE!
~ Jennifer, The Power of Three Readers

I was totally gripped to this story. For the first time ever the Kindle came into the bath with me. This book is unputdownable. I absolutely loved it.
~ Philomena (Two Friends, Read Along with Us)

Very rarely does a book make me literally hold my breath or has me feeling that actual ache in my heart for a character, but I did both." *~ Three Chicks Review for Netgalley*

Also Available

ROMANTIC COMEDIES by Melanie Summers

The Crown Jewels Series

The Royal Treatment

The Royal Wedding

The Royal Delivery

Paradise Bay Series

The Honeymooner

Whisked Away

The Suite Life

WOMEN'S FICTION by Melanie Summers

The After Wife

STEAMY OFFERINGS by MJ Summers

The Full Hearts Series

Break in Two

Don't Let Go – Prequel to Breaking Love - E-book only

Breaking Love

Dedication

For medical professionals the world over:

While the rest of us sit on our couches and whine about feeling 'cooped up,' you're showing up every day, whether at a hospital or a converted hotel, working yourselves to exhaustion.

You show up, even though there will be too many patients, too many horrific decisions, and too many tears.

You show up knowing there won't be nearly enough of everything you need to save each person who looks up at you with fear and hope in their eyes.

You show up knowing you're risking your own life and whatever beautiful future lies ahead for you.

I hope when this nightmare ends, you'll still be here so the rest of us can thank you in person.

With immeasurable gratitude,
  Melanie

Dear Reader,

It's been just over two years since we left the Langdon family —Prince Arthur, Tessa, Princess Arabella, Gran, and King Winston. I knew I wanted to write a book (or two) about the lovely, sweet Arabella, who desperately needs to break out of her shell. But for the life of me, I couldn't figure out who her perfect match would be. Then one day, while working on the *Paradise Bay* series, it struck me like lightning—Will Banks! And I just knew.

I had planned on making the third *Paradise Bay* book about him, but as soon as I knew who he was meant for, it was also clear to me that these two would need their own series. There is just too much deliciously rich conflict for them to sort through. #evilauthorfun

Anyhoo, you can most definitely read this book as a stand-alone. No problem with that at all. It should make you laugh, swoon a little, and feel good. BUT, if you're a person who likes to read in order so you're in on all the private jokes, and can say to yourself, "Well, that comment is just *so* Gran, isn't it?" then I recommend going back and reading the following books in the following order first: *The Royal Treatment, The Royal Wedding, The Royal Delivery, The Honeymooner, Whisked Away,* and *The Suite Life.* That will bring you up to speed on everything that's happened in the crazy, fun, romantic world I've created. But if you're all, "Hey, Mel, that's too many books, and I just want to read this one, mmkay?" that's cool too. You go, girl. Or boy. Or they. You go, too. Do your thang. Read what you want to read in whatever order you want to read it. S'all good.

Okay, I'll sign off now because you didn't buy this book so you could read some boring letter from me. You bought it so you can escape the real world, which can be kind of scary and sometimes a little nasty. And escape you shall, my friend …

All the very best in life to you and yours,
Melanie

P.S. I've read that the prince formerly known as Prince Harry had a nickname given to him by his friends from school. Apparently, they call him Spike, which is something you'll need to know in about two pages. ;)

Avonian Broadcast Network Morning Newscast
Featuring Veronica Platt

Tuesday, April 7th - Valcourt, Avonia

"Good day and welcome to *Avonia This Morning*. I'm Veronica Platt. Today's top story—the global toilet paper shortage is causing bidets to go flying off shelves at hardware stores all over Europe, and things are about to get messy." Veronica, the beautiful brunette anchor dressed in a white button-up shirt and ivory pearls, pauses dramatically. "But first, the entire kingdom has wedding fever, and no, it's not a royal wedding this time, but it might as well be, because Avonia's own king of fiction, Pierce Davenport, is set to marry here in Valcourt in just four days' time. Giles Bigly is live on location in front of St. Stephen's Church. Giles, would you like to tell us what's going on?"

The screen splits into two halves, showing Giles on the left and Veronica on the right.

"Well, Veronica, as usual, you just did." Giles laughs maniacally. "Yes, the big news around the kingdom is the wedding of the second son of Lord Alistair and Lady Bunny Davenport. His grandfather, of course, was the founder of Davenport Communications, the U.K.'s largest telecom, digital cable, and satellite provider. He may come from one of the most powerful families in the kingdom, but Pierce is a force to be reckoned with in his own right. He's the author of the immensely popular *Clash of Crowns* fantasy series that has been turned into one of the world's most-watched television series. This Saturday, he'll be right here in St. Stephen's behind me, marrying his long-time girl-friend, Emma Banks, renowned chef and inventor of the Carib-Asian food craze. The happy couple live in the Benavente islands near her family's resort, where she works as head chef."

"Yes, Giles, I know that," Veronica says in a sugary tone. "I've actually been there to feature the Paradise Bay Resort, as well as Emma Banks, on our show."

Giles stiffens slightly. "I'm fully aware of that, Veronica. It was the one time you agreed to go live on location. In the Caribbean. Instead of, say, that time I had to go to the Canadian Arctic in the dead of winter to do that piece on the effects of climate change on polar bears. I was merely providing Ms. Banks's backstory to our viewers who may have missed your hard-hitting piece on an all-inclusive resort."

Veronica laughs gaily. "Righto. Of course. Now, Giles, any word as to why they decided to get married here, rather than in Emma's home country?" Veronica asks.

"Actually, Veronica, Ms. Banks was born here in Avonia. She moved to the Caribbean at the age of seven when her parents were killed in an automobile accident. Her uncle, the original owner of the resort, took her and her brothers in, and raised them."

"Oh, how sad. Is that why they've come back here for the big day? To bring Emma back in touch with her roots?"

"Not sure, really. Pierce Davenport is notoriously private, so the couple hasn't made any type of public statement. But one could speculate that it's perhaps a way to appease the Davenports since Pierce and Emma live full time on Santa Valentina Island. Or it could simply be that it's much easier to have a few people travel halfway across the world than to expect hundreds of people to do so. It's rumoured that several members of the royal family will be in attendance, as well as the entire cast and crew of NBO's *Clash of Crowns*, which will make Valcourt quite the spot for stargazing, if you will."

"Speaking of stars, we here at ABN have a special connection with Ms. Banks's younger brother, Will. He's the host of *The Wild World*, which, for those who haven't seen it yet, offers an exciting blend of extreme sports, survival tips, and a chance to get a look at some of the most remote and dangerous places on the planet." Veronica grins at the camera. "Will can really do it all—with his in-depth knowledge of nature and his penchant for risk-taking. They start filming the third season in the next few weeks, and I, for one, cannot wait to see what death-defying things he'll get up to this time around."

"If you're lucky, perhaps he'll pop into the studio to say hello," Giles says. "I'm sure you'd love that, Veronica."

"Not sure exactly what that's supposed to mean, Giles, but I see I'm out of time to unpack your latest passive-aggressive comment."

"If either of us is passive-aggressive, it's definitely—"

Feed cuts and commercial for Unicorn Gold Toilet Spray starts up.

From One Spare to Another ...

Princess Arabella

Valcourt Palace, Valcourt, Kingdom of Avonia

FROM: sparegirl@rmail.com
   To: spareone@rmail.com

Dear Spike,

Sorry it's been so long since I've been in touch. I'm sure you won't hold it against me, since you're one of very few people on the planet who understand a life of constantly running from pointless thing to pointless thing, morning, noon, and night.

Anyway, how's my fellow 'just in case' friend? And how is little Archie doing? I bet he's almost ready to walk. And what's life like in Canada? I heard there are no mosquitoes on Vancouver Island. Is that true? Because if it is, that sounds like utter paradise. They're already out in full force this spring, so we're in for another summer of slapping at the little bastards (discreetly, of course, so as to hide the fact that they like blue blood as much as the red variety).

Cone of Silence: Now that you live among the Canadians, you probably have a much better idea whether they're *actually* as friendly as they seem or if it's all a big act. I have a secret theory that Canadians are every bit as ornery as the rest of us, but they're much better at hiding it under a cloak of politeness that allows them to be well received wherever they go. Do tell, because I simply must know if I'm right.

I still cannot **BELIEVE** you got out! Seriously! After all these years of talking about it, you finally did it. I bow to you, sir. I'm seriously blown away by your tenacity (and Meghan's as well). You two are the perfect power couple—superheroes fighting injustice, racism, and the paparazzi everywhere you go. Well done to you both. I wish I had one tenth of your courageous spirit. Perhaps you could lend me a bit so I can finally have a taste of freedom.

Life is much the same for me, only worse. I've hit the dreaded phase of 'you're almost thirty and you're a woman so you must find a man to marry before it's too late and you turn into a shriveled up old maid and never procreate on behalf of the monarchy.' It started literally one week after my twenty-ninth birthday, and it seems everyone wants to get in on the fun, from all the senior advisers (who can suck it) to the media (who can also suck it) to my family (who I'm very close to telling to suck it).

I'll be at Pierce Davenport's wedding this weekend and have already been given dossiers on six eligible men that will be in attendance. SMH. I don't know who put the list together, but honestly, *horrid*! Remember the fellow we nick-named Hal, as in halitosis? Yeah, he's on the list. Quite a mystery as to why he's still single. Although I guess I'm single, too, so I shouldn't talk.

To update you, I submitted the proposal we discussed for me to serve as patron for the Avonian Mental Wellness and Suicide Prevention Foundation, but was told it would be 'too challenging for someone of my delicate disposition and sensitivities.' Instead, they've added the Valcourt Civil Service Sports Council to my duties. It's an organization that provides sporting opportunities for civil servants (which I find confusing because, surely if they have the mental capacity to get a job, they can also sort out their own exercise requirements). In light of being turned down for the wellness initiative, I thought I might put in that proposal about the Equal Everywhere Campaign that Meghan and I were chatting about. Hopefully they won't think me too delicate to work on that project.

As you wrote, the hours truly do turn into weeks of following the same routine and attending the same annual events until each year becomes a replica of the last one. I chuckled at your analogy about it being like the movie *Groundhog Day*, only it's an entire year that repeats itself rather than one day. Unlike Bill Murray (and you, you brave soul), I will *never* get out of it. I'm terrified that one day I'll die, having never breathed a single breath on my own terms.

Can you imagine if anyone intercepted these emails? They'd hate us for whining when our lives are filled with such privilege (and they wouldn't be wrong). We never have to hold a real job or worry about money. But if only they understood the flipside of it—that we *can* never hold a job, even if we're wildly passionate about something.

Speaking of which, what are you going to do now that you're out? Military consultant? Paid spokesperson for a charity? Stay-at-home dad while Megs heads back to Hollywood to rake in the big bucks? I'll be watching with bated breath to see how it all turns out for you. Who knows? Maybe someday I'll get out of it, too. But for now, I must go. I have to attend a formal tea for The Friends of the Valcourt United Cathedral's Platinum Fund for Choristers, where I'll be subjected to the never-ending debate on the difference between the mandate of the Platinum Fund vs. that of the Friends of the Platinum Fund. Honestly, who gives a rat's arse? Not me.

Say hello to Celine Dion for me,

Airy

2

Beauty is in the Eye of the Beholder. Except Sometimes, When It's Obvious to Everyone...

Will Banks

Paradise Bay, Santa Valentina Island, Benavente Islands, Caribbean

"OH WILL, JUST LOOK AT HER," my brother, Harrison, says, pointing out toward the calm early morning sea. "She's every bit as beautiful today as she always was."

My eyes land on a bikini-clad senior citizen strolling along the shore. I reach up and put my hand on my brother's forehead, checking for heatstroke. "You don't feel feverish. Is everything okay with you and Libby?"

"Of course. Why?" Harrison says, giving me a strange look.

"You're ogling a woman who I'm pretty sure is somebody's great-grandmother."

"Not her, you jackass," he says. "Matilda."

I look again, this time past the woman and out to sea, spotting *Waltzing Matilda*, the ninety-foot schooner that used to belong to our Uncle Oscar. Harrison had to sell her to a greasy businessman (who we call Stogie Stew) a couple of years back to save our family's resort from going under. The yacht glides along in the turquoise water, and even though I don't glance over at my brother, I know his expression is a mixture of longing and grief. Harrison would give his left nut to have her back so he could take his own family on the same kind of adventures our uncle took us on.

I fight the urge to smile. Not because I'm a prick who likes seeing my brother upset, but because very soon, I'm going to surprise him by purchasing Matilda back for him. Honestly, I've never been so excited about anything in my entire life—which is saying something because I've spent the last several years on an adrenaline high. I've bungee jumped from the skid of a helicopter over the bubbling crater of Villarrica Volcano in Chile. I've gone cage diving with great whites off the coast of Gansbaai, South Africa—*without* the cage. I've traversed the icy crests and rocky pyramids of the Ellsworth Mountains in Antarctica. But none of it compares with what I'm about to achieve.

You see, Matilda represents one of a million sacrifices Harrison has made, not only for my sister, Emma, and I, but for the entire Paradise Bay Resort staff. Harrison was all set to take off to California to join the pro-surf tour when Uncle Oscar died. He could have sold off the resort, pocketed the cash, and taken off to live his dreams, and no one would have blamed him. After all, he was only twenty-one at the time, and had already been raising Emma and I for an entire decade. Our parents were killed in a collision when I was six, leaving us to our uncle to finish raising us. Since Oscar wasn't exactly a 'hands on' caregiver, Harrison stepped into that role, making sure we went to bed on time, ate at least a few veggies, and finished our homework at night.

But did Harrison do the easy thing and leave? No, he did not. He gave up pro-surfing and took on the massive challenge of running a 274-room resort with five swimming pools, seven restaurants, and a fleet of catamarans, speedboats, and jet skiis. He kept everything running like clockwork until Hurricane Irene came along and wiped us out. Did he throw in the towel? Newp. Did he complain? No. Did he ask my sister to quit culinary school or me to give up my fledgling TV career to come back and help? No, he did not. He quietly sold off *Matilda* and used the cash to turn Paradise Bay into one of the top resorts in the Caribbean. The guy is a living saint. If he weren't my own flesh and blood, I'd probably find him supremely irritating. But, having been on the receiving end of his generosity my entire life, I find myself in a constant state of awe of my big brother. Which is why I'm going to get his boat back for him.

"We'll get her back," I say, with a confident smile. I'm about to start filming the third season of The Wild World, my adventure/nature docu-series. (If you haven't seen or heard of it, think Bear Grylls, only much, much better.) As soon as we wrap for the season, I'll get my danger bonus, and the deal will be as good as done.

"Maybe someday," Harrison says with a shrug. "If not, life's pretty damn great, anyway."

Glancing to my right, I see our sister, Emma, heading our way on her old-timey bicycle. "It was," I say, pointing down the beach in her direction.

She lives at the far end of the bay with her fiancé—soon to be husband—Pierce Davenport. Emma-the-chef is a strong, fun, capable professional who can run a hectic kitchen without breaking a sweat. Emma-the-bride, however, has a temperament and bite force quotient equivalent to a Tasmanian Devil. According to National Geographic, devils are "notoriously cantankerous and will fly into a maniacal rage when threatened by a predator, fighting for a mate, or defending a meal." And that's exactly how I'd describe my sister lately. A terrifying and unpredictable ball of bridal stress that pretty much everyone, including the love of her life, has been avoiding whenever possible over the last two months. "Let's finish up so we can hide before Emma spots us."

Harrison and I pick up our pace, setting up the last few lounge chairs and umbrellas as Emma's legs propel her bike quickly down the path that runs along the beach.

"Hey, you two goofballs!" Emma's voice rings out, competing with the sound of the gentle tide and the calls of the seagulls. She hops off her bike. "Glad I caught you. We need to talk."

"Hi," I wave and smile, even though my lips have gone instantly dry due to terror.

Narrowing her eyes, Emma says, "Why are you staring at me like that? Are you scared? You look scared."

I nod instinctively, which negates the fact that I'm simultaneously saying, "No. Not at all. You look lovely this morning. Did you do something different with your hair?"

"Same ponytail I've worn since third grade."

"Oh, well, something's different." I chuckle nervously.

"Must be that bridal glow you hear so much about," Harrison adds.

"That's not a thing," she says. "Relax. I'm not going to bite your heads off. I just wanted to give Will his packing list." She hands me a thick envelope.

"Just for me? Why doesn't he get one?" I ask, gesturing toward Harrison with my head.

"He doesn't need a list. He's got Libby."

Makes sense. Libby is Harrison's super-organized wife. Squeezing the envelope, I say, "Must be quite the list."

"It's also your flight itinerary, and a shaving schedule so you won't have …" She gestures toward my chin. "*This* going on. I've also included a daily schedule for our time in Avonia. Any items on the agenda with a star next to them are required, okay? I know you have some meetings while we're there, but the whole reason for the trip is my wedding, so I expect you to make it to all the important stuff."

"Of course. Wouldn't miss a moment of it." I give her a wide grin she could interpret as either sincere or sincerely sarcastic.

The scowl on her face shows me she knew which way I meant it. My mobile phone buzzes in the pocket of my shorts. *Yes! I can get out of this conversation before I say something to set her off.* Pulling it out of my pocket, I see Dwight Anderson's name across the screen. "Hey, Dwight, how are things?"

"Horrific," Dwight says, but don't get too alarmed because this is a standard response for my manager/agent. Don't get me wrong, the guy is a terrific manager, but he also suffers from a severe case of Chicken Little Syndrome, and I'm about to find out why the sky is falling today. "Worst news possible."

"That doesn't sound good." I take a few steps away from Harrison and Emma, who is now listing topics of conversation that will be unacceptable in front of her fiancé's hoity-toity family.

Dwight pauses for a second, then I hear a crunching sound, which means his heartburn is acting up again. He inhales Tums faster than Scarface inhaled cocaine. But, not through his nose, obviously. "Allan got fired this morning."

"Fired?" I plunk myself down onto one of the lounge chairs and rub my scruffy beard with one hand. "Oh ... Is this about—?"

"—Yes. I tried to tell him shaboinking the new wife of the head of the network wasn't exactly a great career move, but you know him."

I glance out to the water and the sight of Matilda causes my stomach to tighten. "Shit. Does this mean we have to delay filming?"

"Possibly." Crunch, crunch, crunch. "But I've heard rumblings ABN found a new showrunner before they fired him."

"Any idea who?"

"Some guy named Dylan Sinclair. I looked him up and I can't find him on IMDb."

"So he's a total greenhorn?"

"Quite probably, yes. If that's the case, he's likely some executive producer's loser nephew. Frankly, it's not a great sign, William. It means ABN is giving up on the show."

My heart falls to my stomach so fast, I can actually hear it land. "Is there anything in my contract that gives me a veto?"

Dwight lets out a hard sigh. "You mean you still haven't—?"

"—No, I haven't read the contract yet. That's what I pay you for." I make the mistake of glancing at Emma, who taps her wristwatch and mouths 'hurry up!' to me. Suddenly I realize Dwight is still talking and I've completely zoned out.

I focus in time to hear "... no say whatsoever in crew members."

"Seriously?"

"You want more say? Get better ratings," Dwight quips.

"Like that's so easy. You've seen what we're up against. YouTube, Pornhub ..." I answer.

"... Not to mention BBC's *Newlyweds in the Wild*."

I sigh, wishing he hadn't brought up the bane of my existence. It's a one-hour show featuring a couple who met on
Love Match. They do lame, fake stunts in places that are not
wild at all, but because they're both willing to run around in
very little clothing the entire time, they're killing it. "Clearly
what I do and what they do isn't at all the same thing. I'm not
just prancing around some set in Hollywood. We film in the
most remote and dangerous places on the planet. The four of
us rely on each other to make it out alive."

"I know that. You don't think I know that?" Crunch,
crunch. "Who do you think negotiated the danger bonus into
your last contract?"

"Good, then you can help the network see the importance
of a seasoned director-slash-show runner."

"Listen, William, there's one concept you need to wrap
your head around. You're one little rating point from being
dropped on your arse. When you get here on Thursday for
the meeting, it better be hat in hand: *yes, sir, no, sir, I'll do whatever I have to do to make this work.* If there's even a hint of dissen-
sion among the ranks, they'll pull the plug."

My other line rings and I hold my phone away to see who
it is. Stew Milner calling.

"Dammit, I have to go, Dwight. I'm getting a call I can't
ignore."

"Hat in hand."

"Yes, sir. See you Thursday."

I swipe the screen, hurrying farther down the beach so
Harrison won't overhear me. "Will here."

"Who's the hottie with the body?" Stew asks.

I squint out to the yacht and see him standing on the deck with binoculars on.

"I hope you're not referring to my sister."

"No, the one in the bikini." He means Grandma Bikini. There's a lid for every pot, I guess. "Not sure. I think she's a guest of the hotel. Is that why you're calling? Because I'm really busy this morning."

"No, I wanted to talk to you about Matilda. There's another man who's interested in her."

Shit. "We had a deal, Stew."

"That was before this bloke from Australia came by yesterday. He's desperate for her. Wants to return her to her homeland," he says, making a puffing sound that tells me he's got a juicy cigar in his mouth. "He wanted to pay me right then. Said he'd add ten thousand to your offer."

My shoulders drop. "Are you calling to tell me the deal's off?"

I glance down the beach and see Emma glaring at me and gesturing wildly for me to get over there now. Holding up my hand, I nod quickly, then turn away.

"No. I like you, Will. I want to sell her to you."

"Thank you."

"Having said that, I've got my eye on a property on the west side of the island. I'm not supposed to say anything, but it belongs to a certain television network owner from the US who is putting her house up for sale."

He means Oprah.

"A certain famous American talk show host who runs her own media empire?" Stew asks.

"Yeah, everybody knows Oprah has a place on the island."

"Oh, well then," he says, sounding taken aback.

"I'm going to start filming the next season in a couple of weeks. I get my danger bonus as soon as we wrap up. If you can just give me another month, I'll have the cash."

He makes a clicking sound with his teeth, then sighs. "All right. I'll give you thirty days. Oprah's getting her place re-carpeted so I doubt it'll go on the market for a few weeks, anyway."

"Thanks, Stew," I say, relief flooding my veins. "I'll get you the money. I promise."

"Honestly, I don't care. Either way, the boat'll be sold," he says. "Now, if you could do me a favour and put that little hottie on the phone, I'd appreciate it."

"Sorry, my battery's dying."

With that, I hang up and shove my phone back in my pocket.

"I don't have all damn day!" Emma yells at me.

Letting out a long sigh, I walk toward Bridezilla. One problem at a time. First Emma, then the network, then *Matilda*.

———

Wednesday Evening - 9 p.m.

. . .

Text from Emma to Me: *Do you need me to come by and help you pack?*

Me (after some serious eye-rolling): *No need, I'm already done.*

Emma: *Did you use the list?*

Me: *What list?*

My phone rings and I see Emma's name. Damn, I took it too far. We leave first thing tomorrow morning, which means I should probably start packing, especially since I won't be coming back until after I film the next season of my show. I sit on the bed and swipe the screen to answer. "Heya, sis."

"Don't mess with me, Will. I'm not above murder at this point," Emma says.

"Jokes! I have the list, I've checked it twice," I say, walking over to the desk that sits in the far corner of my bedroom. I pick up the envelope and open it for the first time.

"No more jokes. The shuttle leaves at seven a.m. SHARP. You'll be in front of the lobby on time, yes?"

"You can count on it."

"You sure you don't need a wake-up call?"

"I already set my bedside alarm *and* the alarm on my mobile phone," I say, leaning over to my nightstand and setting my alarm.

"Did you shave yet?"

"No, but only because I want to have the freshest shave possible when I meet your future in-laws," I say, walking into my bathroom and grabbing my razor and a can of shaving cream. I deposit them in my toiletries kit and zip it up. "Don't worry. I promise I'll be my most presentable self when we go see the fancy-schmancies."

Emma sighs and when she speaks, her voice cracks a bit. "I know this is a joke to you, but I'm really nervous about this. We're not like them, Will. They're all so posh and … elegant."

"You're every bit as good as they are, Em."

"Ha! Not exactly."

"What are you talking about? You're a world-renowned chef, you're well-educated, and, despite what I used to tell you when we were growing up, you're not all that ugly."

She laughs a little. "Gee, thanks."

"Any time," I say, opening my closet and pulling out my suitcase. "Listen, I know this'll be hard for you—a big wedding with hundreds of people you don't know, but the truth is, all that matters is that Pierce is madly in love with you, and when this one day is over, you two will be together forever." I put on a mock-dreamy tone on the words 'together forever' to keep things appropriately brother-sister light.

"Thanks, you bonehead."

"You're welcome, Bridezilla. Okay, I better get going. I should really read over this list and start packing." I quickly say, "Last joke, I promise," before hanging up.

Tossing my phone onto the bed, I walk to the kitchen of the small staff villa that has become my home. Other than my surfboard leaned up against the wall, there's nothing personal in it. No family photos, no mementos of my life. Just a small bedroom, one bathroom, and a kitchen/living room combo, which is where my surfboard lives. It's enough for me though, especially because I'm not here much.

I open the fridge and take out a can of beer, then crack it open. For the first time, I'm not excited about leaving home to go explore some new part of the world. I spot a sippy cup under my coffee table and smile to myself as I pick it up. My one-year-old niece Clara was here this afternoon for a few hours. I babysat her while Libby and Harrison were busy with a staff meeting. Man, she's adorable. The way she runs every-where, her little diaper-clad bottom swinging from side-to-side. Her little giggle. The way she holds her arms up to me and says, "Up." I'm going to miss that little tyke for the next however-many weeks or months that I'm gone. But it'll all be worth it.

I hope.

3

Nasty Nonagenarians in Turquoise Track Suits

Arabella

"WELCOME, LADIES AND GENTLEMEN." I smile as I stare into the crinkly faces of the eight remaining members of the Nonagenarian Mall Walkers Club. They've been invited to the palace for a special tour to celebrate one hundred miles of mall walking this year—a vitally important milestone that only a senior-ranking royal can properly acknowledge (or so I'm told). As much as I wish I cared, I have bigger fish to fry today.

Last week, I submitted a proposal to the senior staff, and my father, to become an ambassador for the United Nations Equal Everywhere campaign—an organization aimed at making girls and women equal to boys and men everywhere on the planet. Important work that would allow me to travel the globe, making it a more fair and just place. (I can almost feel my cape flapping in the wind behind me as I hurry down the halls of injustice).

Anyway, in exactly ninety minutes, a meeting will be held to discuss it, and I am *desperate* to be in that room. Not because I actually think they'll listen to me, but because the chances my father will say no are far greater when he doesn't have to risk seeing the disappointment on my face. I've also requested permission to wear a red minidress to the Davenport wedding this weekend, which is purely strategic on my part. There's no way in hell they'll allow me to wear red to anything—especially not a formal event with tons of press. According to royal protocol, red and jewel tones are not for ladies. They're for ladies of the night. Princesses must choose muted pastels. Think cupcakes, a table set for Easter dinner, or better yet, Easter cupcakes, and you'll have it spot on.

I'm currently dressed in a skirt suit in passionless peach, and for tonight's Annual Avonian Medical Association Gala, I'll be dressed in a mind-numbing mint chiffon gown. But I digress, because I was talking about the meeting. The purpose of asking to wear something I know they'll never allow is to increase the probability of a yes for the thing I really want (to be a UN Ambassador).

I glance at my watch, then look at the group, confident in their ability to traverse the width of the palace in under an hour. They may be a little older, but they're also elite athletes. They're even dressed in matching turquoise track suits with red piping, and turquoise jackets that bear the words 'Ninety is nifty!' in bold letters on the front. The back reads 'Nonage-narian Mall Walkers. Get Walkin' or Start Dyin.'

They must be a peppy bunch, no?

Hmmm. None of them are smiling back at me. I wonder if I'm talking too quietly. "For those who don't know me, I am Princess Arabella, and I'm delighted to welcome you today to the palace on behalf of the entire Langdon family."

A tall thin lady with a tight, grey bun holds up one hand. "There's no need to shout, dear. We're not the Nearly Deaf Mall Walkers."

A short, plump woman with blue hair jabs the tall one in the ribs. "We're the *Nearly Dead* Walkers."

A few of them break into laughter, while a lady toward the back says, "Could you speak up, please, miss? We can't hear you."

Blue Hair rolls her eyes and sighs loudly.

"I'm sorry," I say, gesturing for her to come closer. "Would you like to come to the front?"

"Oh yes, that would be lovely." She inches her way toward me while I wait. *Crap, this is taking her quite a while.*

"Shall we get started?" I say.

"Pardon me?" the one man in the group asks, turning his head so his right ear is facing me.

"She asked if we should get started," Blue Hair shouts at him.

"Where's the king? I was hoping we could meet him this time," Tall Thin Lady asks.

"Yes, why isn't he doing the tour?" the man says. "Or *at*

least Prince Arthur? We had a woman last time, too."

"Last time we had his pretty wife, Princess Tessa," Blue Hair tells me.

"Yes, the *people's* princess," a curly-hair woman with the thickest glasses I've ever seen adds. "Where is *she* today?"

I pause, then force a smile. "She's probably around here somewhere."

"Oh, I hope we'll come across her! She's *lovely*."

"Princess Arabella is lovely, too!" Tall Thin Lady, who is quickly becoming my favourite, says. "She looks exactly like her mum."

Oh. Great.

"Queen Cecily," Blue Hair says, clutching her saggy bosom. "I do miss her so. Such grace." Turning to me she adds, "You would have loved her."

Well, since she was my mother, I suppose that makes sense. "Yes, I'm sure I would have."

"I wish *she* were giving our tour."

"As do I," I say, nodding serenely.

"Oh! What about that buff manny for the twins! Maybe he could show us around?"

So, in other words, they'd prefer anyone *but* me.

"What's his name again?"

"Arnold."

"No, it's not Arnold. It starts with a Y, doesn't it?"

"Xavier," I say.

"No, that's not it," Blue Hair says. "It's something very manly, like Jack."

"His name is Xavier," I say. "Trust me, I know him personally."

"*How* personally?" Tall Thin Lady asks, raising and lowering her eyebrows.

I feel my face heating up and I shake my head quickly. "Not *that* personally! Shall we get started?"

"I think she's lying. Look how pink her face has gotten at the mention of him!"

"I'm not …"

"Now, don't be ashamed! He's irresistible. All that muscle *and* he loves children. A girl could do a lot worse."

"Yes, but we're not—"

"Why ever not? Don't tell me he's not good enough for you!"

Holding up one hand, I say, "No, I never said—"

"At your age, love, you should really find a man already."

At my *age? Is she kidding me?* "I'm only twenty-nine. Anyway, should we get—"

"Twenty-nine? And you're still single?! Ridiculous. By the time I was your age, I had already had four children," Tight White Curls says.

"Ask her how many of them come to visit her," Tall Thin Lady whispers to me.

Blue Hair pipes up with, "Oh, yes, you're getting a bit old to stay on the shelf, Your Highness."

"It's true. Don't put it off. Finding a man after you turn thirty is an absolute nightmare," Tight White Curls says. "My granddaughter—lovely thing, but *far* too picky. She had all these crazy notions about getting her Ph.D. first. Well, now she's a forty-two-year-old Doctor of Music, whatever that means. She's fat as a house and lives alone with her six cats."

"Her sex cats?" the man shouts.

"SIX!" Tall Thin Lady yells at him. "One, two, three, four, five, six. Helen's fat granddaughter has six cats!"

"You don't want to end up like that," Blue Hair adds.

"It's true," Tight White Curls says. "Men don't want you once you're over thirty. Your eggs are getting too old, so your currency drops exponentially."

My eggs? Oh, this is awful. I have a strong notion to abandon the group and sprint off to my apartment. There's clearly no way they could catch me. Instead, I speak louder than is probably necessary, even with this group. "Today, we'll be visiting the west wing of the palace which includes the library, the gold drawing room, the throne room, the grand ballroom, as well as the main dining hall."

One of them raises her hand, but I ignore her and continue. Pointing to the ceiling, I say, "These are the murals painted by Giovanni Canaletto in the sixteenth century. Few people know this, but back in the 1980s, a fire broke out in the kitchen and we almost lost these beautiful works of art to smoke damage. After that, the entire palace was fitted with sprinklers and sliding fire doors were added to each side of the Grande Hall."

"How much did that cost the taxpayers?" one of them quips.

"Shut up. You're being rude."

"What did you say?" the man asks me. "I can't hear you at all." He turns to a woman with bright red lipstick, some of it smeared on her straight, white teeth. "Is she speaking English?"

"Oh, I'm sorry," I say, raising my voice and moving closer to him.

"Don't bother." Blue Hair shakes her head. Turning to him, she shouts, "She said these paintings are almost as old as you."

This earns her a laugh from the rest of the group. I take a few steps, then turn back to them, my heart sinking when I see the snail's pace at which we're about to embark on our tour. There is literally no way we'll finish in under an hour. I'd be shocked if we were done by teatime. Double damn. "So, we're celebrating one hundred miles of mall walking," I say, smiling and nodding in a way that says, 'please be much faster than this.'

"That's right, Your Highness," a woman with a short fringe says. "And not one single mile with the use of aids."

"Not so much as a cane," Tall Thin Lady adds.

"Canes are for candy asses," one of the ladies at the back says.

"And walkers are for wimps!" one of them adds.

Grinning, I say, "My goodness, I hope I have your strong constitutions when I'm your age."

"I doubt it," Blue Hair says, wrinkling her face up even more than it already was. "You seem pretty soft. No offense."

"She *always* means to offend," the woman with red lipstick

adds.

Blue Hair glares at Red Lipstick. "Oh, don't mind her, she's just sore because the rest of us don't want her here. She's not a *real* nonagenarian."

"Let it go already, Betty. I'll be ninety next week!" Red Lipstick says. "It's not my fault the rest of the octogenarian walkers died!"

Tight White Curls leans in and gives her a steely glare. "That's not what I heard."

"Hey, leave her alone, you bunch of old hags," the man says.

Oh, dear. That's not going to go over well.

"Of course you would defend *her*. You men! Always chasing around the young tarts!"

"Oh, for God's sake! Just let it go, woman."

Tight White Curls scowls at him. "You don't actually think those are *real*, do you?"

I find myself glancing at her boobs, even though part of me is screaming that it's a bad idea. They're pretty much what I'd expect eighty-nine-year-old breasts to look like—two oranges in a pair of socks.

"Pathetic," Blue Hair says, shaking her head. "Those are dentures if I've ever seen them!"

Oh, her *teeth* are fake.

Tall Thin Lady shuffles closer to me and cups her hand over the side of her mouth. "Don't mind them. His wife died two months ago, so the race is on to snag him before it's too late."

"Okkaayy, shall we continue?" I ask. I pick up my pace a little, hoping they can match it. Without looking back, I make my way across the Grande Hall, distancing myself from the scent of BenGay. When I reach the entrance to the west wing, I turn and see them all shuffling toward me, some of them furiously pumping with their arms, although it doesn't seem to propel their wobbly legs any faster.

"What's the rush? Have you got a hot date after this?" Tight White Curls asks.

"Get off her back," Blue Hair says firmly. "She's just new at this."

"You're right, she's a goddamn nuisance," Single Guy says.

———

It is now 10:34. On the other side of the palace, the meeting has just started, and we've only gotten as far as the library, which is the second room on our tour. Three of the nonagenarians are now napping in armchairs while Red Lipstick makes time with Mr. Popular. Huh, those really must be dentures. They're unnaturally white.

I stand near the door and tap my foot on the plush carpet, not even caring if I seem impatient at this point. *I have got to get out of this, now.* I pull my phone out of my pocket and text Tessa as discreetly as possible. *You wouldn't happen to have an hour free to finish a tour with some delightful athletic senior citizens, would you?*

Tessa: *You're not referring to the Nonagenarian Mall Walkers, are you?*

Me: *Yes, I am! :-)*

Tessa: *I got stuck doing that tour last year. If memory serves, it took over four hours and by the time we were done, my ego had been shredded. Nastiest people on the planet. Don't show any signs of weakness.*

Me: *So, that's a no, then?*

Tessa: *It's a hard no, but please don't think I don't love you. I just don't have time for the PTSD therapy this year.*

Bugger. I slide my mobile back into my pocket and stare around at them. "Who wants to see the throne room?"

———

By the time the shuttle bus is loaded and all the turquoise track suits are gone, it's half past noon. I've missed the entire meeting, having instead spent the morning being reminded of my aging eggs by a bunch of women who haven't dropped any since The Beatles were still together. My stomach growls as I make my way to my office, and when I get there, I see that Mrs. Chapman, my assistant, has gone for lunch.

I'm glad, to be honest. She's extremely formal, extremely experienced, and extremely cold. Think Prof. McGonagall from Harry Potter, except without the pointy hat, the ability to perform magic, or any type of soft spot for anyone. Ever. Mrs. Chapman has been my assistant/taskmaster since I was seventeen and I still don't even know her first name.

I open the tall wooden door to my tastefully decorated

office, then slump my shoulders as I walk to my two-hundred-year-old white French provincial desk. I kick off my heels and plunk myself into my muted olive velvet chair and stare at the vase overflowing with hydrangeas. They've gone with pink hydrangeas this week. Normally, this would make me smile, as would a glance out the large windows to the view of the sun-drenched gardens behind the palace.

But not today. Today, it feels like the walls are slowly sliding toward me. I open the bottom drawer and pull out a bag of Jelly Babies, a treat Tessa got me hooked on. Popping one into my mouth, I spot a note on my desk in Mrs. Chapman's perfect, tight handwriting.

Princess Arabella,

I've gone for a quick bite of lunch. It's a no to the red dress, obviously, and to the equal rights thing. Your father and the advisers thought it too emotional a cause for you. Also, it will interfere with your ability to meet a man, since you'd be working with women all day. They thought perhaps instead you might like to become the patron of The Avonian Bankers Association. Plenty of eligible men there.

Mrs. C

P.S. Be ready to leave by one o'clock for the fundraiser for hamster wheelchairs.

P.P.S. I've ordered you a salad - it's in the bar fridge. Maybe eat that instead of having another meal of Jelly Babies.

4

Red Bull Strikes Again...

Will Banks

Valcourt, Avonia

"I REALLY HAVE to be out of here in under an hour," I say to Dwight as we hurry down the hall of the Avonian Broadcast Network building to the conference room. "Emma said if I'm not freshly shaved and at her future in-laws' for cocktails by six, she'll kill me, cut me up, and use my limbs to beat you until you're dead."

"Delightful," Dwight says. "She's right about the beard though. I can't even believe you would allow that to grow so close to where you eat. Have you not heard of beard ringworm?"

"First of all, gross. Second, no, I haven't."

"Google it. It's a thing."

"Yeah, I'm not going to Google that."

Dwight is a bit of a germaphobe. Well, I could be understating the case. He shaves his head completely bald even though he has a full head of thick brown hair. He says hair hides all sorts of fungus, and he prefers to keep his scalp clean enough to perform an appendectomy on. When one would ever do that, I don't know, but his scalp is surgery-ready. He also keeps a fanny pack hidden under his slightly oversized jacket, containing everything from his Tums to his disinfectant wipes to his tea tree oil spray in case someone sneezes one town over.

We reach the conference room door and he waits for me to open it so he can avoid what he calls 'handle germs.' As soon as I open it, I hear a whirring sound, indicating he's getting out his hand sanitizer which he keeps clipped to himself at all times on a retractable leash. "Hands," he says, opening the bottle.

There's no use arguing so I hold my palms up while he squirts them, then he squirts his own. The two of us avoid eye contact while we silently rub the cool, slippery substance into our skin in front of the slightly ajar wooden door.

When we walk in, I see we are the last people to arrive. The two executives that head up the unscripted division— Victor Petty and Kira Taylor—are already here, along with their interns. Victor and Kira could be their own reality show called 'People Who Think No One Knows They're Sleeping

Together.' What remains of my crew, Toshiro Fukuhara (or Tosh, as we call him) and Callum MacKenzie (who hails from Scotland and goes by Mac), are standing at the back of the room near the snack table. I start toward them but am interrupted by a middle-aged woman holding a can of Red Bull.

She rushes toward me, holding out her free hand. "There he is—the star of the soon-to-be most popular nature-slash-adventure docu-series in the entire universe! I'm Dylan Sinclair, the starmaker." She gives my hand two firm pumps, lets go, and sucks back a few more gulps of her drink. "Oh, and your new showrunner-slash-director."

I stand in place, completely frozen as my brain slowly processes what she's just said. Glancing up and down her navy-blue high-powered suit and stiletto-clad feet, I try to imagine her jumping out of a helicopter into the Amazon River. Nope. Can't picture it. "You're Dylan Sinclair."

"I certainly am." Slamming back the remainder of her can, she tosses it with an impressive overhand shot into the garbage bin, then immediately produces another one from the side pocket of her suit jacket. "Red Bull?"

"Thanks, but my mind is already racing fast enough."

Snapping her fingers, Dylan shouts, "Let's get this meeting started, shall we, people?" She walks over to the head of the table and starts fiddling with an iPad as the rest of us take our seats.

I pull my phone out of my pocket and send a group text to Tosh and Mac. *WTF?*

Tosh glances at his smart watch, then looks at me and shrugs.

"You are probably thinking to yourself 'what the farts,'" Dylan says, giving me a knowing look.

My face heats up and I suddenly panic that she might have somehow seen what I typed.

"First off, let me say I was up literally all night watching every episode of your show, plus all of the extras, and every interview you've ever given. And not to gush, but I loved every second of it. Love, love, *loved* it all!"

Okay, maybe this won't be so bad after all. "Well, thank you. I really feel like we've got a winning formula here," I say. "With a solid marketing push, we should be able to up our ratings."

"Yes. Yes!" Dylan yells, startling everyone at the table. She points at me. "*This* is the enthusiasm I'm looking for! This is exactly what is going to make you a star, mister! We take your natural rugged good looks and your penchant for adventure, and we revamp everything—except the beard. The beard stays, but everything else goes. And I mean everything."

"Excuse me?" I ask. "But if you love it so much, why would we have to change everything?"

"Excellent question! It's because what you've been doing has been done, William. People have already seen Bear Grylls and … and Jacques Cousteau … and that Jane Goodall woman doing what you do."

"Jane Goodall didn't have a show. She studied chimps."

"But some of it was filmed," she says dismissively. "Here's

the thing, and I really need you to hear me now, Will. We are not in a world where people watch what they've already seen. They want new. They want sexy. They want exciting. And that is exactly what we are going to give them."

My Spidey senses are tingling. I do not like the sound of this. "Umm, sorry, Dylan, I don't want to come off as rude here. It's just that, I only met you a few minutes ago, and you're already talking about reinventing our entire show."

"Oh God. I've done it again, haven't I?" She laughs, looking at Victor and Kira. "I have a tendency to jump in with both feet and forget I need to give other people time to catch up with me." She finally sits down. "Let me give you a bit of background about me. I'm what you call a 'fixer,' which means when something is broken beyond what any other human considers repairable, they bring me in. I've made a career out of turning the biggest stink bombs in the U.K. into rose bushes. I can't tell you about most of my clients because of confidentiality, but I can say I singlehandedly restored the reputation of a certain consort to a certain crown prince of a certain kingdom that we happen to be in at the moment. And that was *after* she kicked a one-legged man off a bar-top, causing him to need hundreds of stitches." Lowering her voice to a whisper, she adds, "Hundreds. And now, she's known across the land as the People's Princess. It's true. I'm that good."

Dylan stands suddenly. "More recently, I zipped over to the US to help a certain celebrity couple after the husband was photographed holding hands with his beautiful co-star at a restaurant in New Orleans. When I got back, I was offered Prince Andrew, but I said no way, too easy. I need a *real challenge.* I'm going to resurrect the career of a hot, young, adventurous TV host who has an ocean full of potential but doesn't have the first clue what to do with it."

"So, I'm more broken than Prince Andrew?"

"No! That's not what I meant!" She says with a laugh.

"But you said I was a tougher challenge than—"

She waves off my words. "Forget all that. Not important. What's important is sling-shotting you to the top of non-scripted television."

"Have you directed a documentary before?"

"Nah-uh."

"A reality show?" I ask.

"Nope."

"Sitcom?"

Dylan shakes her head.

"Newscast?"

"I see where you're going with this."

I should hope so.

Dylan sits sideways on the table. "Listen, William. Wills. No, let's go with Will. That works best. Anyway, I get it. You're worried that I can't pull this off, or that I'll somehow get in the way. But I won't. I've been taking Ron Howard's Master Class online. And guess what? Directing could not be easier!"

I turn to Kira, expecting her to come to the same conclusion I've already reached—that this woman is completely unsuitable as a director for our series, or any series for that matter. But instead of looking horrified, Kira's smiling at Dylan and nodding. *What the …?*

"Oh, I get it," I say, chuckling. "You guys are pranking me." I stand and start examining the walls.

"What are you doing?" Victor asks.

"I'm looking for the hidden cameras, but I don't see any." I turn to Tosh. "You're getting good at this. Where'd you put them?"

"There's no camera," Tosh murmurs, shaking his head.

I stand, staring back between him and Mac, but neither of them are smiling.

Dylan springs out of her chair and walks over to me, looping her arm through mine and leading me back to the table like I'm a confused child. "Okay, let's talk about the elephant in the room."

Is she the elephant in the room or am I?

She pats the back of my chair. I sit and try to calm down while she returns to the head of the table. "This is hard. I get it. I mean we all only just found out about Alex—"

"Allan," I say.

"Right … Allan. It's been what? Less than a week? I'm sure you're at least as shocked as I was, but let's see this for what it is—an opportunity. This is your chance to turn things around and make this show what it really should be—the most widely watched and heavily syndicated television series on the planet. Think bigger than *Survivor*. Bigger than *Clash of Clans*. Hotter than *The Thorn Birds*—oh, you're probably too young to know that one. Whatever, think *Lost* meets *Survivor* meets *Big Brother* meets *Temptation Island*. Total show makeover —new name, new format."

Dylan taps on her iPad causing Madonna's "Justify My Love" to start up. On the screen behind her, a video starts with photos and video clips of me—mostly shirtless—interspersed with videos of bikini-clad young women.

I sit with my mouth hanging open as I watch the women slide down ropes, splash in the ocean, and stare seductively at the camera while their hair blows in the wind. Dylan dances along with her shoulders and mouths the words. The video ends with Madonna's voice saying, "Are you scared?"

Yes, Madonna, I am really fucking scared.

Beaming around the room, Dylan says, "Yes? Yes, right? This is it. The secret sauce."

I shake my head. "No, sorry, but I don't do reality porn. I do adventures in nature. It's about survival and pushing the limits of what a human can do—"

"Not anymore, Will. Now it's about sex. And sex sells," she says. "Consider this—we bring on ten to fifteen women who all want nothing more than to marry you. We make them do all kinds of terrifying and disgusting survival things to win the chance at a proposal."

I glance at Dwight who is quietly sucking on a Tums, then say, "I'm not ... there's absolutely no possible way in hell I'm doing that."

Dylan nods quickly. "It's okay. I figured you might be

resistant to this idea at first glance, but trust me, you'll warm up to it when you see these numbers."

She taps her iPad again, and a chart appears on the large screen. Standing, she walks over to the wall. "We showed a thousand women ages nineteen to thirty-four photos and video of you, and asked them to rate you on scales of how interesting and exciting they found you, hotness, and marriageability, etc."

I hold up one hand. "This is ridiculous. I'm not interested—"

"Sixty-eight percent of them considered you equal to or hotter than Henry Cavill. Eighty-two percent considered you highly desirable for a one-night-stand, and twenty-six percent considered you marriage material."

Well that's a little insulting. "Why only twenty-six?"

"Mainly because of your risky lifestyle. A few said you don't look all that bright, but forget about that because they were basing it on your physique, which ninety-eight said was as good as Alexander Skarsgård in *Tarzan*."

"Really? Huh," I smile for a second, then shake my head. "It doesn't matter because I'm not doing this to be sexy. I'm doing it because I want to showcase parts of the planet most people will never see, and to inspire others to get out there and test their limits."

"You can still do all that *and* add the sex factor." Clapping her hands, Dylan shouts, "Winning combination!"

I look at Tosh and Mac. "Guys? Do you want to help me out here?"

Mac tilts his head. "Not really. To be honest, I wouldn't hate being stuck out in the jungle with fifteen hotties."

"Yeah, Mac and I would be there to comfort them when they get rejected by you," Tosh says with a half-grin.

The two of them fist-pump while I scowl.

Turning to Kira and Victor, I say, "Is this really the kind of show ABN wants to produce?"

"You mean one that people watch?" Victor lets out a high-pitched giggle.

"It's a terrific format," Kira adds. "And it's exactly what our division needs—a massive hit."

I fold my arms across my chest. "So, what happens after the first season, when I've picked a wife? Is my career finished?"

Dylan empties her can of Red Bull. "Of course not! You and your wife become hosts of the show and we have new contestants on every season."

"Nope. Sorry. I know you've put a lot of work into this ... research and everything ... but I can't do it."

"Yeah, but here's the thing," Victor says, scratching his head. "According to your contract, you will do it or you'll get fired and we'll sue you for breach of contract."

Kira makes a clicking sound with her tongue. "Oooh, that would bad."

I turn and glare at Dwight, waiting for him to say something, but he's fully engrossed in opening a new package of antacids. I clear my throat and stare at him until he finally makes eye contact.

"Uh, okay," he says finally. "What if we tweak it a bit? Have one female co-host and go for the 'will they or won't they' vibe?"

Dylan slams her hand on the table and shouts, "Yes! That! Love it! Love the creative flow in the room right now. We pick one gorgeous woman and set you two loose in the forest … or wherever."

Victor nods enthusiastically. "I've never met anyone as positive as you, Dylan. You say yes to everything."

"Thanks," she says with a wink. "That's my motto, actually."

Kira looks down the table at me. "You should really take a page out of her book, Will. Be a little more open to new ideas."

"Take some risks in your young life!" Dylan says with a grin.

I stare at her for a moment, trying to process what is happening. I'm totally fucked. That's what's happening. "I don't want to sound difficult here, but what I do is legitimately dangerous. You can't just bring in someone with no survival experience and no … physical strength or stamina. It would be extremely reckless."

"Of course we would never risk anyone's life," Kira adds. "We'll make sure everything is completely safe."

"Absolutely!" Dylan adds. "Safety first. That's my motto."

"I thought it was …" I start, then give up.

"I can make this work," she says. "Trust me. I'll find the perfect woman and the perfect situation to put you two in. It's going to be *epic*. The build-up to the show will be *beyond incredible*. By the time it airs, Will Banks will grace the cover of *People* magazine on their Sexiest Man Alive edition."

Dwight nods. "I think I speak for both Will and myself when I say how exciting this is. Truly a great opportunity for him."

"Right?" Dylan asks. "Isn't this what he deserves? To be at the top of the unscripted heap for years to come?"

"He certainly does."

"He's got what it takes."

"But, I don't—"

"Now, don't you dare be modest, young man!" Dylan clap her hands along with her words, shouting, "You. Are. A. Star." She holds her hands together and says, "You just don't know it yet."

5

Whiny Princesses and the People Who Love Them...

Arabella

"Oh, bugger," I say, staring at my mobile phone screen at a Google alert concerning me. It's an article about the eerie resemblance I bear to my dead mother, Queen Cecily. "I should've known they wouldn't let this anniversary pass us by without pouring salt on the wound."

Arthur, who clearly just got the same alert as me, says, "Bastards."

"I'm sorry, hon," Tessa says, patting me on the knee.

We're in the back of the limo, waiting for Gran, who, in spite of being in her eighties, insists on wearing high heels to every event. I swear she does this just to get the bodyguards to hold her arm wherever she goes. Gran has a thing for strapping younger men with guns. Anyway, we're on our way to the wedding of the season at which I'm supposed to be hunting down the dull men from the dossiers so I can be the bride at the biggest wedding *next* season. Spoiler alert: I'm not going to look for any of them, and if one of them does somehow approach me, I'm going to brush him off like a piece of lint on a pair of black pants. I'm not in the mood for love.

The truth is, I was already fuming before this article came out. I'm still raw about not being allowed to become the ambassador for the Equal Everywhere campaign. Also, now that I've been told I can't wear my non-existent red dress, it's all I want to wear. Instead, I'm in a chiffon robin's egg blue gown with a modest (read boring) boat neck. I've paired it with extremely dull two-inch beige heels. *Oooh, beige. Who's the sex cat now?*

But it honestly won't matter what I'm wearing because all that will matter is this stupid article. "Why couldn't they have released this a few hours from now?" I sigh. "Now all I'm going to hear about for the rest of the day is how I'm the reincarnation of my mother. As if I don't get that enough."

Gran slides into the limo wearing a sparkling gold Dior dress. She's so tiny that if she wears anything drab, people barely know she's there and if there's one thing Gran likes, it's for people to know when she's arrived. She settles herself in, then looks at me and narrows her eyes. "What's up your royal tush today?"

"Nothing. I'm absolutely thrilled to be attending yet

another function with my foulmouthed, feisty grandmother as my plus one."

"You should be thanking me. I turned down several offers just so you wouldn't have to go alone," she says.

"Of course you did," I say, feeling like even more of a loser than I did when I woke up this morning.

"Go easy on her, Gran. The media is making quite a fuss about what would've been our mother's fiftieth birthday." Arthur shoots her a look that says our little Arabella can't handle any type of criticism. I know he's doing it to be nice, but it irritates the living shit out of me.

"Don't patronize her," Gran says. "It's the last thing she needs."

I'm about to thank her when she adds this little gem. "She'll always be a baby if you treat her like one."

"Thanks for that," I say.

"You're most welcome."

"I was being sarcastic. Just because I resemble her, everyone assumes I can't handle more than some weak tea and light conversation."

"Oh, sweetie," Gran says, patting me on the hand. "Is that what you believe?"

"Yes. And to be honest, I'm sick to death of being ordered around and underestimated by everyone." I give Arthur a dirty look. "Including you."

"Arabella," Gran begins in a tone that says I'm about to be subjected to her off-the-cuff wisdom. "If you don't like being ordered around, underestimated, and compared to your mother, do something about it."

"And exactly what am I supposed to do? Die my hair black or get a 'Not Cecily' tattoo on my face?"

"You needn't go to that much trouble," she says. "You only need to stop being so very unremarkable."

I slump down in my seat, and turn to face the window, blinking the tears back.

"Gran, that was offside, even for you," Arthur says quietly. "You should apologize."

"And you should not make a habit of telling me what to do," Gran answers.

An uncomfortable silence fills the limo as we cross the river to the city. In a few minutes, we'll reach the church, where I'll be repeatedly asked if I've seen the article and told how the resemblance between my mother and I is absolutely uncanny—spooky even. They'll stare at me, leaning in with wide eyes and shaking their heads in disbelief. "I've never noticed." "Oh, I have. I've always thought she looks exactly like her mother." Perhaps I should get my own booth at a freak show.

"Arthur's man crush is going to be at the wedding today," Tessa says suddenly. She's clearly trying to brighten the mood in the car by embarrassing my brother. I love her for it, but I'm not up for making fun of him today.

"I don't have a crush on him," he says. "I merely enjoy watching his show."

44

"It's a man crush, dear. Deal with it." Turning to me, she says, "Have you seen *The Wild World* with Will Banks?"

I shake my head.

"Oh, you'd love it. Will is like David Attenborough meets Chris Pratt from *Jurassic World,* except picture him with his body from *Guardians of the Galaxy.*"

Arthur scoffs. "If anyone in this limo has a crush on Will Banks, I'd say it's my wife."

"I'm just painting an accurate picture for Arabella. Besides, *I'm* not the one who is going to make a beeline for him the moment the ceremony ends—unlike you," Tessa says, giving Arthur a teasing smile. She snaps her fingers together suddenly and says, "Oh! You should take Arabella with you so she can meet him."

Turning to me, she whispers, "He's a total hottie."

"Yes, well, as much of a hottie as he is, I don't see a future between someone like him and my sister, thank you very much," Arthur says.

"Who said anything about a future?" Tessa asks. "I just think she could use a good shag to cheer her up."

Arthur stiffens visibly. "Perhaps I should ride up front so as to skip out on the horrifying girl talk."

"Oh, suck it up, Princess," Gran says to him. "Your sister is an adult who can shag whomever she wants."

"I doubt he'd want to shag someone as unremarkable as me," I grumble, giving Gran a glare.

"Oh, Christ, you're not going to pout all day, are you?"

she asks. "Because if so, I really will call one of my many man friends and offer him the position of my date."

"Go ahead. I'd rather be alone than stuck with someone who feels the need to pile on when I'm already having a shit day."

We pull up in front of the church, and a moment later, the back door opens. Tessa gives Arthur the 'they need to talk' face and gestures toward the door with her head.

Clearing his throat, Arthur says, "We'll see you inside."

When they get out, I hear Arthur tell his driver, Ben, to close the door and that we'll need a minute.

When Gran and I are alone, she scooches closer to me on the cream-colored leather bench. Taking my hand in hers, she says, "You are Arabella Florence…a bunch of names I can't remember, Duchess of Bainbridge, Princess of Avonia. You are a sensitive, kind, beautiful, and intelligent young woman. But you're also a total pussy—"

My mouth drops open and she holds up one hand to stop me from interrupting. "—which is not entirely your fault. It's a bit of a vicious circle because people have always treated you like you're made of porcelain, so that is how you act. Yes, half of your genes are from your mother who was as weak as a kitten, but half are from your father. And that means you have more than a little bit of *me* in you. And I'm tough as balls."

I chuckle in spite of myself.

"And I know that deep, deep, deep, *deep* down inside of you is a very strong woman just dying to come out."

"I don't know if that's true," I say, shaking my head.

"You won't know until you test it out. So, my advice is for you to take a risk. Anything at all. The next big thing that comes your way. Don't think about it. Just do it. Give them something more to write about than your good looks."

"Like what?"

"Doesn't matter, really. Just pick something wild and go for it."

"I can't … what if I'm a disaster?"

"Then you'll be Arabella the disaster, which in my books is far better than Arabella the clone. Be bold, child." She stares deep into my eyes, then shrugs. "Or continue to be a timid, cowardly girl. Just pick one and stick with it. And whatever you do, stop complaining, because if there's one thing that can't be tolerated in this world, it's a princess who feels sorry for herself."

With that, she knocks on the window. The door opens and Ben helps her out, leaving me there to marinate in her bitter medicine.

6

Double-Fisting Booze and Mystery Beauties

Will

I AM NEVER GOING to do this, as long as I live. That is a guarantee you can take to the bank, too, because after being part of my sister's wedding fiasco, I can say with certainty it's not worth it. It's been a steady stream of dinners, cocktail parties, 'pre-wedding gift openings,' tux fittings, and don't even get me started on the dress rehearsal last night.

Today, I'm wearing a horribly restrictive rented monkey suit. It's got these stupid tails on the jacket and I feel like a complete idiot with this ridiculous top hat on. I'm standing at the front of the church as the fourth groomsman, along with Pierce's best man, who is also his editor, and his brothers, Leo (a great guy), and Grayson (a total wanker). Harrison isn't one of the groomsmen but that's only because Emma has asked him to walk her down the aisle.

The truth is, a big wedding like this only makes the three of us more keenly aware of the loss of our parents, and I know that part of Emma's sour mood has been the absence of our loving mum and dad to see her through what is likely the most stressful time of her life.

Harrison has had his own troubles to deal with since we got here. Their daughter Clara has a wicked cold and I'm not sure how familiar you are with toddlers, but it turns out they do *not* know how to wipe their noses (or even have any aware-ness that they have number elevens hanging from their tiny noses to their top lips). Also, this church is the exact one at which Libby was jilted a few years ago, so even though Libby is most certainly madly in love with my brother, the building itself does hold some rather humiliating memories for her. And since, as Emma's maid of honor, she's trying to take all the strain off the bride's shoulders today, she's more on edge than I've ever seen her. Libby also has the strange affliction of suffering from stress nosebleeds. When I left the vestibule a few minutes ago, she was well into her second box of tissues.

How can it be worth it to go through any of this? Seriously?

This is why I'm never getting married. And if I somehow did get tricked into proposing, my wedding would be a simple affair on a beach somewhere, or maybe at city hall.

I shift restlessly from foot to foot, wishing this day would be over so I can have some time to figure out what to do about my career, which is about to go up in flames. Dylan has been sending me head shots of potential co-hosts with subject lines like 'Would you do her?' in an attempt to create a show rife with sexual tension. So far, I have yet to respond to any of them, even though I know Dylan is not the type to give up.

I look around the crowded church, my eyes landing on the pews on which the cast of NBO's *Clash of Crowns* are seated. Then a wide smile crosses my face because I realize that the man sitting at the end is the network COO, and this will be the perfect opportunity to schmooze him into creating a show with yours truly sans the sexy co-host.

My mobile phone buzzes in my inside pocket of my rented suit. I pull it out as discreetly as possible only to see it's a text from Dwight. *Don't even think about trying to jump ship to NBO. You will be sued.*

Bugger, how the hell did he know?

I glance up, only to be on the receiving end of a sharp glare from Rosy, my surrogate mum. I slide my phone back into my pocket and give her a guilty smile. She shakes her head at me with pursed lips, but her eyes are still twinkling for her favourite child.

The fifteen-member musical ensemble starts playing "Trumpet Voluntary" and the back doors of the chapel swing open, flooding the space with sunlight. Moments later, the procession of adorable flower girls, lovely bridesmaids, and my sister begins. Thank God this will all be over soon. I tug at my tie, wishing I were scuba diving with tiger sharks or scrubbing barnacles off the bottom of one of the resort's catamarans. Anything is better than wearing a double Windsor knot.

Come on, ladies, hightail it up here so we can get to the part with the open bar already.

Finally, Emma and Harrison come into the church. Well, what do you know? Emma looks beautiful—all teary eyed and smiling as they make their way toward us.

Pierce sucks in a long breath, and when I glance at him, the look on his face stuns me. It's like he's been hit by a truck, only it's the sight of Emma, my grumpy big sister, who's done this to him. I swear he could be knocked on his arse by the slightest flick right now. I look back at Emma and I feel ... almost ... emotional. Maybe this wouldn't be the worst thing in the world to do.

Okay, I'm clearly suffering from jetlag. Or maybe it's the stress from my work situation.

The minutes crawl by like a super-high three-toed sloth. Finally, we get to the vows, which if memory serves from the rehearsal, means we're almost at the end. The minister smiles at my sister and Pierce. "The happy couple has written their own vows and Pierce is going to go first. This gives Emma the advantage because if his aren't good enough, she can still back out."

The crowd chuckles, then when the room grows silent, Pierce takes a deep breath, looking nervous. "Emma, when I think of who I was before you, I have nothing but pity for that lonely, pathetic man hiding from love and life. I never thought I would have what I have with you, which is the perfection that comes with a full life and a happy home. I wish I could say that when I first laid eyes on you I knew, but that would mean I was a much smarter man than I am. A lot of people here probably think that it was your culinary skills that won me over. But it was your beautiful, fierce spirit. There is no other woman like you—one who can hop into a speedboat, drive it out into the middle of the sea, cut the engine, and dive into the water, only to come up with a pair of live lobsters in your bare hands. Then come back to shore and cook them up as part of a four-course meal."

He smiles and pauses for a second while the two gaze into each other's eyes. Seriously? Can you save the gazing for the next fifty years?

"I wish the first time I saw you do that I'd known, but again, not that bright. It took me another few weeks to realize exactly how truly extraordinary you are, and even then, I wasted months before I could finally admit the truth—that I was completely and utterly in love with you.

"You have filled my life with the adventure that I only used to know in my imagination. Every day with you is something new, something fresh, something free, and something wonderful. And I stand before everyone we know today to promise that I will spend the rest of my life trying to be good enough for you. Emma Josephine Banks, I promise to love and care for you, I promise to be your partner, to support you in your dreams and hopes, and to lift you up when you are down. I promise to be faithful to you and not just because you would kick my ass if I wasn't, but because I don't want anyone else. You are the only woman I will ever love. You are the only one who really knows me. You have given me the greatest gift I can imagine—you've given me a home."

Well, that doesn't sound as bad as I thought it would. Mind you, he is a talented writer so he could probably make rolling around in pig shit sound appealing. Marriage is definitely not for me, but I'm glad they're happy.

————

I've been a very good groomsman. I've smiled for all the photos. I laughed through the many toasts and I've done a bang-up job of pretending life couldn't be better for me all day, even though there is a boulder of worry lodged in my chest. And now, it's time for me to get piss-stinking drunk.

The trick with over-imbibing at a wedding is to make it look like you're carrying drinks for other people. In this case, four flutes of champagne from the champagne fountain. Two could still possibly look like I'm going to drink them myself, but four seems far too ridiculous for anyone to suspect me of what I'm actually doing, which is filling them, then carrying them through the hotel ballroom with a purposeful look on my face, stopping periodically to down one and leave the glass.

I'm just filling up the last flute when I hear a woman's voice behind me. "Rough day?"

Glancing over my shoulder, I see a lovely blonde in a blue gown. Her hair is up in some sort of complicated fancy do, and she has the most mesmerizing light blue eyes I think I've ever seen.

My jaw goes slack for an instant before I pull myself together. "These aren't all for me."

Taking one from my hand, she says, "Sure they're not. I saw you earlier crossing the room with your first four glasses. Excellent trick. No one would ever imagine someone making such a pig of himself."

"No offense, though, right?" I say, tipping back my glass and downing it. I set the glass down and hold my right hand out. "Will Banks."

She shakes my hand even though she seems like the type of woman who's more used to men kissing her knuckles lightly. "Yes, I know who you are."

I blush a little and get that slightly squishy feeling that comes along with being sort of famous. "Right, sorry, it's hard for me to wrap my head around people knowing who I am everywhere I go."

"Occupational hazard, I guess," she says with a grin.

"And what are the hazards of your occupation?" I ask. *Oooh, that was pretty smooth, if I do say so myself.*

She stares at me for a second, then says, "It's a bit difficult to put a finger on it, but I suppose you could say I'm in public relations."

"I'll try not to hate you for it," I say with a wink.

"I'm assuming there's some sort of delicious backstory to that comment. Perhaps something that requires eight glasses of champagne to forget."

"Something like that." I watch, thoroughly engrossed as she takes a dainty sip. "Not that I'd ever complain, because believe me, I know how lucky I am to be doing the work I do, but there are aspects of it I could do without."

She nods, a look of understanding crossing her face that makes me want to continue the conversation. I stare at her for a moment and can't help but feel like she's somehow familiar. "Have we met before?"

"No."

"Are you sure?"

"You'd remember me," she says with a little smile.

"Ha! Good one," I say, having a swig of my drink. "Did you enjoy the wedding?"

"It was quite lovely."

"Whose side are you on? The bride or the groom?"

"The groom," she says. "He's a friend of my older brother."

"Your brother must be quite the person. Pierce is very selective with who he allows in his inner circle."

"Yes, you could say that." She glances around, then looks back at me. "What about you? Are you a fan of weddings in general?"

"For other people. You?"

"Agreed. Marriage is definitely not for me."

"So, it's a life of public relations for you, is it?"

"It's what I was born to do."

"Well, I hope whoever you work for, they're good to you—not all stuffy like this lot. All the wannabe royals thinking they're so very important when the truth is nobody outside this ballroom knows who they are, and if they did, they wouldn't care."

"Or worse, the *actual* royals," she says with a knowing look.

"God, yes. What a useless existence that would be. I mean, they're not even in charge of anything *real* anymore. It's just a whole life of pomp and ceremony."

"Pathetic, right?" she answers, rolling her eyes.

"I actually heard someone earlier saying they feel sorry for them."

"Absurd."

"Yeah, honestly. They went on and on about how hard it would be to live in the spotlight your entire life." I take a sip of my drink. "As someone with a bit of fame, I can tell you, there's very little to complain about."

"Well, of course there wouldn't be anything to whine about. Not with all the perks and privileges."

"Exactly. If they want to do something hard, they should get dropped off in Siberia in the dead of winter and try to survive for a week without their chefs and maids and heated toilet seats."

"Ha!" she says. *God, I like her. She gets me. I wonder if she'd be up for a shag?*

"They'd be calling for a helicopter in under an hour, I can guarantee it."

"Probably even less," she agrees, giving me a conspiratorial look.

I glance down at her full lips, then lower my voice. "Say, you wouldn't want to get out of here, would you? Somewhere not quite so stuffy."

She leans in close enough that I can smell her perfume. I have no idea what it is, but it smells like money. She must do really well for herself in the public relations biz. "Somewhere that I could let my hair down and we could get to know each other better."

This is actually going to happen, isn't it? I nod. "Exactly."

She opens her mouth, but before she can answer, an older man in a grey suit taps her on the shoulder. "Princess Arabella, delightful to see you again. My wife and I would love to talk to you about a foundation we're starting for homeless birds."

Shit. Shit. Shit. Shock vibrates through me as my words about her family echo through my brain. *Pomp and ceremony. Not in charge of anything real anymore.* I am *so* not getting lucky tonight. I give her a sheepish look, wishing I could think of a clever way to make it all better, but I've got nothing. Just embarrassment and regret. "So … you're … I did not … I am so …"

"I am, I know you didn't, and I'm sure you are," Princess Arabella says with an amused smile. "Lovely to meet you, Mr. Banks." She holds up her glass to me. "But I'm afraid it's time to get back to my useless existence."

7

Maybe Being a Princess Isn't the Worst Thing in the World ...

Arabella

"GOOD NIGHT, GRAN." I kiss her on the cheek. It's late in the evening and we're standing at the door to her apartment. "Have a good rest."

"I'm not going to bed," she says, looking slightly disgusted. "I'm going to get into my lucky pantsuit. It's poker night."

"Right. Of course it is," I say with a smile. "I hope I have as much fun as you when I'm ... slightly older."

"I highly doubt it. You're not even thirty and you don't have it now." She pats me on the cheek. "Would you like to come with me? It's a $500 buy-in, and the guys down in the garage are a real hoot. You'd love them."

"Thank you, but I'm afraid I have the world's worst poker face. You'd clean me out in under an hour."

Gran grins up at me. "Don't be silly, dear. I'd clean you out much faster than that."

"Thanks."

"Anytime, dear." She opens the door to her apartment and steps inside. When she turns to shut it, she says, "I'm just teasing, of course. But I want you to think about what I said today. Make your own way in this world."

"I will, Gran."

"Promise me you'll take the next big risk that comes your way. Just do it without thinking. Have a little fun in your young life."

"I'll try."

"You can do better than that."

—————

When I get back to my apartment, the smell of lavender tickles my nostrils. The lights have been dimmed by Delilah, my weekend maid, and I know she has drawn me a bath and prepared some chamomile tea to help me unwind. The moment we left the reception, our driver would have called the head butler who notifies the rest of the staff.

I undress and step into the enormous white tub. As I sink into the hot water, I suddenly feel silly about all my whining. This life comes with some wonderful perks. Like this moment, right now.

I lay my head back against the bath pillow and close my eyes, but instead of feeling relaxed, I find myself feeling slightly tipsy and very restless. I smile and touch my lips with one finger as I think about my conversation with Will Banks. I definitely channeled Gran in my saucy responses to him. And the look of horror on his face when he realized who I was—priceless. I let out a laugh at the memory. I can see why Arthur has a man crush on him—he's positively dreamy. The way all those muscles filled in that tuxedo, that strong jawline, and his gorgeous eyes the color of perfectly brewed coffee. Devastatingly dreamy. Sigh …

I wonder what kind of woman he would want. Probably someone totally kickass like his sister—although not *exactly* like his sister because that would be eww. But someone adventurous, I'm sure, and brave, like the wife of the late Crocodile Hunter. Now those two were a great match. Will needs to find his Terri.

Although he was certainly attracted to me, wasn't he? He obviously wanted to sleep with me. But that was before he knew who I was. He probably thought I was some super fun woman who goes rock climbing on the weekends, then showers and goes out clubbing all night. Now that he knows the truth, he wouldn't be interested at all.

I slap the water with both hands and watch as it ripples to the end of the tub, then comes back. Why couldn't I be Terri Irwin instead of boring old me?

I try to picture myself grappling up a mountainside, but even in my mind, I slip and plummet to the earth below. I'm not now and never will be the cool, adventurous type, so I might as well forget all about Mr. Tall, Dark and Daring. I sink deeper into the water, trying to find something else to fill my mind.

I end up thinking about Pierce and his vows to Emma. The look on her face is burned into my mind—she seemed so sure it's all going to work out. Like absolutely positive, as though their love is an undeniable fact. And all those things Pierce said about her driving a speedboat and diving into the ocean to catch lobsters with her bare hands? My heavens! I can't even imagine doing that. But, that's the kind of woman men want—daring and fun and carefree. Someone who owns a bikini and has a killer serve. I'm like a middle-aged woman with a boring wardrobe and the world's most boring personality to match. Which is why I have to forget all about Will Banks immediately.

His gorgeous face pops back into my mind. Oh, who am I kidding? I can't forget about him this fast. I'll need at least a few days of fantasizing first. I dry my hands and pluck my mobile phone off the side of the tub, then Google Will Banks. Mmm … there's an entire website devoted to his show called *Will's Wild Fangirls*. They have a most comprehensive photo album of his greatest hits—and by that, I mean a bunch of pictures of him with no shirt on. Yum. I wouldn't kick him off the throne for eating crackers. When I get to the end of the photos, I reach the blog section. Let's see what his stalker has to say.

ABN Searching for Wild World Co-host

.   .   .

Hello fellow fangirls,

I am not sure whether I'm happy or devastated to bring this news, but it seems as though the geniuses over at ABN have decided to add a female co-host to The Wild World *for season three (which is set to start filming in the next few weeks). I'd be thrilled if they chose me—and believe me, I was likely the first person to apply. I'll be wrecked if they don't pick me, opting for some skanky ho instead.*

My sources at ABN tell me they're looking for someone to help spice up the format a bit, although if you ask me, Will alone is spicy enough for this blogger. Applications will be open for another three days, but don't even think about applying because this is my destiny. Seriously, don't bother because this one's mine, ladies.

Peace Out Bitches,

The Future Mrs. Will Banks

"Well, Gran, I think I may have just found a big risk to which I'll say yes," I mutter. "And to you, the future Ms. Jailbird Stalker, you're about to have one more skanky ho with whom to compete." Although I don't know how many skanky hos use phrases like 'with whom.' Whatever. I'm going for it.

No, I shouldn't. That's insane. And I'm drunk.

I put my phone down and slide under the water until the top of my head is soaked. *But, I did promise Gran, didn't I?*

And it would be very wrong of me to break a promise.

Sitting up, I pat my hands and face dry with my towel, then grab my phone again. I search my contacts and text Kira

Taylor, one of the directors of unscripted television and a fellow board member of Avonian Women in The Arts.

Kira, I'm looking to shake things up a little. Have you found a co-host for Will Banks yet?

It doesn't take more than twenty seconds for me to get a reply. *Are you serious? Because if you're serious, the job is yours.*

I grin and duck under the water to scream like an excited Julia Roberts as *Pretty Woman*.

What can I say? Royalty has its privileges.

8

A Flurry of Uninformative Information

Will

EMAIL TO WILL BANKS CC. Dwight Anderson, Victor Petty, Kira Taylor, Toshiro Fukuhara, Callum MacKenzie
From: Dylan Sinclair
Subject Line: INCREDIBLE NEWS - TOP SECRET!!!

Good Morning All!
I have what is quite possibly the most epically amazing news you will ever receive. Last night, we snagged one of the biggest celebrities in the entire kingdom for the show. The contract has been signed and she's good to go! In the interest of great television, I am not sharing her identity with you because the big reveal is a thrilling moment that needs to be

caught on film. Suffice it to say, you are going to flip when you find out who I've managed to secure.

She's so big, we may need to alter the name of the show—but I won't tell you what I'm thinking of just yet because it will spoil the surprise.

Here's our new format:

1) We pick you up and zip you to the airport where you will fly to an undisclosed location. You take nothing with you (other than your enthusiasm).

2) You will then meet your co-host—on film.

3) We reveal the new rules of the show.

4) The two of you hop into a waiting helicopter that will drop you into the wilderness fitted with GoPros.

5) You two work together to find your way back to civilization using only the tools and equipment provided.

Since I've also managed to get an incredible advertising deal from GoPro, this show is making money and we haven't even started yet. See? Thrilling, right?

Also, the new format sidesteps that little issue of me having no directing experience. As I got farther along in the Ron Howard Master Class, I realized there may be more to the whole thing than I thought. There will be extensive post-production work in editing, etc., but not to worry because there is literally no way this plan can fail. We'll only need Tosh and Mac at the first location, then they'll wait in town to film you when you arrive. It'll just be Will, our gorgeously fabulous celebrity, and your wits.

Let the games begin!

Dylan

P.S. A car will pick you up next Friday at six a.m. sharp to take you to the airport. Make sure you don't shave.

———

Text from me to Dwight: *Please call me immediately regarding Dylan's ridiculous plan.*

Dwight: *In an important client meeting at the moment. The answers to your questions are as follows: 1) No, you can't, 2) Yes, you must, 3) There is no such clause, and, 4) Don't even think about it if you want to have a career beyond today.*

———

Email to Dylan Sinclair, cc. Dwight Anderson, Victor Petty, Kira Taylor, Toshiro Fukuhara, Callum MacKenzie
From: Will Banks

Subject Line: RE: INCREDIBLE NEWS - TOP SECRET!!!

Dylan,

· · ·

Thanks for your enthusiasm about this project. However, I do have a few major concerns.

1) For obvious safety reasons, I require an in-depth knowledge of where we're going, including which plants are edible vs. poisonous, what types of dangerous animals we'll be facing, etc.

2) I cannot in good conscience take an inexperienced person out into the wilderness unprepared. That would put both our lives at risk, and I'm not sure, but I'd guess that one or both of us dying won't make for great television. Maybe Victor and/or Kira can comment on that.

Regards,
Will

———

Email to Will Banks, cc. Dwight Anderson, Victor Petty, Kira Taylor, Toshiro Fukuhara, Callum MacKenzie
    From: Dylan Sinclair

Subject Line: RE: RE: INCREDIBLE NEWS - TOP SECRET!!!

Will,

You are SO right. Death does not make for good reality television. It would totally 'kill' the sex vibe we're going for. Also, we'd NEVER put your lives at risk! Trust me when I say any and all safety precautions have been taken. We'll be using a location you're personally familiar with, so not to worry.

You'll be given all the supplies needed to survive in this environment. Even though your co-host doesn't have a great deal of experience in the wilderness, she's had years of managing difficult situations. Trust me, nothing can possibly go wrong.

Ciao,

Dylan

———

Email to Will Banks, cc. Dwight Anderson, Kira Taylor, Toshiro Fukuhara, Callum MacKenzie, Dylan Sinclair

From: Victor Petty

Subject Line: RE: RE: RE: INCREDIBLE NEWS - TOP SECRET!!

Will,

To reiterate what Dylan is saying, we at ABN would never put any of our employees' lives at risk. We're committed to upholding the highest safety and wellness standards for every member of the ABN family, so please relax and enjoy this new adventure.

We've got you covered,

Victor

———

Text from Dwight to me: *Sounds like they've got it all under control. Have a wonderful trip!*

Me: *You better hope they do because you won't make any money from my corpse.*

9

Awful P.R. People and the Princesses Who Hate Them

Arabella

IT'S TUESDAY MORNING. Gran and I are having an early breakfast in the warmth of the solarium before we both begin our various functions for the rest of the day. The servers have finally left so we can speak freely among the lush, exotic greenery. Since Saturday night, I've been waiting for the perfect opportunity to tell her about my gargantuan secret, needing us to be completely alone and for her to be in a mood that lends itself to helping her youngest grandchild. And if there's anything that puts Gran in a generous frame of mind, it's eggs Benedict day. It's her favourite meal, but since her heart attack, she can only eat it once a month. Lucky for me, today is that day.

I wait until she's had a few bites and her face has settled

into a satisfied bliss before I speak up. "Gran, remember the other day when you told me to make this life my own and to take the next big risk that comes my way?"

Raising one eyebrow, Gran puts down her fork and knife. "What did you do?"

Oh dear. The raised eyebrow is never a good sign. "Before I tell you I need you to promise you won't say a word to Father—or anyone else, for that matter."

"I'll make no such promise."

"Fine." I shrug as though the conversation is over, then slice into a strawberry and take a small bite.

"If you don't tell me, I'll go straight to your father and let him know you're keeping a secret that will likely prove to be catastrophic."

I'm about to say, 'you wouldn't,' when I realize she most certainly would. I let out a sigh. "Do you remember that Will Banks fellow at the wedding? The one Tessa was teasing Arthur about?"

"The James Bond-esque man you were shamelessly flirting with at the champagne fountain?"

"I wasn't flirting," I say, feeling my cheeks warm. "And even if I was flirting a little, I would never do so in a shameless manner."

"You absolutely were. Now, out with it. What did you do?"

"You'll recall Mr. Banks hosts a nature documentary, and I thought it might be exciting to serve as a … co-host." I pop a tiny piece of honeydew into my mouth and attempt to chew it casually. "I think it would be a real confidence boost, which is exactly what you said I needed—an opportunity to spread my wings and test my mettle."

Sitting back in her chair, Gran runs her tongue over her front teeth. "Are you insane? You know you're not permitted to hold a job."

"What if all the money goes directly to charity?" I take a sip of tea. "In that case, it's not a job, but a charitable act— and a considerable one at that, I might add."

"As fun as that sounds, and as attractive as Mr. Banks is, this is entirely out of the question. There is no way the powers that be will allow it."

"Yes, I know," I say, my heart pounding in my chest. "That's why I already signed the contract."

Gran's jaw drops, and she stares at me. For what may be the first time in her eighty-seven years, she seems speechless.

"I leave on Thursday for filming in a secret location. I'll be gone for a week, maybe two, then I'll come home and get back to business as usual, only I'll have shown the world I'm not nearly as soft as they believe me to be."

"A secret location? What is that supposed to mean?"

"Somewhere secret," I answer.

"Where? Here in Avonia?"

"I don't think so. The show generally films in rather … remote places like Antarctica or the Amazon rainforest."

Tilting her head, she says, "So, you're expecting to up and disappear *in two days*? Just wipe your schedule of everything, leaving all those foundations in the lurch—with no notice—so you can go off gallivanting in the wilderness with some man we don't know from Adam."

"I'm sure it can all be sorted out. Tessa and Arthur could each take on a few of my events … and I thought you might be willing to help, since this was your idea in the first place."

"It most certainly was not! I meant paint your nails dark green or … or wear three-inch heels and see if you can get away with it. Not go live out in the wilderness somewhere eating bugs and trekking through swamp-infested, disease-ridden forests and contract malaria while simultaneously humiliating the family."

"Oh." My shoulders drop. "I thought you meant a real risk."

"Well for you, green nail polish *would've been* a real risk. You're quite possibly the most sheltered and conservative person I've ever met. Why would you even consider this?"

He's cute. And he made me laugh. "You told me to do something big."

Pursing her lips, Gran says, "Do you mean some*one* big?"

"Gran!"

"Oh please. Tell me the thought didn't cross your mind. He's hot as hell."

"Is he?" I shrug, picking up my teacup. "I hadn't noticed."

"Right, and I've just been chosen to be the next team captain for Valcourt United."

Rolling my eyes, I sigh. "It doesn't matter how handsome he is because I'm not looking for love. I'm looking for adventure, for some freedom for a change." I pick at my mushroom galette with my fork, suddenly feeling full. "Besides, I'd never be interested in some man who fancies himself to be Tarzan and goes around eating grubs like they're popping corn. This is about proving myself to the family and showing that I can handle difficult challenges and …"

"… And seeing what Tarzan has under his loincloth."

I sit back in my chair and lift my chin. "Since you seem to fancy him so much, maybe *you* should do the show."

"It's not the *show* I'd want to do. Besides, with my heart condition, I suppose I'll have to leave him for you. Although, that would be quite a nice way to go out …"

I laugh and shake my head. "You're terrible."

"I'm honest," she says, picking up her fork and knife again. "And to be honest, this is without a doubt the worst idea you've ever had. Call the producer and back out. Tell them you're not allowed and that it would be an unmitigated disaster for your family—which it would be, by the way."

Disappointment creeps up from my toes to my throat. "You're right. I'll call them and cancel it."

"Good girl. We'll think of a more suitable opportunity for you to test yourself. Something that doesn't involve eating bugs or getting killed."

———

I stare at my phone, dreading what I'm about to do. I have to call Dylan Sinclair, one of the most awful human beings on the planet. She worked for my family for a time, making

Tessa's life a living hell before moving on to torture her next victim. Somehow, she must have squirmed her way in at ABN and managed to get herself hired as a showrunner.

If I had known she was on this project, I *never* would have agreed to it. When I called Kira to say I needed to get out of the contract, she told me I'd have to deal with Dylan directly. So that's what I guess I'll do. Misery weighs me down until even the tiny act of pressing send on my mobile feels difficult.

"This is Dylan. How can I improve your day?"

Blech. "Dylan, hello. It's Princess Arabella."

"Your Highness, hello! I was just about to call you. Everything is on schedule for us to leave Thursday morning," she says, speaking so fast I can barely process her words. "I was absolutely thrilled to discover you were going to be our co-host. Beyond thrilled actually. I literally jumped for joy and spilled my energy drink all over myself." She laughs, then quickly continues. "This is going to be epic. No, bigger than epic. I don't even have a word for it."

"Yes, here's the thing—"

"—You were always one of my favourite royals when I worked for your family. You're just so lovely—you're like if Grace Kelly and your mother had a child."

"Thank you." I think. "But—"

"You are the perfect foil for Will. Elegant and refined princess meets wild, ruggedly handsome outdoorsman. It'll be the greatest 'will they or won't they' of all time!"

"About that. As it turns out, they won't be."

She laughs. "Yes! Perfect. The more you try to resist, the more the delicious sexual tension is going to build!"

"That's not what I meant. I meant I won't be able to co-host the show after all. I'm extremely sorry, but after some thought, I realize I'll never be given permission to do—"

"Do *not* finish that sentence. No need. Who's the fly in the ointment, Your Highness? It's that Phillip Crawford, your father's senior advisor, isn't it? He's such a stick in the mud. Let me talk to the king. Winston loves me. I can get him to say yes to anything."

I don't even want to know what that means. "It's … well … I'm afraid it's not going to happen, and you won't be able to convince him. Again, I apologize for wasting your time."

"You haven't wasted my time," she says in an airy voice.

"I haven't?"

"No, my dear, of course not. Because you're *doing* the show and it'll turn out beautifully."

"It will?"

"Yes, of course. Much better than if you try to back out, and your family's sued for millions of dollars, and your People for Animals foundation loses out on all that sweet network cash."

Bollocks.

"I know they'll be reluctant to let you go, but there's an *easy* way around it. Instead of asking for permission, you just go, then later, when you've made all that money for your charity, proved yourself to be a fierce and amazing nature-lover, and made your family proud, they'll forgive all."

"I don't think they'll see it like that."

"Of course they will! Think of how you'll raise your family's profile! They'll be thrilled. Absolutely thrilled. This will be *the best thing* to happen to the Langdons since the birth of those adorable babies," she says. "*So much better* than being sued. Your family has been scandal-free for nearly two years, and I know you do not want to be the one to break that streak. Especially since the last time you made headlines it was for kicking a one-legged man off a bar and causing him massive injuries."

"I'm not actually the one who—"

"Doesn't matter. What matters is that people remember you were involved and that you nearly caused a trade war between Spain and Avonia. Don't be the royal nightmare. It'll do irreparable harm to your family."

My entire body feels heavy with despair. "I would never want to hurt my family."

"Exactly. And as much *doing* the show will create quite a stir, it'll be infinitely better than backing out and hurting the good people of the Avonian Broadcast Network, which, incidentally, is the largest news and entertainment company in the kingdom."

"Right."

"Right. So, all you have to do is find a way to sneak out and get to the airport where a private jet will be waiting. Easy peasy lemon squeezy!"

———

I'm now in my apartment. It's late on Wednesday night, and I've been writing notes to my family and staff to say goodbye, just in case I don't make it back. The hardest letters were for the babies. It would absolutely gut me if I didn't get to watch them grow up. Although if I'm dead, I suppose I won't know I'm missing out. Not that I want to die.

Why did I do this?! Stupid, Arabella. Stupid. If I get out of this alive, I promise to never have another sip of champagne ever again. In fact, no more weddings either. And no baths. And … and … no talking to Gran. And no shameless flirting with adventurous men.

Oh God, I'm going to die out there in the wilderness, aren't I?

I spent a few hours looking up the most dangerous places on the planet, and it turns out, there's danger everywhere. *Everywhere.* Even the crime rate in the mountains of Tibet where those Buddhist monks live is up. Petty theft. Can you imagine? What would they even steal? One of those bells they use to end a meditation session? I doubt they're worth much. Certainly not enough to hike up a bloody mountain and snatch one, then run back down.

Anyway, it turns out the only truly safe place is here in my apartment with my guards posted outside the door and the sprinkler system to protect me from fires.

Why did I ever want to leave? It must be because I'm utterly insane. Yes, that's the answer, isn't it? Instead of sneaking off into the wild, I should be starting intensive work with a therapist to uncover why I have a death wish.

I've been crying and writing letters for over three hours now, but I'm finally finished. The only thing left to do is get some sleep, then shower. Oh, and take out my earrings because I've been instructed to leave all jewelry at home. No jewelry. Can you imagine?

Tomorrow morning, I'll get up at five a.m. and sneak down to the garage where Tony, one of the mechanics Gran plays poker with, will help me make my escape in the boot of his car. The boot! Where's the dignity in that? I might as well become a pole dancer. Well, not really, obviously pole dancing would be much worse. First of all, I'd be crap at it on account of having no upper body strength. Second ... oh my God! Why am I actually thinking about that? Pole dancing's got nothing to do with this!

In a few short hours, I'm going to ride in the pitch darkness along with an old dirty spare tire and some of those electric cables they use to fix a dead car while Tony drives me to a private hanger at the Valcourt Airport. I approached him this morning and offered him a cool five hundred bucks to help me out, no questions asked. Since he's in deep to Gran for a round of Texas Hold 'Em that went sour, he agreed to my terms.

I stare at the letters on the table, knowing Yvonne will find them when she brings in my breakfast tray. My heart squeezes with sentiment and trepidation.

Oh, Arabella, you dumb twat. What have you done?

10

Private Jets, Defiantly Smooth Skin, and Friends Who Think This is Funny ...

Will

Friday Morning 6:18 a.m.
Valcourt Airport, Valcourt, Avonia

I HAVE NEVER BEEN SO miserable about getting on a private jet in my life. Normally, I'd be taking the stairs two at a time, adrenaline pumping through my veins at what lies ahead, knowing I'm doing exactly what I was put on this planet to do. Usually, I'm over-prepared, having memorized every possible detail about the terrain, the climate, the flora, and fauna of the area. But not this time. This time, I'm dragging my feet like a surly teenager on the first day of school—powerless and clueless. This time, I have to hope I can remember all the details from the last time I was wherever I'm going now.

When I get aboard, I see Tosh and Mac sitting at the table for four. Mac looks like he just rolled out of bed—his red hair sticking up in the back and his beard smooshed in on the right side of his face, whereas Tosh looks like he just stepped out of a GAP ad.

Tosh squints his eyes. "Your beard is gone. I thought you were supposed to keep it."

"This smooth shave is an act of defiance," I say, flopping down onto the white leather seat next to Mac.

Tosh gives me a concerned look. "I was about to ask how you're doing with all of this, but I have a feeling I know."

I nod. "Yup, I'm sure you do. I'm pissed. Really fucking pissed. They're turning our show into some reality bullshit. We had a perfect formula. Why would we add some hot airhead to it?"

"I'm pretty sure you just answered your own question," Tosh says.

I glare at him, then roll my eyes.

"She might not be an airhead, you know. What if she's a super hot sporty scientist?" Mac asks.

"Do you think that combination exists? Really?" I ask.

"In my dreams, she does." Mac smiles wistfully. "She wears glasses and a lab coat all day, but then after work, when she takes both off and lets her hair down … it's on."

"Okay, that just doesn't help me at all, but good luck finding her," I say, rubbing my chin. "How are you guys not upset about this? Dylan has cut you out of the show."

Mac shakes his head. "That's not how I see it. We're getting paid full salary to do a few minutes of filming when we touch down, then hang around drinking by the hotel pool and sleeping in a real bed while you fight your way out of whatever mess they put you in."

I glance at Tosh. "Can you believe this guy?"

Tosh shrugs and gives me an apologetic look. "Truthfully, it sounds a hell of a lot better than sleeping on the forest floor wrapped up in mosquito netting."

"The forest? Is that where we're going?" I ask.

"I have no idea. It was just an example."

"Damn. I hoped you might have some clue as to what I'm about to walk into."

"Well, we do know it's somewhere we've been, so at least there's that," Mac says.

"Oh! I hope we're going to Iceland." Tosh's eyes light up. "I love Icelandic women."

"As hot as they are, I'm hoping for Brazil." Mac grins. "Nothing beats Brazil for women."

"Yes, they're so spicy."

"Well, I'm glad you two are enjoying this!" I snap.

The flight attendant, a tall woman with long black hair and a name tag that reads Lamai, walks up to us. "Good morning, gentlemen. Breakfast will be served shortly after takeoff. In the meantime, I'm supposed to give you this video to watch."

She sets a tablet on the table and walks away. On the screen is Dylan's smiling face. Tosh pushes play, and her piercing voice fills the cabin.

"Who's ready for an epic adventure? YOU are!" she yells with an open-mouthed smile. "William, make sure you get some sleep because you're not only about to go on the adventure of a lifetime, but you're about to start a whole new chapter of your life—one filled with fortune and fame like nothing you've ever imagined.

Now, I know you're probably dying to find out where you're going and with whom you're going to be spending the next however many days, but I'm not giving any hints. You'll find out everything during the big reveal.

"And don't bother asking the flight crew where you're going. They're under strict instructions not to answer any questions. When you land, Tosh and Mac will be exiting the plane first and setting up audio and video while you spend your last few minutes relaxing and making yourself look ruggedly handsome." Dylan winks into the camera.

"Once we're all set to go, you'll be allowed off, and we'll bring out our mystery co-host. I cannot wait for you to meet her. You are going to love her. Or hate her. One of the two. She's your perfect foil. Or your perfect match. We'll see!"

She claps her hands a few times, then says, "Try to fuel up and get some sleep because as soon as you step off that plane there will be no stopping—possibly for several years as you ride the fame dragon. See you on the other side. Ciao!"

. . .

The video ends, but I continue to glare at the black screen.

"Do you think it's just the Red Bull or is she maybe taking Ritalin without a prescription?" Mac asks.

"Oh, she's taking something," I say. "And whatever she's on, she's clearly dealing it to Victor and Kira for them to go along with this insanity."

"This thing's got you rattled," Tosh says. "I've never seen you like this before, even when we were cage diving with great whites and your cage opened."

"Sharks are like dogs of the sea," I say with a shrug. "*Humans* are the most dangerous animal, and Dylan is the worst of them all. I used to be the master of my fate, but she's turned me into a pawn. A pawn, Tosh! I'm just going along for the ride like some schmuck."

"You mean like us?" Mac asks.

"That's not what I meant." I shake my head, desperate for a way out of this. "I meant that *this* …" I point to the screen, "isn't my show. It's embarrassing, phony trash. I might as well see if I can guest star on *Real Housewives*."

"It's not *that* bad," Tosh says. "At least you'll be out doing what you love."

"I'm about to be stuck out in the middle of nowhere trying to drag around some woman who likely has no clue what she's doing and will end up getting us both killed. To be totally honest, I spent the last few days feeling very sure I should just quit."

"What if it turns out they're pairing you up with someone really qualified?" Tosh asks. "She could be a former Navy

SEAL who was raised in a cabin in the woods and can whittle utensils out of birch wood."

"Yeah, put everything you just said together with the word sexy, and see if it fits to you."

"Good point," Tosh says. "Now I can see why you're panicking."

"Damn right I'm panicking. What if she turns out to be some kind of psycho like that woman in *Single White Female* or that one from *The Hand That Rocks the Cradle*? Women can be scary, you know. Have you met my sister?"

The jet starts to back out of its stall and makes a slow, wide turn onto the runway.

"You're in it now," Mac says. "I think you pretty much have to see it through."

"No, I won't," I say. "If I don't think she can handle it, I'm pulling the plug on the whole thing."

Seven hours of me nervously bouncing my leg later, the plane finally lands. I watch as Mac and Tosh fling their backpacks over their shoulders, and it's all I can do to stop myself from hugging them each goodbye.

"See you out there, man," Tosh says, giving me a thumbs up.

"You'll be fine, Sally," Mac says with a wink.

The door opens and they disappear down the steps, leaving me with my heart pounding so hard, I can hear my pulse in my ears. The second I get off this jet, I'll have a life-changing decision to make. Either go along and humiliate myself—and possibly die—or quit, which will not only end my dream career, but it'll mean I can forget ever getting Matilda back.

Oh, and I'll get sued. Let's not forget that.

I rub my face with both hands, then sigh. I'll have to quit. If the mystery guest doesn't seem one hundred percent up to the task, I'll just say no. I'm not putting someone else's life at risk just for some ad revenue.

I hear Dylan calling my name and I stand, forcing my lead feet to make the twenty steps to the door of the plane. I'm instantly hit with the humidity and heat only found in a jungle region. The flight was too short to be South America, so I'm guessing I'm somewhere in Africa.

The afternoon sun blinds me, and I shield my eyes, waiting for them to adjust. As I stand at the top of the steps, I see Dylan and the guys on the tarmac. Dylan has the last thing she needs in one hand—a megaphone. *Oh, please do not lift that thing to your mouth.*

Forcing a relaxed smile, I jog down the metal steps into the searing heat. By the time my hiking boots touch the steamy asphalt, my grey T-shirt is already sticking to my chest. Dylan is facing away from me, talking into the camera so I can't hear what she's saying. Not that I want to.

She turns to me, holds her arms out to the sides and shouts, "Welcome to Zamunda! Are you ready to meet your mystery co-host?"

Plastering a grin on my face, I say through gritted teeth, "Am I?"

Picking up the bullhorn, she yells, "Come on out, mystery guest!"

I look to my left in time to see a woman in very short khaki shorts, hiking boots, and a white tank top stepping out of a luggage carrier. I'm torn—my body very much wants to say yes to spending a few nights alone with her, but my sense of logic is screaming at me to say 'no way.' Her face is shadowed by the bright sun behind her, and her blonde ponytail swings as she walks closer.

It takes a few more seconds before I realize who she is.

"Hi, Will," Princess Arabella says with a small wave.

No fucking way.

11

Famous Last Words

Arabella

Oh DEAR, this is not good. Not good at all. Will *was* smiling, but now he's not. And I'm pretty sure that gorgeous grin faded precisely at the moment he recognized me. Nuts.

Now, he's standing perfectly still, looking ridiculously handsome and utterly angry in a fitted grey T-shirt and blue cargo pants. And I'm standing here like a complete moron in these stupid short shorts while I smile like one of those beer tub girls—you know, the ones at nightclubs dressed very much like I am now, only in front of a tub of ice and beer bottles. Except, in this case, my sole customer does not want to buy what I'm selling. Not that I'm selling anything, but you get the idea.

This is bad. Very, very bad. I'm not sure I've ever felt this humiliated in my life. Or rejected. This feels like having a group of nonagenarians tell you they want your brother's manny to take them on a palace tour instead of you. It reminds me of my school days waiting for the team captains to pick players for a game of field hockey in gym class. You beg them with your eyes to choose you, but deep down you know they'd both be happy to be a player short than to have to pass to you. Will would rather be a player short. Oh Zeus, please strike me down with a bolt of lightning right now.

Dylan breaks the awful silence. "Haha! Perfect! You're in shock, which is *exactly* what I was going for." She turns to the camera. "He can't even believe his eyes, folks. To be standing face-to-face with the beautiful, elegant, dare I say *sexy*, Princess Arabella, fourth in line for the Avonian throne! Will, say hello to your new co-host!"

"Hello," he says, setting his jaw.

Dylan keeps smiling back and forth between us. "Are you two ready to be dropped into the jungle with only each other to rely on for your very survival?"

Instead of answering her, Will starts toward me, his legs moving fast. "Can I talk to you for a second, please?"

"Yes, of course," I say, feeling slightly worried, super embarrassed, and also horrifyingly turned on.

When he reaches me, he takes my hand and starts walking me away from Dylan and the crew, but the sound guy and the cameraman hustle to keep up with us, capturing our every move as we hurry to the chain link fence. When we reach it, he drops my hand and lowers his voice, keeping his back to the camera. "Is this some kind of joke? Because if it is, I don't find it very funny."

Yup. This makes sense. He doesn't want me here. He assumes I'm weak and useless. Well, screw him. "Of course it's not," I say in a haughty tone. "I applied for the show and they chose me. If you don't like it, too bad."

"This is ... You don't ... You have no business—" He stops himself and lets out a frustrated sigh. "Did someone force you into this? Because I swear to God, if someone forced you into this, I will ... well, I don't know what I'll do, but whoever it is won't like it."

Oh, well, that was sort of chivalrous in a weird way. *No, Arabella! It was chauvinistic. He's a gorgeous, gorgeous chauvinist.* "No," I say, straightening my back. "No one coerced me. It was entirely my choice, and quite frankly I don't appreciate the assumption."

"So, if you weren't coerced, that either makes you extremely naïve or completely insane."

"I am *neither*, thank you very much," I quip. *Don't cry. Do not cry, whatever you do.* I dig my nails into my palms and lift my chin.

"Listen, *Princess*, you don't have the first clue what you're getting yourself into out there. This isn't like some luxury safari you may have gone on in the past."

What an arsehole! "I know that."

"Then ... why?" he asks, throwing his hands up.

"To prove I can."

He stares at me for a second, then shakes his head. "Look,

I'm sorry I insulted you at my sister's wedding, really. I didn't mean any of it. I was jetlagged, and I had a little too much to drink, and I don't remember exactly what I said, but I'm sure I implied people from your class are soft or … or something to that effect. And I was way out of line. Okay?" he says, every word sounding sincere. "Way out of line. But trust me when I tell you this is *not* the way you want to prove me wrong. It's life or death out there."

Life or death? That doesn't sound very comforting.

"I'm sorry, Your Highness. I can't let you do this. There's no way you can handle life in the jungle."

Okay, that did it. "You can't *let me* do this? I'm sorry, but I seem to have missed the part where you were put in charge of my life."

"That's not what I—"

Holding up one hand, I say, "You don't know me. You have no idea what I can do or where I've been. For all you know, I was raised in the jungle."

"Were you?" he asks, narrowing his eyes.

I pause for a moment, then say, "No, but I've done … plenty of difficult things. Plenty of really … big, challenging things. So trust me when I tell you I can handle myself."

He barks out a frustrated laugh, then turns and stalks back over to Dylan, who has a gleeful look on her face. The crew follows him, and I hurry after them.

"It's off," Will says. "I'm out. There is *no way* I'm going out there with her."

"Well, I have a contract right here that says you are." Dylan waves a stack of papers at him.

The two argue quietly for a few minutes and I overhear words like giant rats and lethal spiders. *Oh dear, he's totally right about this. I have absolutely no business being out here. I'm actually cheering for him to win this argument so I can go right home and forget all about this stupid idea.*

Dylan raises her voice. "Would you like to hear the two options for show titles? It'll either be *A Princess in the Wild World*, if she films with you, or it'll be *The Princess and the Bear* because I can have Bear Grylls here by tomorrow morning. Either way, I get my show."

"Oh really?"

"Yes. Really," she says, crossing her arms.

"You called him? You called that hack to take over my show?"

Shrugging, Dylan says, "I always have a Plan B. And in this case, it's 'B' as in Bear."

Turning to me, he's says, "This is really what you want? You want to be out in the Congo with giant rats, venomous snakes, and spiders the size of your face?"

My knees are shaking. Literally shaking. Swallowing hard, I squeak out a yes which causes him to scoff.

He shakes his head. "Do you see that helicopter over there? The one with the ropes next to it?" He points at it, and my gaze follows his finger.

"You know what the ropes are for?"

"Obviously." I shrug, when in truth, I have no idea what they're for, and honestly, I don't even want to know.

He smiles down at me—and it's not a particularly nice smile. "So, you're keen to stand on that skid at two hundred feet above the jungle canopy and rappel to the ground?"

Oh, fuck me. "Definitely."

"Good, because that'll be the easiest thing we do out here."

Shit fuck.

———

I'm going to vomit. Or pee. Or pee and vomit. This is really happening. The helicopter pilot, a wall of a man dressed in shorts and a white tee, just arrived. Now that he's here, we'll be able to leave soon. Oh, Lord in Heaven help me, I'm about to get into an aircraft with no sides and be dropped into the jungle. And that's the *easy* part. How can that be the easy part?

Oh, I know. It's because then I'm going to be stuck out there alone with a man who hates the very sight of me.

Will and the pilot give each other a quick man-hug. "Will Banks, my favourite crazy person," he says, in a thick Zamundan accent.

"Idriss, my friend. How have you been?" Will asks. "Crashed lately?"

"Not since last time we were out here."

The two laugh and I stand by, trying to figure out what exactly is so damn funny about crashing.

"We got lucky," Idriss says, shaking his head. "Whew, that was a close one." Glancing at me, he smiles. "Is this your leading lady?"

"Yup, I'll be dragging her around the jungle." Turning to me, Will points. "This is Princess Arabella of Avonia."

Idriss smiles broadly and holds his hand out to me. I take it and we shake. "This guy, with the jokes," he says with a deep chuckle. "Princess!"

Will shakes his head. "This time I'm serious."

His face falls. "You're a real princess?"

"Yes, I'm afraid so," I say with a polite smile.

He gives me a quick once-over. "Have you been out in the jungle before?"

"First time, actually, but don't worry," I answer, trying my best to sound brave. "I ate at the Rainforest Cafe when I was in the US."

Dylan laughs like it's the funniest thing she's ever heard. "Okay, now would be a good time to go over the rules. Come on," she says, leading us into the hanger where a table with supplies and a map wait. She picks up an envelope and holds it up to the camera dramatically. "This envelope contains all the rules of your adventure. Take it with you in case you need to refer to it."

Will snatches it out of her hand, but she doesn't seem put off by his attitude. She grins and shouts, "Are you ready to hear about your challenge?"

We both nod and I'm not sure which one of us is less enthusiastic. He's beyond angry and I'm too terrified to pretend I'm okay.

"You'll be dropped somewhere into the red zone marked there on the map." She points at it. "Tosh, can you get a shot of this?"

He moves in closer while she continues. "You will need to get all the way from here to ..." She moves her finger to a town on the edge of the jungle that looks really frigging far away to me. "Here. The village of Mbambole, taking only these terrific backpacks made by Bearz, the official line of outdoor gear by Bear Grylls, that have been packed for you. As you know, you can't take anything from home. Only what we provide you with, and what you find, of course, so you'll need to be resourceful.

"For safety, you'll have a satellite phone with you, so if something goes wrong, you can call for help. The phone is equipped with GPS so a rescue team will be able to find you within, hopefully, just a couple of hours, depending on where you are. Idriss here will be on call the entire time to bring help straight away, but there's a catch."

Of course there is.

"Of course there is," Will mutters.

Ignoring him, Dylan says, "If you use the phone, you lose the danger bonuses and a special surprise brought to you by the good people at GoPro. GoPro has offered a one-hundred-thousand-dollar prize to be split between the two of you if you can make it out of the jungle in under ten days!"

She shouts, "Can you believe it? An extra fifty-thousand for you, Will, and for your charity, People for Animals, Your Highness!"

"Brilliant," I say, attempting to smile.

Will says nothing, but just stares.

"Yes! Exciting, right?!" She smiles into the camera. "GoPro, be a hero!"

When neither of us start jumping for joy, she lowers her voice. "Well, that's okay. You're obviously too thrilled to speak. Anyway, I'll give you ten minutes to figure out where you want to be dropped, then we're going to start the count-down clock and you'll have exactly two hundred and forty hours to make it to Mbambole!"

Two hundred and forty hours sounds like a very long time.

"Two hundred and forty hours?" Will asks her. Turning to me, he says, "That sounds like a very long time, doesn't it?"

I shrug as if I'm a hardened criminal who just had another life sentence handed down to make an even hundred years.

Idriss pulls a pack of cigarettes and a lighter out of his pocket, then taking one out, he lights it up as he and Will lean over the map. He sets down the pack and the lighter on the table and takes a casual puff on the cigarette. "So, where to?"

I peer down at the map. To the untrained eye (i.e. mine), it just looks like a bunch of trees with the odd river and some elevation markings. But apparently to them, it all means something. There's a large circle that has been drawn on it with a red marker. Will points to the spot that would bring us closest to our end point. "Is it too much to hope we can land here?"

Shaking his head, Idriss says, "The gorillas have moved down there for the hot season. I don't think they're going to welcome you with open arms."

I gasp. "Guerrillas? Nobody said anything about guerrillas. Are they armed?"

Idriss looks at me like I'm wearing my bra on the outside of my shirt.

"*Go*rillas," Will says with disdain. "As in mountain gorillas. They don't generally carry guns because they don't need them. They could snap your skinny neck with two fingers."

"Oh," I say, my cheeks burning.

The next few minutes are spent with me just trying to breathe in and out in long, slow breaths so as not to hyperventilate. I stand silently, not having anything intelligent to add to the conversation. My mind starts to wander, and I glance at the cigarettes and lighter, wishing I was a ballsy woman who'd take one out and light it up for myself. That would be such a power move if it wouldn't make me turn green and vomit everywhere.

Hmmm … maybe I can't use the cigarettes, but that lighter might come in handy. Dylan did say 'be resourceful.' I lean over the table and nod, pretending I'm following what they're saying. Placing my hands down, I carefully cover the lighter with my right hand.

"How close can you get me to that river?" Will asks.

Idriss squints at it. "About five kilometres."

Huh, they haven't noticed. My heart pounds in my chest as I close my fingers around it and casually lift my hands off the table, putting them into my pockets and saying a "Hmm, five sounds good."

Will stops and looks up at me. "Does it?"

"Yes," I say, wishing I'd kept my mouth shut.

"Glad you approve, Your Highness." He picks up a pencil and draws an 'X.'

Suddenly, I realize how uncomfortably hot I am, even though we're in the shelter of the hanger. Tosh, the camera guy, steps up and starts giving us instructions on how to use the GoPros. I'm so terrified, I'm not taking in anything he's saying, so when he finishes, and asks me if I've "Got it?" I just nod and smile.

"Okay, I guess that's everything," Will says. "The sooner we get going, the more light we'll have to set up camp."

He gives me a long look, then turns to Dylan. "Where are her real clothes?"

"This is it. It's jungle chic."

"She won't last fifteen minutes in this getup. She needs thick pants and a long-sleeved shirt."

"That's not exactly what I had in mind." Dylan lowers her voice. "This outfit has more of the sexy vibe we're going for."

"Well, I don't think dead is very sexy, do you? You've already got footage of her to show off her nice legs, so get her some pants."

Nice legs? I can't say I hate hearing that. *Oh, Arabella, what are you thinking right now? You're about to jump out of a helicopter to your death and you're excited about a tiny compliment? Pathetic. Just pathetic.*

———

By the time I've changed into some baggy pants and a button up khaki shirt, the helicopter has been started, creating a loud, intense wind on the tarmac. Will is seemingly ready to go because he's already wearing a harness around his waist that goes through his legs. On his shoulders, he's got a large backpack. He gestures for me to come over, holding a harness for me. "Last chance to change your mind."

"Last chance for *you* to change *your* mind," I say with a raised eyebrow.

He holds open the harness and crouches in front of me. "I'm assuming you haven't worn one of these before?"

I step in carefully, fully aware of his proximity to my body. "You assume correctly."

He stands, pulling the harness up and fastening it around my waist while I stay perfectly still with my arms up in the air. Oh, he smells yummy. Too bad he's a total arsehole.

"Turn around, please."

I do as he says, and he tugs on the harness, tightening it even more, his fingers dangerously close to the bottom of my bottom. Clearing my throat, I say, "I could probably manage this myself."

"I'm sure you could, but we're in a bit of a rush, and it's not something you want to get wrong."

Fair enough. When he finishes, I turn to find him directly in front of me, holding a backpack. I take it from him, and the weight of it causes my arm to fall to my side. It feels like it's got a bowling ball in it, but I don't dare complain. Instead, I slide it on, wishing I was anywhere but here.

Will gestures with his head, and we start toward the helicopter. I jog along behind him, ducked down like an idiot the entire time, even though we're still a good fifty yards from the helicopter. Once we're on, he attaches two long ropes to my harness and checks to make sure everything is secure, tugging hard enough on the equipment to lift me off my feet.

Mac and Tosh sit across from us, then Dylan gets on. As the helicopter lifts off, my stomach hops up to my throat and I plaster a smile on my face in spite of the fact that I'm positive I'm going to vomit. That lunch was a bad idea.

Tosh points the camera at Will, who puts on an easygoing smile and starts to talk. "We're here in the beautiful jungles of Zamunda—the third-largest untouched rainforest on the planet and also one of the most species-rich habitats on Earth. There are over 10,000 species of tropical plants here, four hundred species of mammals, a whopping eight hundred fish species—including Goliath Tigerfish, which are also known as the African piranha. And for anyone who likes to have a lie-in, this is not the place because these forests are home to over two thousand types of birds. And they like to wake up early. The Zamundan jungle is one of the most dangerous places I've been, and also one of my favourites.

"It's literally teeming with wildlife and danger at every turn. And we are about to be dropped into the heart of it, where we can only hope we don't come across any of the several species of gorillas or chimpanzees, who, from my past experience, I can tell you are *not* big fans of humans venturing into their territory. If we manage to avoid them, we'll still have to worry about the giant rats that call this jungle home. They're roughly the size of a large house cat and they have razor-sharp teeth they use to kill any venomous snakes who try to attack them. But all of that is nothing compared to the deadly spiders we're sure to see. And as if that wasn't enough, it's not just the animals who live here that can kill you—some of the plants can as well."

He stops talking for a second but keeps grinning. What the hell is he grinning about? None of the things he just said sound remotely positive. I glare openly while he continues.

"Venturing out here without a good knowledge of the area is going to get you killed, because even though you're surrounded by food sources and fresh water, if you don't know where to find them, you'll likely succumb to poisoning. That is, if you don't starve to death first. These forests are so dense and the terrain so difficult, it would take a search and rescue team several months to find your body."

Tears spring to my eyes and I quickly look out the side of the helicopter which only causes my stomach to lurch. *It'll be okay. Just don't listen to him, Arabella. He's only saying those things to add to the drama.*

"We're about to rappel down into the canopy of the jungle to start our trek all the way to Mbambole. This is where we have to have an incredible amount of trust in our helicopter pilot because one wrong move by him, and Princess Arabella and I will fall to our deaths or be impaled by one of the thousands of tree branches below. Lucky for us, Idriss is one of the best in the world."

Will casually leans his upper body out of the helicopter, searching for a spot to stop. I have a sudden urge to grab him and pull him back in, but I don't. After a few minutes, he shouts, "This looks good here! There's an opening in the trees directly below us!"

Does it? Does it really look good?

Idriss gives him the thumbs up.

I guess it does.

"All right, Your Highness, are you ready to do this?"

I try to nod, but my head shakes a solid no, instead.

"I thought as much," he says with a look of understanding that I'm positive is totally phony. "It's okay. It's pretty cool that you even got this far. Very few people on the planet have ever seen any of this."

He smiles in a way that is both kind and condescending at the same time.

There's something about it that ignites a fire in my belly. "You'd like that, wouldn't you? If I stayed in the helicopter?"

"To be honest, yes. Then I wouldn't have you to worry

about the entire time," he says. "Think about it—by tonight you could be at home on your thousand-thread-count sheets."

"They're two thousand, actually, and they'll be waiting for me in ten days. Now how do we do this?"

He gives me an exasperated look, then stands up and turns his back to the open side of the helicopter. "Stand here," he says. "Grip this bar. Step back onto this skid. Then step off slowly and you'll start to slide down."

"See you out there. Or not," he says, stepping back and dropping out of sight.

I stand, my entire body feeling wobbly as I reach up and grab hold of the bar next to the door. *Okay, Arabella. You can do this. It's just an easy step back. You are not going to die.*

Yes, you are, you fool. Get back in your seat, where you belong!

I grip the bar so hard, the skin of my palms is being pinched, but I don't dare let go now that I'm here. The wind whips me and the sound of the blades so close to my head makes me feel dizzy and disoriented. I'm now too scared to step back and too scared to let go so I can reach for my seat. I close my eyes, forcing the tears of fear back inside, my breath shaky.

"Will's already disconnected. You've got to go, Your Highness!" Idriss says. "I can't hover so close to these trees much longer."

Right. I need to hurry. But I don't want to hurry because I'm not in any rush to die! Was my life really so bad? Being served every meal and helping charities every day? It wasn't. I don't need to do this. I can't.

"You've got this, Your Highness!" Dylan shouts. "For all women everywhere!"

Yes. Equal Everywhere. I have to do this.

I reach behind me with my right foot, tapping with my toes until I feel the skid.

"It's easier if you do this with your eyes open," Mac shouts at me.

"No, thank you. I'm good like this," I yell back, forcing my foot to land firmly on the skid. *Okay, that's one. Now do the other one. Just do it. For all women everywhere.*

"I want to see you be brave," Dylan screams.

"Yes, I brave," I say. I don't think that made sense. I can't let that be my last words.

"You need to make a decision, Your Highness," Idriss calls.

"All right!" I snap. "I'm going."

My hands are starting to cramp up, but I force my left foot down, then without thinking, I take a deep breath and shift my weight behind me, letting my feet slide off the skid.

And now I'm slowly being lowered to the ground.

And swearing like a sailor the entire way down.

I guess, "Shiiitttttttttt-fuckballs-son-of-a-bitch-fffffffffuuuuuu-ucccccccckkkkkkkk!" will be my last words.

Good thing it's all going to be captured on film for posterity.

12

Don't Lick the Yellow Ones

Will

WELL, bugger, she is actually doing it. I stand, my eyes fixed on her as she drops toward me. I'm seriously torn between being incredibly impressed, super irritated, and wanting to bust out laughing because of the string of fucks and shit fucks and mother fucking fuckers pouring out of her mouth.

I remove my harness, then let go so it can be pulled back up to the helicopter, all the while keeping my eyes on her as she descends.

"FUUUCCKKKKKKKKKKKKING HELLL!" she shouts, clearly not realizing she's almost on the ground.

I reach up and grab her by the waist, then gently lower her. "Welcome to the jungle. I'm going to unhook you now."

She nods slightly, her chest heaving, her face pink. If she

MELANIE SUMMERS

weren't so annoying, I'd say she's cute right now.

"I did it," she whispers. "I didn't die."

She lifts her arms so I can unhook her, and I get started, trying not to think about the lovely figure under her baggy clothes.

"I did it," she says again, this time louder and with a shocked expression.

"You sure did." Crouching, I tug the harness down to her feet.

She steps out of it and I hold it up for Mac, who gives me a salute, then starts pulling up the rope.

When I stand, Arabella grins at me. "I did it," she says again.

Chuckling, I say, "I know. I saw you. And I heard you."

She throws her arms around my neck and hugs me. Mmm ... this feels *way too* nice.

Suddenly seeming to remember herself, she pulls back. "Sorry. I'm just so amazed. I actually stepped off of a helicopter that was *really high* in the air. I did *not* think I was going to do that, but I did. I *rappelled*. And not just off a little wall at a rock-climbing gym. Off an *aircraft*. In the air. Above the jungle." Shaking her head, she smiles. "I didn't think I had that in me."

Neither did I. "And I didn't think you had such a foul mouth. We'll have to bleep the audio of your entire descent."

She gives me a sheepish look. "My deepest apologies. Apparently, I swear like a sailor when I engage in death-defying activities."

106

"Well, try to curb your language a little if you can because we're going for a prime-time slot."

The sound of the helicopter fades, and it hits me that we're actually doing this. We're out here all alone with only the sounds of the birds, the rustling of the gentle breeze through the leaves, and the thick heat.

Arabella looks around, as though just noticing where she is for the first time. She slowly turns, her mouth hanging down while she gazes up and takes in the surroundings. "This is *magnificent!* Have you ever seen anything so lush and wild and free in your entire life?"

Looking back up at me, she blushes. "Of course you have. You've been here."

I can't help but smile, finding her unbridled enthusiasm contagious. "It's incredible, isn't it? There are so few places on the planet untouched by man, and you, Your Highness, are one of a handful of people throughout history who will ever see any of this in person."

She turns to me and smiles, her lovely face lit up with exhilaration. The sight of it makes my heart skip, then quickly reminds me, *I'm* responsible for getting this beautiful-but-clueless woman out of here alive.

My gut hardens at the thought, and my smile fades. "We better get moving. I want to make it to the river before it gets dark."

"Is that where the camp is?" she asks, as we start to walk.

"The camp is wherever we make it."

"Oh," she says, her tone quiet.

"You didn't think there'd be accommodations out here, did you?"

"No, of course not," she answers quickly, avoiding my gaze which means she absolutely one hundred percent thought we were about to take a stroll to some luxury lodge.

"When you signed up for this, what exactly did they tell you about the show?"

"I'm afraid Ms. Sinclair was rather vague about the details, but I gather from the rules she outlined earlier that it's just us, whatever we've got on us, and whatever we can make."

"And what can you make?"

"Whatever you teach me," she says with more than a hint of defiance. "I know you don't want me out here, but I promise I'm a quick learner."

"Yeah, this ain't Girl Scout camp, Your Highness, and we're under a deadline that I intend to beat. I don't have time to teach you anything. All you need to know is to stick close by and follow instructions. I'll do the rest."

A flash of anger crosses her face. "So much for teamwork."

"Let's get one thing straight—*I never wanted* to be part of a team. I work better alone. Now, I'm not trying to be an arse. I'm trying to keep you safe."

She looks down at the forest floor and shakes her head. "If I had a dollar for every time I heard that—"

"—You'd be ridiculously wealthy and never need to work a day in your life?"

Arabella's face turns pink, and her eyes fill with shame. "I suppose that is what you would see."

I start to apologize, but she holds up one hand. "Don't bother. It's best if I know from the start what you think of me." Lifting her chin, she says, "I thought we were in a big hurry?"

"Right, we are." I nod. "We've got about five hours of daylight, which may sound like a lot, but we've got a lot to do in that time." I take off my backpack and set it on the ground. "First, we should have a look at our supplies so we know what we've got and what we'll need to pick up along the way."

We both unpack our bags, then stand, surveying the contents. I attach a selfie stick to my GoPro and turn it toward me. "So, Princess Arabella and I have been dropped into the middle of the Zamundan Congo with supplies that have been chosen for us by the network. While they did a pretty good job of choosing items, there are a couple of things we don't need and a few that we'll definitely miss."

I crouch and aim the camera at our supplies. "Believe it or not, this small pack contains a tent, which in my book is a luxury item that I normally wouldn't bring, but because I think my companion will want it, it comes with us. Toothbrushes and toothpaste—you can survive without, but who would want to? I see they've packed a makeup kit in Princess Arabella's bag. Totally useless, so it stays here."

I pause for a moment, assuming she'll protest, but she doesn't.

"We've got two emergency blankets made by Wellbits.

These guys are super handy, weighing in at less than an ounce. They double as rain ponchos, which, as you might imagine, will be extremely helpful in a rainforest. We've also got our map—again, a nice-to-have item, but because I'm out here with a survival novice, I'm not taking any chances. I'm bringing it."

I point to a metal pot. "Another luxury. If you find yourself stuck in the wild, you can make one out of any number of things found in the forest. Looks like we've also got two head lamps and a super-charged solar power plant."

"Say, that's made by Bear Grylls!" Princess Arabella adds.

I stiffen slightly. "I doubt very much that *he* had any part in the design or manufacturing. It's more likely he just slapped his name on it. Anyway, we've got biodegradable soap shavings in this plastic container, two Ziploc bags which we can definitely use for collecting herbs and sap along the way, four backup batteries for the GoPros, and a machete, which is a must out here. Also, we've got his and hers Swiss army knives with nail clippers and tweezers in case you get a hangnail," I say with a wink in Arabella's direction. Oh, she did *not* like that. "It also comes with scissors, a corkscrew, which we won't need—"

"—Too bad," she interjects. "I, for one, could use a bottle of wine right now."

"Same here, except make it a case." I pick up a small rectangular canvas bag and slide the contents out into my hand. "You've probably seen one of these before, yes? Maybe in the throne room, or your private library."

She says nothing but gives me a look meant to show me she's above pettiness. Huh, that actually worked. I feel bad. I clear my throat. "This is called a Muncher. It's one of the greatest multi-tools ever invented. This end here is called a spork—it's both a spoon and a fork —

"—I know what a spork is."

"Of course. I'm sure you use them at all your state dinners, don't you?" *Dammit, Will. Stop being a prick.*

"I've seen them on the telly," she says.

"Great. Out here in the wild, it's for every course from soup to nuts." I point to the opposite end of the tool. "You'll notice the tip of the serrated knife is flat, so it can be used as a screwdriver. This is a flint, which we'll definitely need—"

"—You will. I won't," she says.

I look up, thoroughly confused as she digs into her shirt. She produces a lighter and spins it in between her forefinger and thumb. "Knicked it off the helicopter pilot."

My mouth hangs open, and I find myself speechless.

She smiles shyly. "I don't normally do things like that, but Dylan did say to be resourceful. Plus, smoking kills so I can justify it."

I fight the surprised laughter inside, reminding myself I don't want her here. Continuing on, I look back at the Muncher. "Potato peeler, can opener, which we won't be using this trip. And finally, this hook here is perfect for cutting cords. We'll use it to cut one of nature's most useful inventions—the vine."

I pick up the empty green backpack that has the word

"Bearz" emblazoned across it. "Huh, this is a lot heavier than it needs to be. I'm surprised he'd put his name on these."

Arabella lifts hers, as though testing its weight, although I don't think she has anything to compare it to. "Doesn't feel bad to me," she says with a satisfied smile.

"Well, that's because you've never used a proper back-pack," I mutter. Turning the camera on myself, I say, "Okay, we're going to get everything packed up and hit the trail. Princess Pickpocket and I have a long trek ahead."

————

Once we start walking, I hold up the selfie stick. "We're going to head east for the next several days until we reach the town of Mbambole. Now is the best time for me to remind my companion not to touch *anything*, and I mean anything, without asking me first. These plants may be beautiful, but many of them are deadly."

I walk quickly, slashing at the heavy brush ahead with the machete. "Stay behind me, okay, and keep up."

"That's what I'm doing," she says, already puffing a bit.

"We'll be hiking downhill for hours and Mother Nature is not going to make it easy for us. The ground is wet and spongy because it's covered in layers of fallen leaves and sedi-ment. It's already tough, but at any moment, it could start pouring, which will make it all the more difficult."

"You're rather dramatic, aren't you? It's not *that* hard," she says.

I slide down a few meters then regain my balance and turn to catch her, knowing she is likely not going to make it. But much to my surprise, she manages to stay on her feet, skidding down toward me like a pro.

"Excellent balance, Your Highness."

"Thanks, but I'm not in need of your approval."

We continue on for another few minutes, now reaching a short drop-off that requires a jump to get down. She almost loses her balance and reaches for a vine, but I grab her palm before she can touch it. She makes the jump, then tugs her hand away. "I'm fine, thank you."

"That vine you were reaching for was an Asian liana. Those thorns would have embedded themselves into your palm and with this humidity and heat, your entire hand would be infected within a few hours." I turn and start through the brush again, slicing a path. "So, when I say don't touch anything, I mean don't touch *anything*. Oh, and if you see any frogs, don't lick the yellow ones."

"Being impolite to each other is hardly going to make anything better," she says in a stiff tone.

I stop and turn to her. "I'm just trying to keep you safe, Your Highness, and if you're doing something that could put your life—and therefore *mine*—at risk, I won't have time for niceties."

"But certainly there was time for it *after* the fact, which is when you snapped at me," she says, sounding irritatingly regal.

Christ. I don't have time for this shit. "If it pleases you, Your

Highness, it would be most wonderful if you could refrain from touching anything without asking, so as not to become infected and die. I'd prefer not to have to carry your lifeless body out of the jungle for a proper royal burial."

She stares at me for a moment with her lips pursed. "You've made it clear you don't want me here. There's really no need to continue hammering once the nail is all the way in the board."

With that, she continues on and I hurry to get in front of her. We hike in silence for a long time, both of us furious. She has no business out here and rather than admitting it, she's pretending like she has every right to be risking both our lives. And that's exactly why I'm going to get us the hell out of here as fast as humanly possible. She doesn't know it, but we're heading to the river to camp for the night. Then, first thing tomorrow morning, I'm building a raft that will get us out of here in under five days flat. It'll also allow me to keep her from getting herself killed. She can just sit in the middle of it and wait while I get us to Mbambole.

The sun starts to go down, so I decide to make the most of the fading light. Holding the selfie stick up, I say, "If you ever find yourself in a jungle such as this one, and if you've got the choice, always cover as much of your body as possible so as to avoid cuts and scratches. Anything that can lead to potential infection is deadly out here." Turning the camera and aiming it in front of me, I say, "When you're lost in the woods, you'll want to look *through* the jungle instead of *at it*. Find a spot about five metres ahead so you can see any movement before it's too late. The tricky part is you also need to remain keenly aware of what's happening on the ground directly in front of you and to your sides in case something is either slithering or creeping up to you, looking for it's lunch."

Flipping the camera back toward me, I see Arabella's face behind me in the screen. She looks unmistakably horrified which, I hate to admit, brings out a pathetic sense of satisfaction. "If you ever find yourself lost in any type of forest setting, one of the first things you have to do is make sure you aren't walking in circles. That's why most people end up dead. The best choice is to stay put until you're rescued, but if you know that's not an option, here's how you get out alive. Pick an object in the distance and follow that. Once you reach it, pick another one ahead of you and keep going. Turn back a few times to make sure the last object is still behind you. That'll keep you going in a nice straight line. If you find a stream or other flowing body of water, follow it. You'll not only have a source of water, but rivers don't run in circles, so eventually, you'll find your way out."

I turn behind me and see that she's quite far back so I stop, sit on a log. While I wait, I take out my canteen and have a few swigs of water.

When she reaches me, she starts to sit down, leaving as much space between us as possible. "Thank God, I need to catch my breath."

I stand quickly, screwing the top on my canteen, and start walking. "No time. You can rest when we get to camp."

Once we're walking again, I say, "What would you guess

the leading cause of death would be in an environment like this?"

"Probably mosquito bite."

"Good guess. That's number two. The leading cause is infection." I stop and point at a tree to my right. "This skinny tree is called an Acacia Giantus. It's one of the most important species for our purposes," I say. "It's got one of Mother Nature's best remedies for cuts and scrapes."

I take a small Ziploc bag out of my backpack, then scrape a large dollop of transparent orange goo off the tree and deposit it carefully into the bag. "We'll save that for later."

"How much further before we find a suitable place to stop?" she asks. "Not that I'm tired or anything. Just curious."

"I'd say another couple of hours."

"Brilliant."

Looking down, I spot some rhino beetle larvae. I aim my camera at them and zoom in. "Are you hungry, Your Highness? Because these little guys are an amazing source of protein. We just have to empty out their digestive tracts first."

I pick one up, twist off its head, then squeeze it, letting a sizable amount of brown goop ooze out onto my palm. Holding it up to her, I say, "Tea break?"

Arabella makes a gagging sound. "Thank you. I had a rather large breakfast."

I shrug and pop it into my mouth, maintaining eye contact while I chew it. It's disgusting and squishy, but I force a satisfied smile on my face anyway. "Mmm. That's good and it'll keep me going for a good long while, unlike my companion who may start to feel fatigued soon."

"I'll take my chances."

We continue on and I pick up the pace now. "Let's move. It gets dark early out here."

As we walk, I continue to narrate. "Now, Princess Arabella and I are lucky because we have a machete. With this handy device, not only can I cut a path through the dense vegetation, I can also turn stalks of bamboo into a torch, a fishing spear, a fresh water source, as well as an effective weapon."

"I had no idea I was out in the wild with MacGyver. By any chance, can you teach me how to make a bomb out of some seeds and a chewing gum wrapper?" she asks, lathering on a sweetness so fake, I should start calling her Splenda.

"If the seeds contain palm oil, sure." I turn back to the camera. "Now that it's starting to get dark, we both need to keep our wits about us and watch for anything that could be a threat. This jungle is home to a variety of snakes, the black button spider, not to mention some large wildcats that might be feeling hungry right about now. Most of the animals out here feed at dusk and dawn, which makes this the most dangerous time of day."

Arabella makes a tiny squeaking noise and I turn to her. "What was that?"

"I didn't say anything," she mutters, raising her eyebrows as if I'm hearing things. "For someone who says he's in such a hurry, you certainly stop a lot to make videos."

"It's part of the job," I say, narrowing my eyes at her.

"Oh, right. Sorry. A *job* is something people do to make money. You see, they have to perform certain tasks as laid out by their employer. If they complete the tasks, they get paid so they can afford things like food and rent."

She ignores my dig and whispers, "Are you still standing there talking?" She wrinkles up her nose and gives me a 'you're not all that bright, are you?' look before she starts walking again.

I catch up with her after a few steps, then zigzag around her so I'm in front again. "I know it's not royal protocol but out here, *you* walk a few steps behind *me*." Now I'm just being a prick.

"Right. I'm happy to let you go first," she says. Dropping her voice, she adds, "If that's what it takes to make you feel like a big man …"

I shake my head, regretting ever getting on that helicopter with her as I slash through the brush with more vigor than needed. After a minute, I turn to her and feign being apologetic. "Oh, I'm sorry, earlier I forgot to explain what rent was. You probably don't know."

"I suddenly understand why you love it so much in the wilderness," Arabella says in a facetious tone. "It's the only place big enough for your giant ego."

"I do *not* have a giant ego."

"You most certainly do." She lifts her chin at me. "You're by far the most arrogant, smug man I've ever met. And I know *Kanye West*."

"Really? Of the two of us, you think *I'm* the one with an

attitude?" I let out a frustrated chuckle. "That's rich coming from someone who's probably never even seen a washing machine."

"You know what?" she asks, her eyes growing wild with rage. "Shut up!"

"Shut up?!"

"Yes. Shut up." She nods once. "I can't bear another word of your self-satisfied, know-it-all commentary about the jungle and survival and … and … *me*! You don't know the first thing about my life, so just shut up already."

"Let's get one thing straight. This is *my show*." I stab my chest with my thumb. "*Mine*. And in case you hadn't noticed, *you* need *me*, and not the other way around, so don't tell me to shut up or to do anything else for that matter. Because if you do, I'll happily leave you here to get eaten by leopards."

Her head snaps back. "Oh really?!"

"Really!"

"You think *that's* going to scare me?" She scoffs. "I'd actually *rather* be torn apart by a pack of hungry leopards than have to suffer through another minute of listening to you drone on and on with that smug smile on your stupid face."

Stupid? Wow. Just wow. "For your information, leopards rarely travel in groups, and if they do, it's either called a leap or a prowl," I yell. "Not a pack!"

With that, I turn on my heel and storm through the brush, whacking at anything in my path with a rage-filled vengeance. I'm getting the hell out of here now—with or without her royal hagness.

13

If a princess poops in the woods, is she still a princess?

Arabella

I STOMP ALONG BEHIND HIM, imitating his voice quietly but furiously, "I'm sorry. You probably don't know what rent is. Oh, that's rich coming from someone who's never seen a washing machine." Holding up both middle fingers, I scowl at his back like the world's most immature woman. "I've seen washing machines, thank you very much. I own a television."

Oh, stop it, Arabella. You're the one who wanted to go on a big, shiny adventure.

We walk along for a long time in silence, and after a while, my anger gives way to exhaustion. Yes, he's an arse, but I'm not exactly Princess Peach at the moment. It's so bloody hot here that every article of clothing I'm wearing is sticking to me. As is my hair. Errant pieces of it keep landing on my face and adhering themselves to my skin like those sticky hand toys kids love so much. You know the ones—they're like tiny neon hands with long stringy handles that you slap against the window, then get yelled at by the maid because it'll leave a mark and she *just cleaned that!*

I'm sure I must be absolutely disgusting. At this point I'm literally dripping with sweat, my antiperspirant doesn't seem to be up to 'jungle standard,' and my mouth is so dry it feels like cotton balls have been stuffed into it, even though the rest of my body is completely moist. And even the fact that I just used the word moist shows you exactly what kind of shape I'm in at the moment because, *moist*. Eww.

I hear the faint sound of running water, maybe a creek or a river or some such, but I'm so close to delirium I assume my mind is playing tricks on me. It seems like we've been walking for years now, even though I know it's all just one horrid, sweat-filled, starving, terrifying, humiliating afternoon. The sound of the water reminds me I haven't gone to the loo in a very long time, which reminds me of something I'm trying very hard to ignore. I need to pee … and do *the other thing* you do in the loo. But since I refuse to ask Mr. Condescending how, I've resigned myself to holding it until we reach the sweet relief of a hotel toilet.

I can hold it for several days, can't I? I'm sure I've heard of people doing it before. I doubt it's advisable, but then again, nothing I've done since my first flute of champagne at that bloody wedding has been in any way a good idea.

It's not just the overwhelming ocean of regret I'm swimming in. I'm drowning in hatred for this man. I can't believe I've chosen to spend the next several days (or the *last* few days of my life, depending on how this works out) with someone like him. All day, he's been providing his ultra-condescending survival commentary. I know he has to do it as part of the show, but there is a definite undercurrent of passive-aggressiveness to it, like everything he's saying is with the express intent of scaring the living shit out of me.

I glare at his back and imagine myself kicking him into a deep ravine, then wiping my hands while my lips curve up into a satisfied smile. But, since he's my only way out of this hell, I suppose I shouldn't try to off him. Bollocks. My feet have never been this sore in my entire life, and I once wore Manolo Blahniks that were two sizes too small to a gala because I loved them so much, but the store didn't have my size. The blisters took weeks to go away. But that was nothing compared to the pain I'm in now. I'm scared to take off my boots in case I have already contracted trench foot. Can you even get trench foot in the heat of the jungle or is that only in cold climates? I should really Google that because I've heard it's a terrible way to go. Except I can't Google anything because I don't have my mobile, and even if I did, I imagine this stupid jungle doesn't have Wi-Fi. Is it still called trench foot if it's in both feet, or is that trench *feet*?

I'm delirious, aren't I?

Will stops suddenly. "All right, normally I'd be farther along by now, but we'll have to stop here for the night."

Oh, would you? You'd normally be farther along because you're a superhuman godly specimen of manliness, stuck with a princess-sized albatross around your neck. Fuck you, you fucking fuckwit. "Brilliant. That actually didn't seem that far now that we're here." I unclip my backpack and it falls to the ground with a thud.

Will shakes his head. "Oh, no. Not here. We need to get down there first."

He points and I peek over the ledge we're standing on, only to see it's a good thirty-foot drop to the riverbank below.

"Of course we do," I murmur, picking up my bag and strapping it back onto my aching torso.

He smiles at the camera. "Lucky for us, these vines should provide a safe and easy way to get down there."

"More rappelling," I say. "Fantastic." *Fan-fucking-tastic.*

He grabs a thick vine growing out of the ground and tugs on it a few times, seeming to decide it's safe. "I'll go first so I can help you if you run into any trouble. Unless you want to go first? I don't want to be sexist about it."

"Just go."

"Gladly. If you could just lean over the edge and film me while I make my descent, that would be very helpful."

I do as he asks and watch as he rappels a little more than halfway down, then jumps to the ground while looking up with a big grin on his face and two thumbs up.

"Show off," I mutter.

"Okay, your turn. I'll film you and you go," he calls.

"Perfect," I murmur. "Make sure you get lots of footage of my sweaty arse in these baggy pants while I slam into the side of the cliff repeatedly. Or better yet, when my arms give out and I fall, killing us both. At this point, I'd welcome death so long as I take you out with me." I crouch and pick up the vine, pulling on it as I turn away from the ravine. "You don't want to be sexist. Sure you do, arsehole," I say, then start imitating his voice as I get my footing. "Everything out here can kill you. Don't touch anything and don't drink anything and don't eat anything except these putrid larvae. Oh, and don't be here because I don't want you here."

I start down the cliff, gripping the slippery vine while I continue muttering to myself. I shut up as I near the ground, not wanting Mr. Thinks His Shit Doesn't Stink to hear my spot-on imitation of him.

When I finally get to the bottom, he says, "Hey, that was pretty good. You didn't shout any curse words that time."

"That's because I've lost my will to live. At this point, between being faced with the prospect of spending another few days out here with you or just ending it all quickly, the second option sounds far more appealing to me."

He stares at me long enough for me to wonder if he's considering drowning me in the river. Then he nods. "The first day is always the worst."

"Oh, is it?" I quip.

I clomp over to the stream and crouch down, plunging my hands into the cool water to refresh my skin. *Aahhh, that's better.*

Except that it's reminding me I really must use the ladies' room. I cup my palms together and am just about to have a sip when he says, "Oh, don't do that. We need to boil that first."

"Obviously I wasn't about to drink it," I lie. "I only meant to splash some on my face."

"Don't do that either. You could get a parasite in your nose or mouth, and it'll be game over."

I stand and shake my hands off without offering a response.

"I can have our camp set up in about fifteen minutes, but it'll be a good two to three hours until we can eat."

"No. That can't be right." I'm too hungry for that to be right. I take my backpack off and drop it, then crouch, unzip it, and start taking everything out even though I already know we don't have anything to eat "We must have some protein bars or something. They wouldn't have sent us out here to starve."

"We're not going to starve. We're going to *survive*. Did you not understand the premise of the show?"

"Yeah, I got it, thank you," I snap, scowling at him. "I'm just a bit hangry right now is all."

Unlike me, he's still in nature documentary host mode. "Well, the good news is we're surrounded by vegetation and protein sources. Since the rhino beetles weren't your thing, I'll catch us some fish and dig up some wild yam tubers. In about three hours, we'll be nice and full."

Three hours? I can't. I just can't. I slump down onto a fallen log and let my body go limp. Tears fill my eyes and I shake my head with what's left of my energy. "Okay, forget it. I'm not meant for this. I give up. Just call the helicopter and have them come get me. I don't want to do this anymore. I thought

I wanted a great adventure, but this is not what I had in mind. You win. My brother wins. My father wins."

I let one arm flail out to the side. "The entire staff at the palace—they all win. I am just a sheltered, spoiled, soft princess who has no business being out here whatsoever. I'm sorry I wasted your time and the time of the network, and I sincerely apologize to the People for Animals Society for losing the funding, but please, I must leave now."

He holds his hand out to me and for the briefest second, I think he's going to say something kind, but he doesn't. Instead he barks, "Get off that log. You're about to be attacked by a colony of bullet ants."

Something pinches my wrist. "Ouch! Shit!"

When I look down, I see an army of enormous red ants, who are marching three by three toward me.

I jump up, screaming. "Get them off me! Get them off me!!!!" while I run to Will.

He stops me with both hands, then brushes the ant off me while I continue to scream.

"It's okay. It's gone now."

"No, it's not okay," I say, shaking my head wildly. "Just call them. Call them and get me out of here now! This is over. You were right. I was wrong. I can admit it, okay. I'll go home and go back to giving tours to those hateful nonagenarians. It's not that bad."

He stares down at me, his face softening. "This is the worst moment. I promise it gets better from here."

"No, it won't." I hear the sound of loud sobs and it takes a moment before I realize they're coming from me. Taking a deep breath, I say, "I thought this was like *Survivor*—if something goes wrong, they always have people nearby to rescue them."

"*Survivor*'s a game show. Have you not watched *The Wild World?*"

"I assumed you didn't show the safety people," I say, sniffling in a most undignified way.

"That's because there *aren't* any safety people," he says, shaking his head. "What did you think the danger bonus was for?"

"I don't know, to make the whole thing more dramatic?" Desperation overtakes me. I close my eyes and start clicking my hiking boots together at the heels, saying, "There's no place like home. There's no place like home."

After a few moments, I open my left eye first, only to find Will staring at me, his mouth agape.

"Oh, dear," he says, his expression somewhere between pity and fear.

"I'm sorry I did this. I never should've applied. I think maybe I'm having some sort of quarter-life crisis or something," I say as I pace back and forth in front of him. "I've just turned twenty-nine ... which would mean I'm planning to live to be almost one-hundred and twenty. Maybe it's a third-life crisis. Is that a thing?"

"Not sure, but the math sounds solid."

"Okay, at least that's something, right? The thing is, I'm under a tremendous amount of pressure to find a husband before I turn thirty. Only all the men I know are complete wankers and I could never be attracted to any of them. They want to set me up with the future Earl of Wimberly, and do you know what his nickname is? Hal, as in halitosis! Yeah, imagine kissing that until death do us part. No, thank you.

"Then I drank too much champagne at your sister's stupid wedding. Who has a champagne fountain? I mean *really*! How irresponsible can you be?! After my third glass, I met you and I thought, 'Yes!'"

His eyes grow wide and I realize what he thinks I just said.

"No, not like *that*. I don't want to marry you. God, no. You're a total prick. I wanted your *life* for a while. The way you were bragging about it, you made it sound so free and easy and wonderful—all lies, by the way—but I thought to myself, 'If I could just be him, even for a few short days, it will all be okay.'

"I just needed a break from constantly being told what to do and how to do it and what to wear and what I can't wear and what to eat and what I can't eat. Did you know we're not even allowed to eat garlic if we're going to see the Queen of England any time in the next month?" I ask, stopping and nodding my head. "Yeah, no garlic! And I'm not allowed to wear heels taller than two inches or miniskirts. In fact, I can't even wear *anything* that cuts off above the knee, as if my bare knees are so scandalous. I've had to dress like I'm some woman in late menopause since I was … well … born, I guess. And honestly, that makes it *really hard* to attract a man."

I step closer to him and put my hands on his upper arms.

Oh, God, those are muscly. Never mind that. "You know when I got to wear those shorts earlier? That is probably the most free I've felt in my entire life. But then *you* said I had to change, and it was over, like that." I snap my fingers in his face. "And now, here we are. I'm in my baggy, ugly communist-chic outfit, and I'm going to get us both killed. I am, Will. We are going to *die out here.* Possibly today, maybe tomorrow, but most certainly before the end of the week. I'm not going to see my niece and nephew grow up. I mean, they're so cute and cuddly, and they adore their Auntie Arabella." I start to cry, my voice going up two octaves as I start to pace again. "And what about Gran? She seems as tough as nails, but honestly, she's been through so much and now with her heart condition. I don't think she could take if something happened to me. I'm her favourite person."

I stop pacing and stand in front of him, then burst into uncontrollable sobs until tears are pouring down my cheeks. I cover my face with my hands and cry into my palms, feeling like Anne of Green Gables when she's in the depths of despair. I feel Will's arms wrap around me and he shushes me while holding the back of my head gently.

"And I've had to use the loo for hours now and I'm afraid to ask how that even works because I hate you so much and I just know it's going to be horrifyingly embarrassing and likely you'll have to stand guard while I squat somewhere only to end up wiping my arse with some sort of plant that will cause a horrible rash!" I sob into his shirt. "An itchy, painful rash. And I'm not allowed to scratch anything, let alone my bottom. It's going to be excruciating!"

"Oh, wow," Will says, letting out a long breath. "When you fall apart, you really go for it."

I nod, pulling back a little, then my face crumples and I wail, "I'm not allowed to fall apart!"

"Okay, Arabella," he says, lowering his face to mine and maintaining direct eye contact. "Let's deal with one problem at a time. Using the loo is pretty simple, really. I'll find some moss for you, then dig a little hole near a log—one *without* bullet ants—then I'll walk away to give you some privacy. You do what you need to do, then you cover the hole and we don't ever have to talk about it again."

I nod and sniffle. "That sounds dreadful."

"It's not all bad. Once we've dealt with that, I'll set up the camp and feed you. I promise, you'll feel a thousand times better once we do those things, okay?"

I sniff again and nod. "Okay."

Wiping my cheeks, I feel my despair give way to shame. I stare at the ground, trying to compose myself. "Sorry. I don't normally fall apart like that."

When I finally look up at him, his face is filled with compassion. "Can I tell you something?"

I nod and dab daintily at my eyes.

"The first night is always the worst. I promise. And it really will get better from here."

"Not if we die."

"We're not going to die. I won't let that happen," he says,

putting both hands on my shoulders. "Now, look around you. We are surrounded by not only one of the most beautiful and untouched places on Earth, we're also surrounded by an abundance of food and water. You're going to be fine, I promise." He rubs my arms up and down reassuringly. Hmm, well that feels rather nice, actually.

"Okay."

"I'm going to get you set up to use the loo. Then, start the fire. Then all you need to do is sit here and keep it going while I get us food. But first, let's get you some fresh water. I'm pretty sure you're dehydrated." With that, he walks over a tall stalk of bamboo and with one quick slice of his machete, cuts it, then holds it sideways while he walks over to me. "Here, open your mouth."

I do as he says, and a second later feel cool refreshing liquid pouring into my mouth. I gulp down as much as I can before I feel like I'm going to choke, then hold my hand up to let him know I need a break. He drinks some, then offers me more, which feels oddly intimate. Once the entire bamboo shoot is emptied of water, he sets it down.

"Thank you. That tasted kind of like carrots."

He grins. "I've never noticed that. But now that you say it, I think you're right."

Twenty minutes later, I've taken care of my biological needs, and am sitting on a rock in front of the fire, watching Will turn the bamboo stick into a spear. He describes what he's doing into the camera while he works quickly. My stomach growls and I feel weak and hungry and tired. But he was right because somehow, sitting here feels infinitely better. He disappears into the bushes for a few minutes, then comes back with the bottom of his shirt flipped up, carrying some fruit. "I thought you could use a little amuse-bouche while I make dinner."

He crouches and unpacks the load onto the ground next to me. Holding up one of the oranges, he says, "These are monkey oranges. They have a tough outer shell, but they're very juicy and full of vitamins. Eat up. Oh, but not the seeds. The seeds'll kill you. I'll see if I can get us a catfish."

When I look up into his eyes, gone is the smug, angry attitude, and in its place is kindness. Something about it makes me feel much worse about my tirade. And about giving him a hard time in the first place when, in reality, I'm making his life much harder. "Thank you," I say with a smile.

"Don't mention it."

Reaching out, I touch his hand, which is resting on his knee. "No, really. Thank you. I'm sorry I imposed myself on you like this."

"That's okay. If you hadn't applied, it could have been someone much worse."

"Like that woman who stalks you online?"

His head snaps back. "Who?"

"She has a website dedicated to you. She and your fellow groupies call themselves Will's Wild Fangirls."

A look of understanding crosses his face. "Oh, right. *Them.*"

Nodding, I say, "The head super fan applied for the show."

He smiles at me. "I suppose I should be happy I'm not stuck out here with her."

"Yes, she seems like the type to go total *Fatal Attraction* on you."

"Good thing I don't have a pet bunny." He chuckles and stands. "Will you be okay for a bit while I go down to the river?"

I nod, and for the first time since this morning, I believe I will be.

Maybe.

————

It's dark by the time we eat, which I don't think is necessarily a bad thing. Dinner is wild yam tubers and bony white fish. We're using banana leaves as plates and our table is the tops of our knees. The outside flesh of the yams are charred black and they smell of coals, but at least they're warm and soft enough to scoop with our sporks. There's plenty for both of us, and with every bite, I feel more like myself again. Instead of feeling angry, I feel grateful for this simple meal. There's a shift in the feeling between us. It's no longer a tension-filled hatefest, but a calm, tentative truce, which feels infinitely better.

"Will, I want you to know I'm sorry about all the awful things I said earlier. It was uncalled for."

"Me too," Will answers, glancing up at me. "I was being a judgmental prick, and I didn't mean any of it. Especially not the bit about leaving you here to get eaten by leopards. I'd never do that to anyone."

"Thank you. That means a lot," I say. "And you're *not* more smug than Kanye." I grin a little, hoping he'll know I'm joking.

He offers me a half-smile in return. "Thanks, that's very kind of you."

I give him a teasing look. "It's close, but he really is more arrogant than you. By a narrow margin, but still…"

We both laugh, and it feels like we're starting over. Relief fills my body as we sit in a comfortable silence watching the fire.

Adding another piece of wood, Will says, "I cried the first time I spent the night out in the wilderness."

"Really?" I ask.

He clearly wants to make me feel better about my melt-down earlier. Huh, that's sort of nice of him. "That surprises me."

"Well, it's true." He gives a little half grin. "Mind you, I was seven at the time."

I roll my eyes and chuckle a little. "Of course you were."

"My parents had died a few months earlier and our uncle took us in. He moved us all the way from Valcourt to the Caribbean—talk about culture shock. He was a real outdoorsman—I think he assumed everybody lived that way —snorkeling, scuba diving, surfing, sailing."

I stare at him, my heart tugging a little at the image of him as a young boy with no parents. I say nothing because I know from experience, there's really nothing to say.

Will continues, shifting his gaze to the fire. "There was this little uninhabited island that we went to one night, not that long after we moved there. He thought it would be a great adventure for us kids, but I was terrified. I'd never slept out under the stars before, and I kept thinking I was going to get eaten by a crocodile, even though he kept telling me there were no crocodiles there. Only iguanas and birds."

He pauses and smiles, seeming to be far away in his mind. "Every little noise woke me for the first part of the night, but then I must have gotten so exhausted, I finally fell asleep, tucked in between my sister and brother, with our uncle sitting by the fire, keeping an eye out for crocs for me. The next morning, we hiked all the way to an amazing waterfall with a lagoon that was like something out of a movie." Will grins at the memory. "We had the greatest time swinging into the pool from vines and splashing around. As an adult, I understood what he was trying to do for us. He wanted to help us return to our roots. Our long-forgotten, cave-person roots. Humans are animals and we're meant to be outside—even the royal ones."

14

Eighties Popstars, Soothing Tree Sap, and the Night Sky

Will

"EVEN THE ROYAL ONES?" she asks. "I find that hard to believe."

She smiles at me and even though her face is only lit by the light of the campfire, it's like the whole jungle has suddenly become brighter. Oh, that thought has no business in my mind. Not with her. Not here. And certainly not now. I clear my throat, then say the least romantic thing I can think of. "We should check your feet for infection."

Her head snaps back and her nose wrinkles up in disgust. "Is that a possibility? I've been wearing my boots all day, and believe me, my personal hygiene is generally quite excellent."

"Sorry, I didn't mean to insult you," I say. "What I meant was, we need to let our feet dry and check them over."

I dig around in the backpack and grab the headlamps, then slide one on, and hand the other one to Arabella. I unlace my boots and take them off, then remove my damp socks. Switching the lamp on, I then set up one of the cameras to point at my feet. "When you're in an extremely humid climate like this one, you need to make sure you allow ample time for the insides of your boots to dry, but also your feet as well. You should carefully check for blisters or sores, and, as gross as this sounds, ensure your skin isn't starting to peel off, because if it is, you're in a lot more trouble than you might think."

"With moves like these, it's a wonder you're single," Arabella says.

I chuckle a little, then watch her remove her boots. Uh-oh. She winced. Once her socks are off, my eyes land on open sores on either side of her ankles. "Shit. Did that just happen today?"

"It's nothing." She gives a quick shake of her head. "You know, breaking in new footwear."

I dig around in my bag and grab out the sap I collected earlier. Pointing the GoPro at my face, I say, "Princess Arabella has got open sores on her ankles from wearing new boots—and in her case, it's not her fault. Her wardrobe was provided by the network, but normally before embarking on a trek like the one we're on, you'll want to break in whatever footwear you have, to avoid these types of blisters. I'm going to pop down to the river, wash this pot out, then boil some water and this bag of sap so I can make the perfect soothing balm to heal those sores in no time."

"Could we not talk about my sores?" she whispers.

"It's an excellent opportunity for learning survival skills."

"That may be, but I prefer not to make a public spectacle of my feet, certainly not when they're in *this* condition."

I tilt my head. "You have really lovely feet. Those are world-class cute toes."

Feeling silly, I toss two more pieces of dead bamboo on the fire to keep it going. "You relax and let the heat dry your skin. I'll be right back."

———

Once the sap has melted, I take the pot off the fire. "You can see the consistency of the salve is a nice thick liquid so it'll glide on smoothly. We'll let it cool for a while before I apply it, but in the interest of allowing my co-host some privacy, I shall now bid you good night and turn off the cameras until morning so the batteries can charge up while we charge our own batteries." I shut off the camera, then mutter, "That was cheesy."

"Just a bit." Arabella removes the holster her GoPro is attached to and hands it, along with the camera to me. "There. Much better."

"Yes, we're alone now."

She nods. "Children behave, that's what they'll say when we're together."

I narrow my eyes in confusion.

"We should probably watch how we play," she adds. "But they don't understand."

"What are you talking about?"

"Come on, Will," she says with a grin. "You know the words."

"Oh, this is a *song*?" I shake my head even though I know exactly what song it is. "I have absolutely no idea what song that is."

"You are *such* a liar. Everybody knows Tiffany."

"Not me." I scratch my chin thoughtfully. "But I do have one question for you."

"Shoot."

"Are we running just as fast as we can? Holding onto one another's hands?"

Arabella bursts out laughing, then sings, "Trying to get away into the night ..."

I join in, unable to resist. We belt out the song together, and I interrupt, only to say things like, "I should put the camera back on. Dylan would call this solid gold television."

Arabella shakes her head while she sings, "... the beating of our hearts is the only sound."

I pick up the camera and she grabs for it, her delicate skin waking me up. "Don't you dare. I'll stop singing."

"Then I won't."

We glance at each other for a moment, then at the exact same time, we both sing out, "I think we're alone now."

Soon, we're both laughing too hard to finish the song. And

when the moment ends, I stare at her longer than I should, but find myself unable to tear my eyes away. A happy version of this pain-in-the-arse princess is sort of irresistible. "You're fun."

"And you're surprised by that," she says. "Of course I can be fun. Well, under the right circumstances, and in the appropriate setting."

"Ah, yes." I put on a posh accent. "The hallmark of uninhibited fun—under the right circumstances and in the appropriate setting."

"Quite," she says, lifting an imaginary tea cup with her pinky out.

I laugh again, then give her an inquisitive look. "By any chance, did you lick one of the yellow frogs earlier when you went to the loo?"

Arabella laughs, a full lovely sound that causes me to join her.

Okay, Will, enough of the gazing at the beautiful princess. You can't have her, so forget about it.

Needing to distract myself, I check the temperature of the salve, finding it just right. Scooping some onto my finger, I hold out my other hand. "Your foot, milady."

"Oh, no, it's fine. I'll do it. I haven't washed my feet, so they're rather yucky at the moment."

"I have news for you. Every part of us is going to be 'rather yucky' until we get out of here," I say. "That's just life in the bush. Now, I offer an all-inclusive service out here in the jungle—delicious warm meals, unlimited fresh larvae, and medical attention."

"All-inclusive? Hmm …" she says with a flirty smile.

Oh wow, do I ever want to find out what she means by that. Instead, I force myself to get back to the matter at hand. "Give me your dainty little foot so I can fix you up."

She reluctantly lifts her foot and sets it down on my waiting palm, the weight of it giving me a hint as to how slight she really is. I switch the headlamp back on and get to work, fixing up her ankles and covering them with bandages.

The fire starts to die down, and I see her yawn, then realize I'm a little disappointed that this evening is coming to an end. Huh. That's weird. "We should get some sleep. It's been a long day."

She glances over at the tent, then at me, and I can't be sure, but it seems as though there is meaning in the expression she's giving me.

No, that can't be right. I'm just tired. But she did make the phrase all-inclusive sound a little dirty …

Which is exactly why I have to sleep out here tonight.

She blinks slowly. "I feel terrible taking the tent while you're out here."

Do not make eye contact. I glance up at the sky. "I actually prefer it out here under the stars."

"And with the brown recluse spiders and Wolverine frog and mosquitoes …"

Is she trying to persuade me to join her? *No. Bad, Will, bad. Do not go there.* "I'll be fine. Maybe if I could keep my boots in the tent with you. That way if it rains, they'll be nice and dry for me."

I stand, and get my sleeping bag out of my backpack, then lay it next to the fire. "Do you know why I picked this spot for the night?"

"Because of the water."

I nod. "Yes, but one of the benefits of being next to a river like this is that there's a break in the trees so you can see all the stars up there."

Arabella leans back and stares up at the night sky. "Well, that is incredible," she whispers.

"Right?" I say, laying back.

"I mean, I knew there were millions of them, but the sky isn't even black. It's absolutely *filled* with twinkling lights," she says. "Hold on a second."

Arabella gets up and unzips the tent, then pulls out her sleeping bag. She sets it down near mine and lays on it. "I'm not ready to sleep just yet. I want to stare at this until I know I'll never forget it."

"It's amazing, isn't it?" I ask with a happy sigh. "People go their whole lives without seeing the Earth and the sky for what they really are. They just stay stuck in their boxes from the moment they are born until they die."

"I've spent my entire life in a box. A very grand, luxurious, safe box," she says quietly.

Glancing at her, I say, "Is that why you came, Arabella? Because you can't stand being confined anymore?"

She nods, turning her head to me. "I needed to get out. I felt like … I might …"

"Die if you didn't?"

Nodding again, she says, "I know it sounds horribly ungrateful. For someone like me to feel any sort of discontentment when my life is one of incredible privilege."

"Not to me, it doesn't," I say, turning onto my side to face her. "To me, your life sounds really sad."

"I don't know if it's sad," she answers, turning her body toward me. "But it comes with a list of dos and don'ts that could fill up that whole night sky."

I stare at her, trying not to memorize her beautiful face. "How did you convince them to let you do this?"

"I didn't." She shuts her eyes tightly. "I approached Kira Taylor in private, then I had to sneak out of the palace without my security following me."

My mouth drops in shock. "Are you serious?"

Arabella nods. "My grandmother plays poker once a month with the guys who work in the garage. One of them is into her for a lot of money, so I was able to offer him a nice wad of cash to hide me in the boot of his car and take me straight to the airport."

"Okay, can I just say how impressed I am?"

"You may," she says in a regal tone. Her smile fades, replaced by a worried expression. "I can't even imagine what's going on back home right now. I left overly sentimental handwritten notes for nearly everyone on staff and in the family."

"Just in case?"

"That probably sounds silly to you."

"Nope. Life is really fucking short," I say, thinking about my parents and Arabella's mother.

"It *is* really fucking short," she says. "You know something funny? You and I both lost people at a very early age, and we've both come to the conclusion that life is short, but the *way* we respond to that knowledge is completely opposite. I never risk anything, and you do nothing but risk everything."

I gaze into her eyes, and for an unexplainable reason, I find myself wanting to risk everything once again. She is so unexpectedly sweet, and vulnerable, and beautiful. *Do not kiss her. Do not even think about it.* I glance down at her full lips and then back up at her eyes. The sound of an owl hooting interrupts the moment.

"If the owls are out, it must be late," she says, biting her bottom lip.

"We should get some rest." As soon as the words leave my mouth, my entire body grows furious with me for saying them.

Not tonight. Not ever.

15

Tiny Tents, Hot Men, and Other Things That Keep You Up at Night

Arabella

WHY CAN'T I SLEEP? I mean, really—why? I've been up since the crack of dawn, have had enough adrenaline flow through me today to revive ten patients in cardiac arrest, I've trekked what feels like a thousand kilometers on uneven terrain. Every muscle in my body is aching, and I am utterly exhausted. I should have fallen straight into a deep sleep. And yet, I'm lying here in this tiny tent, staring up at the fabric above me, listening to the babbling of the river, the hypnotic song of the cicadas, and the gentle snoring coming from just outside the tent (which I must say I find oddly comforting).

And I know what you're thinking, but trust me, you're wrong. I'm not awake because of the man making those comforting snoring sounds, or because I've never felt as safe in my life as I do with him—especially the bit where he held me while I fell apart like a complete baby. Seriously, it's got *nothing* to do with him and everything to do with me knowing that back home, my family, as well as most likely the media, are freaking out wondering what the hell has gotten into me. My father must be through-the-roof mad. And Arthur is going to be furious with me, not that I care.

All right, *fine*. I do care. And it's killing me to know I've upset everyone like this. It feels absolutely selfish for me to have runaway from my duties and the people who love me most.

Good God, Arabella, just close your eyes and go to sleep already. There's nothing you can do to fix any of it. Not from here. The only thing you can do is get out of this jungle as quickly as possible, so you can go home and make everything okay again.

Sigh.

.

.

.

Sigh again.

Okay, but first, I do have to get a few things off my chest. There's no denying that he's absolutely gorgeous, and he smelled quite yummy even though he was wearing bug repellent and was all sweaty when he was hugging me. Also, he said that really sweet thing about how cute my toes are. That was definitely knicker-melting. Plus, he turned the cameras off for me.

I mean, he was totally a dismissive dickhead earlier in the

day, but I'm not sure I can blame him. Imagine what a threat I must be? After all, Dylan did say she was going to rename the program so it'll be about me. That must have stung, no? Plus, he wasn't wrong about the fact that I don't have the first clue what I'm doing out here, and it's entirely possible I'll get us both into some kind of scrape and we'll end up dead. So, I suppose he had reason to be a bit snippy.

Anyway, back to me not sleeping. The fact that I find him attractive beyond what I have ever felt in my life has nothing to do with me lying awake. It's really just all the other things. I'm definitely not thinking about unzipping this tent and crawling into his sleeping bag with him. Because that would be wrong. That would make me the skanky ho that awful blogger was worried about. Well, not really. I'm judging myself rather harshly, aren't I? I can have sex with an available, single, interested man. That's totally fine in this day and age.

Just not *that* man. First of all, how do I know he's interested? Just because he kept glancing at my lips, it doesn't mean he wants to kiss them. So there's that. Besides, we're not meant for each other. There is absolutely no way a relationship with him would work in the long term. Short term out here in the wild where no one would be the wiser, however …

Nope!

I'm out here to test my resolve—not only out here in nature, but my resolve about not becoming physically or romantically involved with someone who is entirely wrong for me. Someone totally sweet who made us dinner, then prepared a warm salve for my ankles, which, I do have to say is making them feel so much better. Someone who's also such a gentleman that he's outside, possibly being feasted on by mosquitoes, while I sleep in this comfy tent. Although, if I'm going to be completely honest, I do miss having a pillow and my Tempur-Pedic mattress.

Oh God, I do fancy him! Shit. Okay, that's it. First thing tomorrow morning, I'm just going to pull it together. No more crying, no more gagging when presented with beetle larvae for lunch. I am just going to woman up, stop whining, and let the inner Xena, Warrior Princess in me come out for the first time ever. Yes, that's it. No flirting, no more being a girly girl. I'm going to earn his respect and the respect of everyone else I know because that is what I'm here to do. I'm not here for love. I'm here for respect.

So, I will not shag him.

Ever. No matter what.

Even if it would be amazing and no one would find out.

No shagging.

None.

Not even a little.

Go to sleep.

———

ABN Morning Newscast – Friday, April 17th

"Good morning, I'm Veronica Platt with the ABN news desk. Our top story this morning is the mystery of the missing princess. Rumblings have been heard throughout the city of Valcourt over the last two days as Princess Arabella has begged off all of her obligations with no explanation. Silence from the palace as she's left twenty-eight charities wondering where their patron is. Giles Bigly is on scene in front of the palace this morning. Giles, what can you tell us about this shocking situation?"

The screen splits in half, and Giles Bigly fills the right side, standing under an umbrella as rain beats down around him. Instead of looking at the camera, he's talking to someone out of the shot. "... because they're a bunch of bloody sadists, that's why." Pause. "There is no good reason to have us out here when it's pissing down like this. I could have just as easily done this in the studio. You can't even see the bloody palace behind me for all the rain."

"Giles! It's Veronica! Can you hear me?" she yells.

Turning to the camera, Giles lifts his microphone. "Yes, I'm here, Veronica. You'll have to speak up. The pounding rain is competing with your voice."

"Righto. Giles, what have you learned about Princess Arabella's disappearance?"

"Not much, Veronica. Palace officials are remaining tight-lipped as to her whereabouts. My sources at the hospital have indicated there's no sign of her at their facilities, so it's unlikely that she has taken ill."

"Thank goodness for that, at least. Could it potentially be some sort of a mental breakdown?" Veronica asks. "After all, she is so much like her mother and her mother definitely had difficulty keeping up with her obligations before her untimely death."

Giles glares at the camera, barely hiding his disdain. "It's hard to say. For all we know, she's got a touch of a flu or some injury—she does a ballet workout every morning, so maybe she pulled a hamstring or tore a ligament. What we do know is that, up until this point, Princess Arabella has always been a steady and reliable patron of all of her charities and her many foundations throughout the kingdom."

"Giles, would you say her reliability makes her sudden disappearance more alarming?" Veronica asks.

"No, not really."

"You don't think so?" Veronica says. "Her disappearance is extremely out of character. There's some buzz around the nation about a possible kidnapping, although none of those rumours have been substantiated."

"I highly doubt it," Giles answers. "I'd say the explanation is likely nothing of consequence and when we do find out why she's taken a few days off, the whole thing will be rather anti-climactic, and certainly not worth having a seasoned jour-nalist standing outside during this frigid rainstorm."

"But, let's imagine for a moment she has been kidnapped. Would you have any idea who might have wanted to kidnap her?"

"Nope. No clue, Veronica. What I do know is that spreading unsubstantiated rumours is not in keeping with any sort of journalistic integrity."

"So true," Veronica answers with a firm nod. "I'd say it's

all the more reason for the palace to make some sort of statement."

"Indeed. That would put a stop to this nonsense."

"Exactly, Giles. Whatever they're hiding, they really do need to come out with it."

"Again, there is likely nothing going on, Veronica. Other than a slow news day, that is."

Veronica shakes her head and purses her lips. "Well, let's just hope wherever Princess Arabella is, she'll return home safely."

"Okay, sure," Giles answers, throwing his free hand up in the air.

The feed cuts and Veronica's face fills the screen. "That was Giles Bigly live on location in front of Valcourt Palace. Stay with us throughout the day as this alarming mystery unfolds. Coming up next, we're going to meet a man who says his turtle is the reincarnation of Albert Einstein. That and more after a word from our sponsors."

16

There's a Thin Line Between Lust and Hate...

Will

I WAKE to the early morning chorus of birds, the thick, humid air, and a sense of panic. Yesterday was an absolute mind bender. I want her, I hate her, I feel sorry for her, I want her again, I think she wants me, then 'Goodnight, William. Sleep well.'

I fell asleep to the mantra of 'you cannot have her,' and now, in the early morning light, I'm even more sure about that. But damn, do I ever want her, which is why I'm going to get us the hell out of this jungle in under four days. And that's a promise. Any more than that, and … well, I don't even want to think about what could happen, but I know it'll be really bad. But also, sssooooo good. So very, very good. Which is why I'm determined to return a certain princess to Mbambole before I end up making a disastrous error, like letting the whole 'opposites attract' thing get in the way of my life.

Her tent is still zipped shut, which is good. She's probably exhausted from yesterday's trek, and to be honest, I could use some time alone to get my head on straight. I stand and quickly roll up my sleeping bag, then brush my teeth for much longer than normal (for no particular reason).

Taking my GoPro, I walk over to the spot where I left our water bottles last night and turn on the video camera. "One of the best ways to get fresh water when you're out in a rain-forest is to use the natural humidity in the air and a big leaf to collect the water for you. Last night, I set up our water bottles under this banana leaf. By now, they should be full."

I check the bottles and smile at the lens. "And it worked again."

I shut off the camera and mutter, "That did sound smug. Huh."

"But not overly so," Arabella says, scaring the hell out of me.

I start, then turn to her with a sheepish expression. "I thought you were still asleep."

"Got up early to collect some breakfast," she says, already looking lovely, with her hair up in a ponytail.

I glance down to her arms and see she's carrying a bunch of bananas and some oranges. "I see you did some early morning foraging."

"I thought it only fair since you provided supper. It's not larvae, but it'll have to do."

Grinning at her, I say, "We can always find some bugs to eat along the way, Your Highness."

"Yum, can't wait."

We sit together and eat our fruit, listening to the water rush down the river.

"Can I ask you something?" she says with a serious expression. "I'd like you to stop calling me Princess Arabella or Your Highness. I'm taking a break from royal life for a few days."

"Sure," I say. "In that case, I need to give you a nickname."

Raising one eyebrow, she gives me a skeptical look. "Like what?"

"I don't know yet, but it's probably going to have something to do with you being a thief."

Arabella gasps dramatically, but her eyes sparkle with laughter. "I am no such thing!"

"That lighter you keep in your bra says otherwise."

She laughs and slaps my arm playfully. "I was being resourceful. Think of a name that has to do with that."

"Nope, you're a bit of a scoundrel. Sticky Fingers?" I ask, then shake my head. "Nah, too weird. Maybe I should go with something to do with your foul-mouth."

"I do not have a—oh wait, I guess I do when I'm rappelling, don't I?"

"Just a bit." I stand and smile down at her. "I'm going to have to put some thought into it, but I'll come up with something just right."

Getting up, Arabella rolls her eyes while she starts to collect the peels from our breakfast. "How about Arabella? You won't have to hurt your brain coming up with a nickname, and it brings with it the added bonus of me answering to it."

"Hurt my brain? Was that an insult?" I ask.

"No, I would never imply that you're not smart," she says. "Just because a good portion of the women Dylan surveyed thought you didn't seem that bright?"

"She told you that?!"

"She may have done, yes," she says with a mischievous grin.

"They only said that because of my physique."

Arabella wrinkles up her nose. "Is that what she told you?"

I burst out laughing. "You're a bit of a badass!"

"A bit, yes," Arabella answers with a hint of pride. "Now, let's get moving. We have miles to go today and I don't need you slowing me down."

I grin down at her for a second, then remember I do not want to fall for this woman. "Speaking of slowing you down, I have a much quicker way for us to get to Mbambole."

"Really?"

"Want to help me build a raft?"

"I'd like that very much."

"Good." I grab the machete and start into the bush with Arabella in tow. "I'm not going to forget about the nickname, you know?"

"Damn."

"You thought you could distract me with the results of that horrible survey and I'd forget, didn't you?" I ask, over my shoulder.

"And I was right. You forgot all about it."

"For about a minute."

"Oh, come on, it was at least two."

17

So, I Do Want to See Under Tarzan's Loincloth. What of It?

Arabella

THE CAMERAS ARE ROLLING AGAIN, which immediately shifts Will's focus, bringing him back to his business as host. The two of us have spent the last hour collecting long, green bamboo shoots and dragging them to the river's edge. Each trip back, I yearn to jump in so I can be refreshed by the cool, fast-flowing water, but instead, I drop what I'm holding, turn, and continue on. I'm already sweaty and tired, my muscles aching from the exertion, but I'm also filled with a sense of hope that propels me forward and gives strength to my arms while we work. Riding the river is going to be heads above cutting a trail through the dense brush.

We reach an impossibly tall tree, where Will stops. "I'll go up and get us some vines. If you can film me, that would be a great help, Mad Dog." He looks at me for a moment, then shakes his head. "Nope, you're not Mad Dog."

"I should hope not," I say, watching as he swiftly starts his ascent. He climbs up a few feet, then turns his head toward me and speaks into the camera. "Now, if you really want to get the strongest and longest vines, you're going to have to climb for them. This is not something you should normally do without a harness because the fall from these heights could be fatal."

"Brilliant," I say. "So, that's exactly what you're going to do."

"Yup. But don't worry, I've never died before." With that, he starts casually climbing, as though he could hang out in that tree all day. I stand on the ground, finding myself simultaneously impressed with his abilities and terrified that he may be overly optimistic about the outcome. A few moments later, he's disappeared into the canopy of the tree. He calls down to me, his voice sounding far too distant for my liking. "You'll want to stand back so that none of these vines land on you."

I back up, then shout up to him. "All clear!"

Crackling and zipping sounds fill the air as the vines drop to the ground, slamming against branches and the trunk on their way down. When they hit the jungle floor, the soft bed of leaves and organic matter fly up and scatter. After several vines have been freed from the tree, I wait, expecting to see him climb down. Instead, he decides to swing down on one, hollering like Tarzan.

I laugh as he lets go of the vine and sticks the landing with his hands in the air. "Not bad, hey?"

I clap and say, "Encore. Encore."

"Glad you enjoyed the show. Don't forget to tip your waitress."

———

The raft is roughly the size of a queen-sized bed when it's all put together, and I cannot wait to get on and rest when we're finished. The impossible humidity makes me feel like I'm sucking in water instead of breathing in air. As we work together tying off the vines, Will teaches me how to make a 'clover hitch connector' by placing one length of bamboo perpendicular to the others at one end of the raft. "We're going to wrap the vine through the connecting piece, then use a simple overhand knot to secure it. The overhand knot is one of the most fundamental of all knots. It's used in everything from fishing to shoelaces to climbing."

"Or in my case," I say, "If I wanted to tie some two-thou-sand-thread-count sheets together and climb out of my bedroom window."

Will laughs. "Sure, or say, if you accidentally drop your tiara down a well."

I grin. "That happens to me all the time. I must have dropped at least a dozen tiaras down the well behind the palace."

"Now, you'll be able to retrieve them yourself," he

answers. "Here, you pull this one. I want to see how tight you can get it."

I take the vine from him, letting my skin brush against his for the briefest second. I yank on it as hard as I can, grunting and struggling while I put my entire body into it. When I finish, I stare at him, hoping I passed the test. "So? Did I do it?"

"You tried. I'll give you that." His face scrunches up a little as he takes the vine with one hand and gives it a quick tug, actually tightening it.

"Oh," I mutter, my shoulders dropping.

"Don't worry about it. By the time we get out of here, you'll have some upper body strength. I'm going to turn you into Lara Croft, Tomb Raider."

He gives me a questioning look. "Hmm, Tomb Raider? Croft?"

"Better than Mad Dog," I say. "But not by much."

"Yeah, still not quite right. I'll figure it out."

As we set to work on the other connector, I find myself wanting to reach out and touch his cheeks. And by cheeks, I don't mean the ones on his face. Those are some taut buttocks. Yum.

Oh, dear, the humidity must be getting to me.

After a quick lunch of leftover cold yams from last night and more fruit, we pack up camp and get ready to float our way down the river. A thought pops into my head that hadn't occurred to me before. "There aren't crocodiles here, right?"

"Not many. I have heard of Nile crocs coming as far west

as this, but don't worry, they mostly hunt at night, and with any luck, we'll be off the water by then."

"Well, that sounds comforting," I say.

"Actually, we were more likely to be attacked by one last night since we were camped so near the river." He gives me a teasing grin and I narrow my eyes, unsure of whether to believe him.

We heave our packs onto the raft, then Will holds it steady while I climb on and sit near the center. He hands me the long bamboo pole he's going to use to guide us downstream, then pushes us away from shore and lightly hops on in one swift move. A rush of excitement fills me as we start down the river. I turn and grin back at him as he kneels behind me.

He takes the pole and says, "What do you think? Does it beat walking?"

I nod. "Yes, my ankles say thank you. Well, actually, my entire sore body thanks you."

"You should thank yourself. You did a lot to build this."

"Thank you, me," I say, feeling surprisingly proud of myself. I smile around at the passing trees and feel the sun on my skin, happy to be able to rest safely here as we make up some miles today. "This is terrific. We should do this until we reach Mbambole."

"If only we could. We'll stay on the river for the next three days, maybe a little more. Then it curves north, so we'll have to hike it out from there. With any luck, you'll be heading back to your palace in under four days," he says.

"Really? But that's five days ahead of schedule."

"Yup! We'll take them all by surprise."

"Brilliant. Can't wait," I say, with a big smile, even though on the inside, that thought makes me anything but happy.

18

A Fork in the River

Will

It's our second day on the river, and I'm having far too much fun, which is why I need to get the hell out of this jungle *now*. If I don't, the consequences will be dire, because for the first time in my life, I think I might be allowing a woman to worm her way into my heart like a skin-penetrating nematode. And it's not just her looks—although she definitely has the most beautiful eyes I've ever gazed into. Gazed into. *Stupid Will, so very stupid*. I've never gazed into anyone's eyes before, and the fact that I'm admitting to it in *this* situation proves that if I don't get us out of here as fast as humanly possible, I'm totally screwed.

I want to hate her. I really do. Or, at the very least, I want a healthy disdain for her that will save me. But the more I get to know her, the more I get *all* the feels. She's funny and quick-witted and smart, and she has the loveliest voice I've ever heard. I could listen to her talk all day long. Or laugh. She has a great laugh, too. It's like this full, feminine sound that is not only contagious, it's addictive. And to be honest, it's so much more fun to be out here with her than I ever would have imagined. She's so enthusiastic about everything she sees, and even though she has a weak stomach, and isn't into eating grubs or larvae, she's up for almost everything else I've asked her to try. For a graceful, gorgeous, pampered princess, she's extremely adventurous. And it's the adventurousness that scares me because it makes me wonder if that trait might possibly carry over into the bedroom. Because if it did, *wow*. I'd be done in.

So, for all of those reasons, plus the whole money thing, I absolutely, positively *must* get us the hell out of this jungle as fast as possible so we can go our separate ways and I can forget all about her. I've done the math, and no matter which way I flip the equations, a relationship between someone like me and someone like her has exactly zero percent chance of working out. Not that I want it to, because I don't. But, if I did and she did, it could never happen. I wouldn't last two days in her boring, stuffy, conservative world without wanting to slit my throat, and it's not like she's going to give up her life and her family for me—nor would I want her to because that kind of sacrifice never works out. No, this is a total dead end, and if there's anything all my travels have taught me, it's that dead ends are a waste of time and effort.

Although she does seem incredibly happy out here. I thought she'd be missing home, but she hasn't mentioned it once. Not that *that* means anything because, as fun as this is for her for a few days, it won't be long before she'll need to go back to everything she knows—the security, the luxury, the ability to eat something other than charred yams and river fish.

Have I considered seeing if she's up for a secret fling? Yes. Yes, I have. But Arabella's not the kind of girl who 'flings.' She's the kind of girl who falls in love for keeps. She has these bursts of courage and strength that seem to take her by surprise, but at the end of the day, she's an extremely vulnerable person. And it's for that very reason I refuse to take advantage of her, not while I know how this ends. There is no future for us. We're just two strangers who are spending a very intimate time together under highly unusual circumstances. It's bound to make you feel things that aren't real and think things that aren't true.

And for all those logical reasons, I'm doing my level best to make as many miles as possible each day. With any luck, I'll only have to resist her for three more nights, then it'll be goodbye Princess and hello *Matilda*.

Last night, when we stopped, I decided we should build a primitive rudder to make steering easier. Arabella thought we should cover the raft with a soft bed of banana leaves and made chairbacks out of bamboo poles wrapped in more leaves. To be honest, I'm kind of excited to try it out, which is what we're going to do in just a few minutes. We've eaten and cleaned up our camp. Now it's time to set off for the day.

"Last chance to use the loo," I say as Arabella sets her pack on the raft.

"I'm good, thank you," she says, her voice growing a little more formal as it does whenever the topic of a bodily function comes up.

"All right, let's test out our top-of-the-line raft." I hold out my hand and help her get on, only to find I don't want to let go when she's seated.

Okay, Will, keep it professional here.

I push away from the shore and hop on, then try the rudder. It does what I hoped it would—and soon we find ourselves in the center of the muddy river. I stretch out my legs and lean back, feeling the warmth of the sun on my face.

"This is so much better than hiking," Arabella says. "It's like being on a holiday."

I glance over at her and see her eyes are closed, and she looks incredibly relaxed, which I imagine is an unusual state for her. We float along in a comfortable silence for a while, and I listen to the calls of the birds and the odd howl of a monkey in the trees.

"Are you missing home yet?" I ask.

"Certain things, of course. My Gran, and my niece and nephew, mainly. And my sister-in-law, Tessa. She's wonderful. Oh, and my brother. He's all right as far as overprotective big brothers go." She pauses for a moment. "I suppose I miss scones, and raspberry-filled crêpes drizzled in chocolate sauce.

Oh, well, obviously I miss my shower and real shampoo, too. And sleeping in a bed. I guess that's something I've always taken for granted, but I don't think I will again." She opens her eyes and looks over at me.

"So the answer is yes, then," I say with a chuckle.

"I suppose, a little. But all of that will be waiting for me when I get back, so I'm not going to waste a second wishing I was home."

"Except for the scones."

"Yes, I would wrestle a gorilla for a warm blueberry scone and some heavy cream right about now."

"Or a guerilla?" I ask with a grin.

She lets out a laugh. "One of those, too. You wouldn't happen to know how to turn some tree bark and leaves into pastry, would you?"

"Afraid not." Bugger. She's being all adorable again. I wish she'd stop that already.

Arabella sits up a bit. "What do you miss when you're out being wild and free?"

"My family. I've been traveling so much over the past few years that sometimes I think I'm skipping their entire lives," I say, then immediately regret it because sharing deep feelings is the last thing you should do when you want to keep your distance from someone.

"Your family seems wonderful."

"They are. I'm lucky to have them. Emma, Harrison, and I are really close."

She nods, understanding filling her eyes. "Tragedy has a way of binding people."

My heart squeezes a little at her words. "Yeah, it's kind of the silver lining that comes with hard times."

"So true," she says.

We're both quiet for a minute, and I wonder if she's thinking about her mum. I won't ask though. Instead I'm going to steer us into safer topics. "I miss cold beer and reggae music."

"Really?"

"Yup. Those are two of my favourite things. They remind me of home. We play it for the resort guests. I used to hate it, but now whenever I hear it, it takes me right back to hanging out at the beach bar with my brother while we serve up drinks to happy people."

Arabella smiles. "That sounds lovely."

"It is. You should visit sometime. I think you'd like it there. We even have a royal suite." *Now, don't go inviting her back to your place. Idiot.*

"Do you now?" she asks, pretending to be impressed.

"Yes, but I'm sure the entire thing would be the size of your closet." *That's better. Convince her not to come.*

"Do you really think I'm the type who needs a giant closet to be happy?" she asks, looking slightly offended. "I'd say I've done quite well living out of a backpack for the past few days."

She's got me there. Damn. "Well, now that's true, isn't it?"

"Yes, it is, so I'm sure I would be more than pleased with

your royal suite," she says. "I just may have to come someday."

"We'd be happy to have you." *As a hotel guest. Not as my future wife.*

"Do you live at the resort? Like in some type of family compound or some such?"

Some such. How cute is that? "No. My brother and his wife have a bungalow tucked away at the back of the resort. Emma and Pierce have their own piece of property and an amazing villa at the end of the bay, so we can walk, bike, or swim over to their house. And when I'm home, I stay in the staff quarters."

"Really? That surprises me. A world-famous television star like yourself living in staff quarters?"

Shrugging, I say, "I'm not famous. I'm also not there much, and I've never seen the point of having a bunch of stuff. It just ties you down." I glance over at her for a second, feeling slightly embarrassed for some reason. "That probably sounds strange to you."

"No, I agree with your philosophy actually," she answers, nodding slowly. "My ancestors have all obsessively guarded their 'things,' if only for the sole purpose of passing them down for the next generation to protect. Eight-hundred-year-old tapestries, thousand-year-old paintings, an enormous vault filled with jewels that require round-the-clock armed guards. There are days when I honestly can't see the point of any of it."

I say nothing, knowing she just needs someone to listen.

"We're just doing what's always been done, for no other reason than because it's what we do." She gives me a smile, but beneath it, I can see she's kind of sad. She turns and looks out at the water. "Sometimes when I'm holding my niece, Flora, I want to cry for her future. She'll be burdened with all of it, whether she wants to be or not."

"You dodged a bullet being born second."

"I suppose I did."

Something in her mood shifts and I want to make her happy again. "What's your favourite place on earth?"

Arabella tilts her head. "Our family home near Didsbury. It's a tiny village on the northernmost tip of Avonia," she says. "Have you been?"

I shake my head.

"Oh, it's lovely. Very relaxed up there, miles of wide-open spaces, and if you walk long enough, you'll end up on the cliffs overlooking the North Sea. That's where we spent every Christmas growing up. Summers too. Playing in the fields and swimming in a pond near the castle." Her face turns slightly red. "I almost managed to share a relatable memory, didn't I?"

Chuckling, I say, "I could totally relate right up to the word castle."

"Says the man who grew up in a resort."

I laugh and nod my head. "Touché. I guess we've both had unusual lives."

"Indeed, we have," she says, then she lets out a long sigh. "Can I ask you a question?"

"Sure."

"Why did you agree to do the show? I mean, when you found out Dylan was changing the entire format and forcing me on you?" Arabella asks.

"Money," I say, hating like hell to admit that to someone like her.

"But surely you could have found another network? You're talented and you have a huge following."

Shaking my head, I say, "Not big enough. The ratings for season two weren't all that stellar, to be honest. And if I turned this down, I don't think I would have gotten picked up by anyone—not quickly enough, anyway." I rub my tongue over my teeth, and for some dumb reason, keep talking. "I'm trying to buy back our family's yacht for my brother. He had to sell it to save our resort, and since then, I've been trying to raise enough cash to surprise him with it. A few weeks ago, someone else made an offer on it, so it's now or never."

"She must be a very special boat for you to be willing to come out here with me."

I nod. "Waltzing Matilda—a ninety-foot schooner. Our Uncle Oscar bought it when he was a young man and sailed it all the way from Australia to the Benavente Islands. Our family's best times were on that yacht and I know Harrison would give anything to have her back."

"To carry on the tradition with his own family?"

"Yup," I turn to her. "I owe him everything and that's the only thing I can think of to pay him back."

"That's beautiful," Arabella says.

I shrug. "Not really. It's just a boat."

"No, it's not. It's a beautiful gesture that will mean a lot to your family," she says. "Which makes me all the more terrified of messing this up for you."

"You won't," I answer.

"How can you be so sure?"

"Because you're tough and you're smart and you also have a lot to lose if we can't make it out of here in time."

Arabella smiles, her back straightening a little at my words. "Thank you, Will. I promise to do my best to help you get Matilda back."

"I know you will."

Uh-oh, we're staring into each other's eyes again. That is *no bueno*. "Okay, truth or dare time," I say, desperate to bring things back to casual acquaintance territory.

Arabella grins and shakes her head. "That sounds like a terrible idea, especially with a man whose middle name is Dare."

"It's Danger, actually, but I promise to go easy on you."

"Oh no, don't do that," she says with a grin. "I'm up first. I choose truth, if only because it seems like the slightly wiser of the two options."

"Okay." I tap my lips for a second, thinking of the perfect question. "What is the worst part about being royal?"

She leans toward me and whispers, "Can we shut off the cameras for this conversation?"

I nod, then do as she asked.

"Thank you," she says. "Now I can speak freely, which is something I normally can never do."

"So, is that the worst bit? Lack of freedom?" I ask, taking the lid off my water bottle.

Arabella nods. "Definitely."

"Huh. I would've thought it was the constant media attention and all the public criticism."

"That bit sucks a big bag of dicks as well," she says, causing me to spit out my water.

I burst out laughing, and she joins in with a satisfied smile. When we're done, I let my smile fade. "But bags of dicks aside, tell me more about this lack of freedom."

"Well," she says with a sigh. "First, I'd like to preface this with my knowledge of how very irritating it would be for most people to listen to someone in a position of considerable privilege complain about how awful their life is. I do understand how lucky I am that I never have to worry where my next meal is coming from or if I can pay the power bill this month. Those are *real* problems compared to mine."

"But?"

"But my … particular situation … has in fact lent itself to a more restricted existence than other royals."

I stare down at her for a second, trying not to think about kissing her. "How so?"

Arabella narrows her eyes, giving me an intense look. "What I'm about to tell you is extremely private, so I must ask you never to share it with anyone."

"Never. Not even if I were tortured."

"Excellent," she says with a grin that quickly fades. "The truth is, as long as I can remember, people have always said how much I resemble my mother—not only in how I look, but how I speak and move. Everything. I know they mean it as a comfort to me, but it has the opposite effect. As far as I can gather, my mother was ... not well, and the royal life proved too difficult for her." Arabella turns her gaze to the shore, and when she speaks again, her voice is quiet. "She couldn't handle it, and it took its toll on her, mentally and physically. Eventually, it was her undoing."

I stare at her for a moment, trying to decipher the meaning behind her words. "But your mum passed on, didn't she?"

She nods. "When I was two months old. Who does that when they have a new baby who needs them?"

My heart squeezes, and instinctively, I reach for her, folding my hand around hers. "I'm so sorry, Arabella. I don't even know what to say."

"It's fine, really," she says, shaking her head quickly. "It's not like I knew her or anything."

"But the fact that you never got a chance to know her, I'm sorry for that."

"Thank you. I used to spend hours at a time secretly watching any footage of her that I could find, trying to imitate the way she walked, or how she spoke. I didn't know then how she died. The official line is that she had sudden heart failure, which is what I believed for most of my childhood."

Well, my idea of steering the conversation into safer waters has failed miserably. We're about to go over a waterfall, aren't we? "When did you find out?"

"When I was twelve. It was the anniversary of her death, and I wanted to do something special for her to mark the occasion—a family dinner in the solarium, which was her favourite place at the palace. Arthur was almost grown by then, but still had that surly teenager in him. When I asked him if he would come, he said 'never,' and told me there was nothing to celebrate. I got angry and pushed the issue until he finally cracked."

A heavy feeling fills me and it's all I can do not to pull her into my arms and hold her until I can take all her pain away. "God, what a burden for a twelve-year-old."

She nods slowly, seeming to be lost in the memory for a moment before she clears her throat and snaps back into being a very formal princess. "I'm sure she didn't realize what legacy she was leaving for me. A lifetime of being surrounded by people who treat me as if I'm the world's most delicate vase. When you grow up that way, you start to believe it yourself."

"So, that's why you're out here," I whisper, rubbing my thumb over the back of her hand.

She nods again.

"To prove to everyone you know that you are a strong person."

Arabella looks up at me and shakes her head. "That's why I *thought* I came, but the longer I'm out here, the more I realize I needed to prove it to myself."

I suddenly remember I'm still holding her hand, and I start to loosen my grip, only to have her flip her palm up and lace her fingers through mine. It's seemingly nothing, and yet it does something to me I can't comprehend. I'm overwhelmed by her—by who she is and what she's been through—and I'm completely unable to do anything about it.

She smiles at me. "Your turn. Truth or dare."

"Dare." I say, grinning back at her.

"I dare you to tell me the truth about one thing."

I laugh and shake my head. "You're a bit of a cheater."

"I take offense to that. I've never cheated at anything in my life."

"I find that hard to believe coming from Princess Pickpocket."

Her eyes light up for a second, then she narrows them. "Don't distract me. I'm going to get the truth out of you."

"Okay. What's your question?"

"What's your greatest fear?"

"Nothing."

Pursing her lips, Arabella says, "It can't be nothing. You must be afraid of something."

"No, seriously, I've been all over the globe and faced death numerous times and so far, nothing has scared me to the point where I wouldn't do it again."

"Okay, let me rephrase the question because clearly you're not capable of allowing yourself to be vulnerable enough to answer it honestly—which could be a clue as to what your true greatest fear is, by the way. But I'll set that aside for the moment and ask what your version of hell would be."

"I suppose my version of hell would be the famous one—you know, Satan and fire and brimstone and all that."

"You're impossible," she says with an exasperated sigh. "Fine then, what type of life would kill you?"

"Yours," I say without thinking about it.

She looks shocked and pulls her hand away, immediately filling me with regret. "Sorry. I didn't mean it like that. I just meant wearing a suit all day and having other people plan every hour of your life for you." I give her a sheepish look. "I'm not making it better, am I?"

She chuckles a little, letting me off the hook. "Not really, but that's okay. You can't play the game unless you're willing to hear the answers."

"I'm sure there are many amazing things about your life that I couldn't even comprehend," I say, desperate to fix what I've done. "It must have a lot of perks—otherwise there wouldn't be so many people wishing they were royals."

She tilts her head. "It did get me to the front of the line to be your co-host."

"Well, in that case, you really *are* privileged." I steer the raft a little to the left to avoid a large rock. "Okay, your turn, if you still want to play, that is."

"I do. I'll go truth again because I have a terrible feeling choosing dare would lead to me balancing in the middle of the river on top of a bamboo pole."

"Oh, I'd think of something much worse than that," I say.

"All right, this is an easy one. What have you always wanted to do, but never have?"

She stares into my eyes, her cheeks turning pink. "It's silly, but the first thing that popped into my mind …" She shakes her head. "Nope. I can't."

I laugh. "You have to, or you'll have to do the dare, which would involve beetle larvae."

She points to something on my side of the raft. "Oh, look, some river otters."

I glance over to see sleek, black otters swimming next to us.

"We should really film them."

I laugh, turning back to her. "Nice try. I think we got enough river otter footage yesterday. Now, answer the question or eat the larva?"

"Fine. Skinny dipping."

"Really?" I ask with a wide grin spreading across my face.

"Any and all outdoor naked activities are most strictly forbidden for members of the royal family. There is never a moment where you're safe from the paparazzi."

"Well, you're definitely safe out here …"

"Oh, marvelous. I'll just strip down right now and go for a dip with the crocodiles."

"Not here on this river, but somewhere out here in the jungle, I'm sure we'll find a picturesque lagoon where you can live out your greatest fantasy."

Rolling her eyes, she slaps me on the chest with the back of her hand. "I never said it was my greatest fantasy. I only said it's something I've never tried that I would like to. But obviously, not with you."

"Obviously not." I make a *ppffftt* sound to let her know I think she's full of it.

"Maybe if I were here with Bear Grylls." She starts out looking very serious, then busts out laughing at my shocked face. "I couldn't help it. It's just so obvious how much you can't stand him."

"That's not true. I don't even know him. I just can't understand why he feels the need to drink his own urine unnecessarily," I say with a casual shrug.

"You're jealous!" she says, laughing.

"Am not. *Anyone* could have their own line of outdoor gear."

Nodding, she says, "Absolutely. And yet, here we are carrying around Bear Grylls backpacks that you can't seem to stop complaining about."

I scowl a little, then say, "Do you know who I *really* would've liked as a princess co-host? Who's that one from England? Kate? Oh yeah, her."

Arabella's eyes grow wide and she reaches over with both hands and starts to tickle me aggressively.

I bust out laughing and grab her hands, tugging her on top of me. "What's the matter, Your Highness? You can dish it out, but you can't take it?"

"Bastard," she says with a grin. Her body is pressed against mine and our mouths are a mere two inches apart right now. I so badly want to close the gap and taste her lips, but my brain is screaming at me to back up and abort the mission. I don't move. Instead, I stay as near to her as I can, hoping she doesn't pull away.

Her eyes flick down to my lips and then back up. "What have you always wanted to do but never have?" she asks me in a breathy tone.

"You have no idea how tempted I am to say have sex on a moving raft."

"Why don't you say it then?" she asks, giving me a sexy look. "I dare you."

My pulse quickens as I stare at her. *Do not say it. For God's sake, Will, do not say it. You cannot have sex with this woman. Not ever. She is not for you.* "I can't," I say with a grin. "I haven't shaved my legs."

She smiles back, but disappointment fills her eyes. Every muscle in my body grows furious with my stupid mouth and I know I will regret not seizing this moment for the rest of my life. She rolls off of me and lays back down, closing her eyes. "It's just as well. I doubt it would have been very good."

"Because of the lack of a mattress?"

"Sure. You tell yourself that if you need to protect your fragile male ego."

19

"Rain" in Your Feelings, You Silly Twat

Arabella

WELL, I figured out why this is called a rain forest. It's because when it decides to rain out here, it doesn't bloody well stop. Ever. Yesterday afternoon, shortly after our almost-sex on the raft—which would have been a terrible idea, by the way, so thank goodness Will came to his senses. Not because sex with Will and/or sex on the raft wouldn't have been good. It likely would've been quite pleasurable considering the firmness of the … Never mind. Anyway, immediately following that *moment*, a loud clap of thunder got both of our attentions.

We got the hell off that river as fast as possible and quickly set up camp, using the raft as a shelter. Will managed to gather more banana leaves to make a floor, and the raft is now one side of a lean-to being held up by bamboo posts. It's large enough that we have an area for a small fire pit, as well as the tent set up along one side.

The rain is pouring down so hard, it's more like a steady stream than drops, and it's the only sound we've heard for quite some time. The chorus of birds and all the howler monkeys have gone silent, having hidden away from the storm. It's late afternoon and we're both hungry, so Will is out gathering food and more material to start a fire. Apparently, you can find dry bits of wood in hollowed-out tree trunks.

To be honest, it's a welcome break from being so near to him. I need to try to get my head on straight. As foolish as this is, I'm almost certain I'm falling for him. He's just so manly and delicious and thoughtful and brave. And he has such a kind heart and such a gloriously hard body and a gorgeous face, even though it's now partially hidden by several days' worth of beard. I've never really been into beards like some other women are, but on him ... *yes, please.*

But never mind that, because beyond some fabulously sexy outdoor sex in the jungle, this would never work out. A shame, really, because in my entire life, I've never felt as confident or as beautiful as I do when he looks at me. Over the past few days, I've gone from being a burden to being his partner. He respects me for my abilities and for who I am, not what I am, which is like the world's strongest aphrodisiac for someone like me.

We built this shelter together, and we built the raft together—both projects that required me to use my muscles for once. And today, he's trusting me to make the fire, which isn't as easy as I thought it would be. It's actually quite hard, even with the lighter. It sounds like a silly thing to feel proud of, but I can't help it. I'm proud of my newfound skills.

I strike my lighter, then set the flame to the bamboo shavings I've made, and gently blow on them until they catch. A few minutes later, I see Will coming through the rain, all wet and manly. Sigh.

"Hey, nice fire, Drew." He crouches down and makes his way under the shelter, and out of the pouring rain. "You're getting good at that."

"Drew?"

"As in Barrymore. You're a lot like her—tougher than you look and she has some serious fire-building skills."

"So, after two days, that's what you've landed on?" I ask. "Giving me the name of a Hollywood actor?"

"You're right. I'll keep thinking." He sets the wet pieces of dead bamboo he's gathered near the fire so they can dry, then starts unpacking his bag. "I'm going to make you a proper high tea today, since we have nothing much else to do."

I grin and fight the compulsion to throw my arms around his neck and kiss him hard on the mouth. Instead, I watch as he sets a large bunch of small leaves and some dark blue berries on the floor.

"I won't be able to make scones, but I almost think I might be able to make you a decent cup of tea with these peppermint pelargonium leaves. Well, it'll be hot water with some colour to it, anyway," he says, shaking his head a little.

I grin up at him. "Sounds lovely."

"These are black nightshade berries. They're kind of like a cross between a tomato and a blueberry. They're rich in vitamin C and antioxidants."

"Nightshade? Why does that sound familiar?"

"Probably because people sometimes get them mixed up with the deadly variety of nightshade berries—*Atropa belladonna*. They look almost identical."

Oh dear. That doesn't sound very reassuring. "You know I have to ask, right?" I say.

Nodding, Will chuckles. "I'd sure as hell ask. The answer is yes, I do know the difference. The safe ones grow in bunches. The poisonous ones grow alone."

"Ah, okay, and these were …"

"Definitely in bunches."

"And if you did somehow mix them up?"

"At best, something we don't discuss in polite society."

"Ah, I see." I wrinkle up my nose a bit.

"Both ends."

Holding up one hand, I say, "No need to go into detail. Worst case scenario?"

"Death."

"So, no berry picking for me then," I say.

"Of course you can pick them. Just don't eat them until you check with your handsome guide."

I look around, craning my neck. "Where is he? I don't think I've met him yet."

"Oh, very funny. Here I am trying to fix you a fancy tea and you're making fun of me."

"But only for my own amusement."

He tilts his head. "In that case, please carry on."

"I think I shall."

"Did you notice the chimps across the river?" he asks.

"No," I say, suddenly feeling very excited. Or scared. So hard to tell sometimes.

"Right there," Will says, pointing to a tall ironwood tree on the other side of the rushing water. I move toward the edge of the lean-to so I'm right next to him, our arms touching. Neither of us makes any effort to pull away. I've noticed this happening more over the last couple of days. We both find little reasons to be close to each other, and it's almost like an unspoken game of chicken to see who will move first. Each round gets longer and longer. A terrible idea, I know, but when you're stuck in a tiny space without much to do, you make your fun however you can.

It takes me a moment to find the chimps among the lush, green branches. It's a small group. One is grooming the other. I pick up the GoPro and turn it on, zooming in as best I can to capture them.

After a moment, I say, "I don't think those are chimps. I think we're actually seeing bonobos."

"Really?" he says, narrowing his eyes to get a better look. "Hey, I think you're right. That's a pretty lucky find."

"Yes, they're extremely rare. I was seated next to a primatologist at a fundraiser once. She did her dissertation on bonobos."

"Tell you what," Will says. "You film them and do some narrating while I put the kettle on."

He sets to work while I swell a little with pride at this small, but meaningful, gesture. It's as though he's actually accepting me as a co-host. Yay, me!

Hmm, but now that I'm in charge of narrating, I don't know what to say. Will must know I'm flustered, because after a minute of me filming without speaking, he says, "Just pretend you're on a call with your Gran and you're describing what you see."

Oh, well, that sounds much easier. "Okay, here we go. We've been camped along the river in a rainstorm that moved in yesterday afternoon. It's afforded us an extremely rare opportunity to observe a small family of what we believe to be bonobos. Bonobos are a very close relative of the chimpanzee and, in fact, for many years, scientists didn't distinguish between them and chimps. But this amazing group of primates has some important differences. First, they only exist in this one small area of the world. They're slightly smaller, for the most part, than chimps. And you can't tell at the moment because they're not walking, but when they do, they tend to use a more upright posture than most other primates."

"Is that so?" Will asks, from the 'kitchen' area of our little home.

"Yes. In fact, they favor walking only with their back legs and swing their arms the way humans do, rather than using them to help propel their bodies forward. They're also known as a peaceful, relaxed animal, which is probably because the females of the species are in charge."

"Really?" Will asks. "I did *not* know that."

"It's true," I say, turning to look back at him for a second. "Primatologists have a motto for the bonobos—make love not war." My cheeks turn red, but I force myself to continue, on the basis of educating people. "They actually use sex to resolve tension within and between groupings."

"You're making that up."

"I swear it. When they meet up with another group, the alpha females will approach each other and then ... well ..." *Oh, God. Why did I bring this up? This is awful. Just stop talking.*

"They what?" he asks, looking very serious even though I can tell he's enjoying making me squirm like this.

Fine, two can play that game. "Touch each other in the ... you-know-where and ..." Nope. I cannot talk about this. And yet, something about the amused expression in his eyes brings out my defiant side. *It's just science, Arabella. Don't be a prude.* "They pleasure each other to reduce tension and show acceptance."

"I really can't help but feel like you're making this all up," Will says.

"No, it's true. They're very sexual. It's why you don't see them in zoos. Because it's far too uncomfortable for people, especially if they're on an outing with their children."

Will busts out laughing, and I see one of the bonobos up in the tree turn her head to look. She stops grooming the other one and stares back at us.

I zoom in on her with the camera, and gasp a little, whispering, "I can't believe this. We're actually *looking at each other*. How amazing is that?"

Will comes to sit next to me and the two of us watch her together.

"This is incredible," I say. "She is staring right at me. It's like she's trying to communicate with me somehow."

The bonobo tilts her head, then starts to … Oh, dear! I quickly put the camera down and turn to face the other direction.

"Is she …?"

"Yep. Let's give her some privacy, shall we?" My entire body feels hot with embarrassment, but Will seems to find the entire thing hilarious.

He's laughing so hard his shoulders are shaking, and silent tears pour down his face. "I think she likes you, Arabella."

"Shut up."

"Maybe she has a thing for royalty," he says, laughing some more.

I fold my arms and glare at him. "It's really not that funny. It's just … nature."

"And that particular bit of nature was absolutely turned on by you. In fact, she's still going for it."

I slap him on the arm. "Stop that. Don't stare at her while she's … you know …"

"What? Take it as a compliment. You're empirically attractive to all species. You should be thrilled."

"All right, that's enough out of you."

"I think you should do it back, so she knows we're friends."

I growl in response.

His smile fades. "I just thought of something," he says. "What if they decide your lack of masturbating is a sign of aggression, and they come over here to attack us?"

"Weren't you making tea? I think you've lost your focus."

"Can you blame me?"

———

Well, this is just ridiculous. There is literally no way I'm going to be able to resist this man now. He has fashioned little teacups and saucers out of bamboo and made stacks of sliced fruit and yam cakes for us to eat. He's even sweetened them with a piece of a honeycomb he managed to procure. When I asked him how he did it, he said, "I don't want to talk about it. Let's just say it was not pretty."

So now, the two of us are sitting near our fire in our cozy, delightfully-dry lean-to, sipping what is quite possibly the most disgusting tea I have ever tasted in my life and eating tiny slices of bananas, oranges, and berries together while the rain falls around us. This is the most romantic moment of my life, and I don't know if that makes me incredibly lucky or extremely pathetic, but at this very second, I feel nothing short of elation. I don't want the rain to ever stop because I just want to stay here with him in this place forever.

"You don't have to drink the tea," he says.

"But I want to. It's so delicious."

"It's disgusting and you know it." He gives me a half grin that I find irresistibly sexy.

"No, it's … amazing."

"Is that why your face winces every time you have a sip?"

"Well, it might be just a tad tart for my taste, but I am rather picky, so I don't want you to feel at all bad. It's the thought and all the effort that counts."

"You're a true diplomat."

"It's one of the few skills I have perfected."

He snaps his fingers. "Let's add some more honey to it."

"Yes, thank God! Because it really is awful."

We both laugh, then share one of those gazing-into-each-other's-eyes-longingly moments that have been happening more and more often over the last two days. I want him so badly, there is literally nothing I can do to keep the thought of our nude bodies doing very naughty things to each other out of my mind.

"I found something while I was out getting that honey. I thought you might like to know about it," he says in a low tone.

"Really?" I swallow hard, finding myself slightly afraid of his answer.

"Remember how, in your entire life, your greatest wish has always been to go skinny dipping?"

"I remember saying something to that effect." My heart pounds in my chest while I wait for what he's about to say next.

"There's an extremely beautiful lagoon about half a mile from here."

"Is there?" I ask in a breathy tone.

Nodding, Will says, "Crystal clear blue water fed by a gentle waterfall, surrounded by lush, green foliage."

"Well, that sounds like the perfect place to …" I pause and stare him, then remembering myself, I say, "Wash our clothes."

He gives me the sexiest look I have ever seen in my entire life. "Definitely. You know, you can wash your clothes in the rain?"

"Can you?" I ask, my voice thick with lust.

"Oh, yes, you definitely can, especially in a nice warm rain like this. You can get everything very clean."

"Well, I do want to be clean again."

"Then maybe we should go wash up…"

Say no, dummy. Say no. This is a terrible, horrible, deliciously wonderful idea. "Okay."

20

Irresistibly Sexy Lagoon Sex

Will

DEAR GOD, please let us be talking about the same thing. Because if she's actually talking about washing out her dirty clothes and giving herself a scrub down, I am going to be *super* disappointed.

We hurry in the direction of the lagoon. The rain has now slowed to a soft patter while I do my best not to seem too eager, even though what I really want to do is toss her over my shoulder and sprint all the way there.

She just smiled at me, and that smile did sort of say 'sex is on the menu for this afternoon.' But honestly, it's so hard to tell. For a woman like her—someone used to being clean and done up at all times--this type of life must be awful for her. Not that she *looks* awful, because she definitely doesn't look even close to what anyone could call awful. And that's saying something because we've been out here for days now and most humans, including me, tend to look pretty rough by this point. But not Arabella. She's got this natural beauty that … I should not be noticing.

"How much farther is it?" she asks.

"Just around this bend. I'll race you," I say, tapping her on her shoulder, then sprinting ahead.

She laughs, then says, "No, thanks, I'm not really a runner."

I stop, doing my best not to seem too disappointed.

Do not blow this, Will. Seriously.

That was a message from my penis, who has been struggling to stay down for the last few days. I mean, think about it —four days alone in the jungle with the most beautiful woman I've ever laid eyes on, and I haven't been able to touch her or even relieve my own 'stress.' It's not like I can leave her alone and disappear into the bush for a quick wank. Because, not only would that be extremely creepy, it also would put her life at risk, so up until a few minutes ago, I had resigned myself to just putting it all off until we got to town and I could be alone in my hotel room.

But maybe I won't have to wait because she has just caught up with me, and taken off ahead, laughing.

"Wha—? You cheater!" I yell, jogging after her. I catch her just as we reach the lagoon, wrapping my arms around her, lifting her off the ground, and setting her down behind me. "I win."

Arabella's eyes grow wide. "Weasel!"

"I'm tempted to say, 'takes one to know one,' only that would sound juvenile."

"Says the man who just challenged me to a race."

I stare down at her, watching drops of rain slide over her ivory skin. "God, you're pretty."

She blushes a little and looks down at the ground—a simple movement that makes me want to have her, but at the same time, makes me positive I shouldn't. I can't use her and say goodbye. I just can't.

My smile fades and I say, "Okay, well, you can go first. I'll turn around and stand guard for you."

Her face falls a little, then she nods. "Righto. That makes sense. I'll go first, then *you* go, and I'll watch for trouble."

"Not that there will be any, I don't think," I say. "It's daytime and most animals prefer to hunt when it's not raining."

I gaze at her, hoping she'll invite me in, but she doesn't, so I turn my back and try not to pout visibly, even though, on the inside, I'm crushed.

Okay, just stand here and don't imagine her taking off her clothes. That would be a horrible, horrible idea.

I hear a splash and I bite the side of my finger. She is definitely naked.

"So? How is it?" I ask over my shoulder. Oops, I just saw some side boob. Some very lovely, perky side boob. *Bad, Will, bad!*

"Amazing. The water's perfect."

"Skinny dipping, right? It's pretty awesome." *Pretty awesome? Smooth, Will. Very fucking smooth.*

"Would you please hand me the soap?" she asks.

"Certainly," I say, turning and taking in the sight of her bare shoulders and her pale skin disappearing into the blue water. Her hair is wet and she's lazily treading water while she smiles at me.

I take a few steps toward the edge of the lagoon, then reach out to hand her a few shavings of soap. "It's biodegradable."

"Is it?"

"Uh-huh," I say, completely mesmerized. "It works as shampoo, too."

"Does it?" she asks with a grin.

I nod, unable to force myself to look away. "I'll just turn around now."

"Okay." She shrugs like she doesn't mind if I don't.

Staying perfectly still, I say, "Because turning around would be the right thing to do."

"Yes, it would," she answers, rubbing soap onto her arms.

Oh, that is so hot. Seriously. I can't even ... "It's ... um ..." I swallow hard. "Important to do the right thing."

"Always." Her hands disappear under the water as she starts soaping other areas.

I turn quickly, my heart pounding in my chest. "I'll just be right here. Let me know if you need more soap. Or if you need a hand for any of your hard-to-reach places."

I glance back in time to see her laugh. "I don't have any

hard to reach places. I do yoga and ballet workouts most days."

"Oh, that's nice," I say, with barely enough brain power to form the words. "Good for you. It's important to stay limber."

"Will," she says, her tone sounding more serious.

I turn my head to face her again. "More soap?"

"Are you going to get in or are you just going to pretend you're not looking at me?"

"Sorry, I didn't mean to … It's just that you're so …"

"Get in."

Did she just say that? The look on her face says she wants me to come in. "I don't do yoga."

Grinning, she says, "Well, then I can help you."

"What about doing the right thing at all times?" I ask.

"Would it really be so wrong? We're both single and, if I'm not mistaken, we both want to."

Yes! Yes! Yes! "I know *I* want to, but I also don't want to be a total scoundrel."

"I don't see how treating me with the respect of letting me make my own decisions is scoundrel-type behaviour."

Shit. I'm totally going to wreck this, aren't I? "It's just that you're *you*, and I'm *me*, and when we're not out here, I'm afraid there wouldn't be much of a future together."

"I'm okay with that, Will," she says with a grin that I have to say looks enticingly naughty. "I came out here looking for adventure. Believe me when I say, I want to try it all."

"Well, when you put it that way, I suppose it would be disrespectful of me not to … get in and let you try it all."

It takes me all of two seconds to strip down and jump in. Arabella covers her mouth with one hand, trying not to laugh at my overly enthusiastic entry. I stay a few feet away from her, treading water, waiting for her to make the next move.

She swims over to the rock and lifts some soap out of the container, then swims back to me. "What can't you reach?"

"Anything. I'm so buff, I have no flexibility anymore."

"Tragic really," she says, rubbing the soap shavings over my skin, starting with my shoulders and down my arms. Her touch stirs something inside me I've never felt before and a desperation to have her takes over every thought. She smiles as she moves her hands over my chest and abs until the soap has dissolved. "I'll go get some more."

I reach around behind her and pull her to me, unable to stand the torture of not holding her for even a second longer. She looks up, her expression filled with lust as she wraps her arms around my neck and presses herself against me. She brushes her lips against mine, and oh, do those ever feel soft and perfect. Closing her eyes, she does it again, and I respond with a gentle kiss, slow and cautious to make sure it's what she wants.

I move my hands down to her waist and pull her closer, then let my lips hover over hers. "You are just so damn gorgeous."

"You're not so bad yourself."

"No, but I mean, you are *stunning*. Just like this. With no makeup and wet hair. Just you."

"You're the only person who will ever see me like this."

"In that case, I'll have to burn the memory of you into my brain on behalf of everyone who doesn't get to see this for themselves." I nip at her bottom lip with my teeth, then kiss her again, gripping her hips with both hands.

She wraps her legs around my waist, and I let my hands slide around to her bottom to hold her up. Oh, we are so doing this …

———

Wow, so lagoon sex turned into up-against-a-tree-in-the-rain-on-the-way-back-to-camp sex, which lead to tent sex, and now we've just finished by-the-fire sex (which got started when we were waiting for some water to boil). And now, we're wrapped up in each other's arms, panting and recovering while the rain falls.

"That was … quite nice," Arabella says.

"Oh, quite nice, was it? Like a mincemeat tart or a Christmas card from an elderly auntie."

"Well, not *that* nice. But lovely, all the same," she says with a wicked grin.

I lift my head off the ground and narrow my eyes at her. "So, how loud do you scream when you open your Christmas cards?"

"Much, much louder." Arabella laughs, tucking her face into my chest.

I laugh, then say, "In that case, I should scarf down a few

bananas. I'll need my potassium if I'm going to truly satisfy you."

"Yes, you will," she answers, giving me a lingering kiss that wakes me up out of my post-sex haze.

I lay my head back down and snuggle her close to me, caressing the length of her arm with my fingertips.

"I want to stay here forever," she whispers, closing her eyes.

"Me too," I say, kissing her on the forehead and inhaling the scent of her skin.

"I know we can't, but maybe … could we stay for a few days?" she asks, and there's something so vulnerable about her voice I can't bring myself to say no, but I know I can't say yes either.

"I know we can't stay long," she says. "And I'd never want to cost you your chance at getting your brother's boat back. I was just thinking maybe because we made up some time using the raft, we could give ourselves this little break from the world."

I prop my head up on one arm and look into her impossibly blue eyes. "Is that what you need, Arabella?"

She nods. "Desperately."

My brain tells me to say no, but my mouth ignores it. "Then that's what we'll do."

21

Deliciously Scandalous Outdoor Nude Activities

Arabella - Three Days Later

I PRAY for rain before I open my eyes. More rain means more sexy sex with the sexiest sex god of all of Sexlandia. That's what I've secretly named this entire area of the jungle. Sexlandia. A fitting name for it because between us and those dirty bonobos on the other side of the river, there's a whole lot of fooling around happening day and night. It stopped raining yesterday morning, and when Will suggested that the smart thing to do would be to get back on the river, I talked him into staying for one more day. Well, I didn't so much as talk him into it, but rather *showed* him several fun reasons to put off leaving. After a quick look at the map and some calculations, he decided we could risk another day and still make it back in time.

Speaking of time, the first time we *you-know-what* in the lagoon was a-MAZ-ing with a capital amazing. Like mind-blowingly wonderful, multi-orgasmic, wet and wild and free. There's something about being in the great outdoors that really heightened the experience for me. Or maybe it's him and his huge … personality and the way he touches me. It's like he's gentle and generous and in control the whole time. He's like a competitive sexlete (which is similar to an athlete or a mathlete, but for sex, obviously). He makes sure I 'enjoy' myself at least twice for every one time he has a happy ending. Before Will, I could add up the number of orgasms I'd had with a partner on one hand. But in four days of Wild World sex, I've had … well, I've lost count already. I honestly don't know where this is going, but I *do* know I'm desperate for more. I want us to forget the show all together and just … live right here eating berries and fish and having sex morning, noon, and night.

Although I suppose that's not an option because they'll come looking for us. But what if they couldn't find us? Hmmm … the jungle is a very big place. Maybe the bonobos would accept us into their clan and help us hide out for the next several years.

Okay, even the fact that I'm thinking that is bad. Really very bad indeed, because we definitely should not be doing this. I mean, there is literally no future for the two of us. Out in the real world, we have basically nothing in common. Whereas out here, we connect on such a primal level. We're like two ultra-horny chimps just doing it everywhere we can.

Maybe, as a society, we've got it all wrong. Maybe this is what life is supposed to be like—just two people foraging for food, building shelter, and enjoying each other. No thinking about status or money or any other type of obligations of any sort. No letting anybody else decide who you are or what you should do with your days. We wake up and eat and talk and talk and talk and have sex and swim in that beautiful lagoon. Then we eat some more, and have more sex, have a little campfire and we laugh and tell each other everything and have more sex and it's all so amazing.

The truth is, Will gets me. I mean, he *really understands* who I am and who I could be. I am Terri Irwin when I'm around him—confident and happy and fearless. I've even started swinging into the lagoon on a vine. A slippery, wet vine. I run at it, grab hold and swing as hard as I can, then drop into the water, all the while screaming and laughing like a fool. Or an utterly blissful person.

I've done things I never would've even thought about doing before, because unlike everyone else I know, Will doesn't have the preformed opinion that I am incapable of anything that presents even the slightest challenge. Not that this type of existence is easy, because it's not, but it is *infinitely* better than my real life.

Urgh, the thought of my real life gives me chest pains. It was bad before, but that's nothing compared to what it'll be like when I get home. Arabella before she went adventuring with a hot, hot man didn't have a clue what she was missing. She wanted to know what it would be like to be wild and free and utterly uninhibited. But *imagining* something will be wonderful and actually experiencing it (and finding out it's ssoooo much better than you even thought it would be) are two entirely different things. The shit part is that as soon as I step on that plane to go home, I'll be whisked back into a world I don't want be part of anymore. Only it'll be much, much worse because: a) I've caused a horrible scandal that I'm sure will follow me for the rest of my life, and more importantly, b) I'll be alone and confined to my stupid luxury box forever without a certain sexlete.

For the first time, I'm completely free and completely happy all day and all night. I'm absolutely, stupidly, crazy in love.

Oh, bugger.

I'm in love.

With a completely unsuitable man who already told me that my life is his version of hell. Those were his actual words. Well, when I asked him what his version of hell was, anyway. It's not like he said it out of the blue, but still, he did say it. He is *never* going to want to get married and have adorable little adventure babies, so if that's what I'm thinking, I better just forget it.

I turn over and watch him sleep, reaching out and tracing his beard with my fingertip. I whisper, "Please don't break my heart."

But he will. And it'll be my own damn fault for getting so wrapped up in someone I can't have. So far, we've been playing it casual, like we both know this is just a quick fling that doesn't mean anything, but the truth is, I want him to be my forever. And that is not going to happen. As soon as we walk out of this jungle, I'm going to get my heart stomped on like a grape in a winery barrel.

He opens his eyes and grins at me, pulling me to his deliciously warm, naked body.

Oh, that is very nice. You know what? For once, I won't overthink what I'm doing. I'm just going to enjoy it, and if it ends the second we get to Mbambole, well then, I am going to have an entire lifetime of remembering this moment right now while he, oh, my, *that's* why he woke up. Mmm …

What happens in a few days is Future Arabella's problem, and I refuse to worry about her. Not when he's doing *that*.

"I thought of the perfect nickname for you," he says, nuzzling my neck.

"You did?" I ask in a breathy voice.

He kisses my collar bone. "Belle."

"So, after all that thinking, you just shortened my name?" I give him a teasing smile.

He shakes his head. "Belle, as in the bravest of all the Disney princesses."

"I thought that was Mulan. Or Merida, you know, the one from *Brave*?"

"They're fine, too, but you remind me of Belle. When the movie starts, everyone underestimates her, but deep down she's fierce—like you." He nibbles on my ear lobe, making it impossible to concentrate on what he's saying. Will props himself up on one arm and traces my lips with his finger.

"The way she sacrificed herself for her father and stood up to the Beast? Come *on*."

I lift my head and give him a kiss. "Are you secretly a big fan of Disney cartoon princesses?"

"Emma made me watch those movies over and over when we were kids," he says.

"They are great movies."

"Yes, they are, but don't ever tell anyone I said that."

"What you would do if I told someone?"

He looks up for a second as though considering the question, then grins. "It's more like what would I stop doing…"

"Which would be?"

Oh, he's going to *show* me his answer instead of telling me. Mmm. "I'll never say a word."

———

ABN Nooner Newscast – Tuesday Edition

"Good afternoon, I'm Veronica Platt with the ABN Nooner News. Our top story this lunch hour remains the mystery of the missing princess. It's been seven harrowing days for the people of Avonia without any sign of Princess Arabella. Although palace officials put out a brief statement yesterday morning, hoping to put a stop to the myriad of rumors throughout the kingdom, it seems for many, it's a case of too little, too late." Veronica stares into the camera with a stern expression. "Giles Bigly, our man on the scene, joins us live from the Langdon library, where a meeting of the

Avonian Introverts Society was just held without their patron."

The screen splits into two and Giles is seen standing next to a middle-aged man wearing a button-up shirt, a brown bowtie, and a tweed jacket.

"Giles, can you tell us what the impact is on the Avonian Introverts with regard to this shocking story?"

"Yes, Veronica, I'm here with Mr. Fred Bundy, president of the—"

"I'm sorry. Did you say *Fred* Bundy?" Veronica asks, cutting Giles off mid-sentence.

Mr. Bundy rolls his eyes and lets out a sigh while Giles says, "That's right, Fred, as in Frederick."

"Bundy," Veronica says.

"Let's move on from that, Veronica. I gather it's a bit of a sore spot. Anyway, Mr. Bundy is the president of the Avonian Introverts Society, a small group who have enjoyed Princess Arabella's patronage for the past three years. He's one of many Avonians growing increasingly concerned and frustrated with the palace's vague statement regarding her whereabouts."

"Yes, Giles, I'm going to read that statement out for those of our viewers who haven't heard it yet. It was sent to the various news outlets yesterday, and it reads, quote, 'Princess Arabella is fine and accounted for. There is no reason for alarm, and we assure you she will be returning to public life shortly.' Mr. Bundy, can you hear me?" Veronica asks.

The man nods once and mumbles, "Yes."

"Excellent," Veronica says. "Were you given any prior notice of Princess Arabella's disappearance or did you find out at the same time as the rest of us?"

Giles holds the microphone to him while he speaks quietly. "We got a call on Monday to say she couldn't make it."

Veronica nods gravely. "And if I may, who exactly placed that call?"

"Her assistant, Mrs. Chapman."

"And how are the good people of the Avonian Introverts Society handling this alarming news?"

"Veronica," Giles cuts in. "Perhaps I could interview my guest since I am the man on the scene."

"Of course, Giles," Veronica says. "Go ahead."

"Thanks." Giles turns to Fred Bundy. "So, how are the folks at the Avonian Introverts Society handling this news?"

Fred shrugs. "The meeting was pretty quiet because she usually does most of the talking. She's not an introvert, really."

Turning to the camera, Giles says, "There you have it, Veronica. One very quiet meeting."

"Giles, have you heard anything at all about her whereabouts, or if she's, in fact, alive at this point?" Veronica asks.

"Well, based on yesterday's statement from the palace, I'd say we can safely rule out her death."

"Can we?" Veronica asks.

"Yes."

"Mr. Bundy," Veronica says. "Would you agree with Giles in his assessment that the princess is indeed alive at this time?"

"I would," Fred answers with a nod. Turning to Giles, he mutters, "Okay, are we done here? Because I'm going to miss my chance to bring home the extra donuts if I don't get back in there. And Eli brought Krispy Kreme this time."

Veronica speaks up quickly. "Would that have been the donut Princess Arabella would have eaten?"

"One of them, yes," Fred says.

Veronica makes a *tsk*ing sound. "A donut with no princess to eat it. Could this story get any more tragic?"

22

Time to Say Goodbye ... to Sexlandia

Will

THE SUN IS out in full force this morning as I crawl out of the tent, and although everything looks bright and shiny, the world feels like a much darker place because, as much as I wish I could hold it off, we have to get back on our way. Arabella is up already and has gone to 'pick berries,' which is our euphemism for her needing to go to the loo. You can take the princess out of the palace, but you can't take the palace out of the ... okay, that was a crappy analogy, but you get the idea.

The last few days of being together flow through my mind, and even though I know it won't happen, I find myself wishing she and I could somehow make this work on a long-term basis. And believe me when I say that's not something I *ever* thought I'd entertain. *Especially* not with someone like her.

After I brush my teeth, I pull out the map again, feeling more than a little worried. We should have left twenty-four hours ago, but after a particularly wonderful round of wake-up sex, I calculated our estimated distance to Mbambole again, and decided we could squeeze in one more night. But because my calculations were done with a ratio of maximum sex to bonus money as the parameter, I'm now realizing I may have been overly optimistic. But what's done is done, and believe me, it was done well.

As I pore over the map, I realize we must leave this morning. Anything beyond that will be disastrous. We're already cutting it too close, because we've used up ninety-six of our two hundred-forty hours having wild monkey sex. Add that to the time it took to get to Sexlandia, and we're only left with fifty-six hours until I have to kiss that sweet bonus and *Matilda* goodbye.

I'm just folding up the map when I hear Arabella humming happily. The sound squeezes my heart, knowing I have to put an end to the only precious few days of freedom she's had in her entire life. But as much as I want to give her a longer escape, I can't. When she comes around the corner, she smiles at me, looking absolutely gorgeous in the early sunlight.

Well, maybe we could leave this afternoon …

She holds up the cooking pot. "I actually did pick berries this morning."

Chuckling, I say, "I thought you royals didn't talk about things like that."

"We don't." Arabella grins and sets the pot down on the rock we've been using as a table. When she glances at the map in my hand, her smile fades. "I guess it's time, right? I've kept you here too long already."

Putting my arms around her waist, I give her a lingering kiss. "We really should get going, but if you promise to hike very fast, I think we can get away with another few hours in Sexlandia."

She nods and forces a bright smile on her face, even though I can tell she doesn't mean it. "Brilliant. As wonderful as this has been, I am looking forward to a hot shower and a proper bed."

"Are you sure you want to go back to your real life?" I ask, pretending I'm joking. "I thought maybe I'd converted you by now, and that you'd be keen to live out in the jungle for the rest of our lives eating fish and berries."

"Don't forget the grubs. There are plenty of those for both of us to live on for years."

I lean in and kiss her again. "Don't tempt me. I just might burn the map."

My stomach growls loudly, interrupting the moment.

Arabella pulls back and says, "I've got a cure for that." She picks up the pot and puts it in my hands. "Dig in. I've already rinsed them," she says proudly.

I look down at the berries for a second, then narrow my

eyes and pick up the top few. "Black nightshade berries. Yum! Just to make sure, these were in bunches, right?"

"I thought the ones in bunches were the poisonous ones."

"Nope, those are the singletons."

"Damn."

"You didn't eat any, did you?"

Her cheeks flush, but she shakes her head. "Of course not."

I stare at her for a moment, trying to assess whether she's being entirely truthful. She's not making eye contact, so my gut is telling me she may have eaten some, but I can't exactly accuse her of it, now can I? "Thank God, because if you had, in about six to twelve hours, you'd be sicker than you've ever been in your life."

She grabs the pot out of my hands and tosses the berries into the brush, then turns back with an overly enthusiastic smile. "Good thing I didn't eat them, then."

"You sure you didn't try even one? You can tell me if you did."

"I'm not so stupid that I'd eat something without checking with you first," she says, looking thoroughly offended.

"Sorry. I know you wouldn't." I give her an apology kiss, but her response seems stiff. "You okay?"

"Terrific." Closing her eyes, she brushes her lips against mine. "How about we make use of our last few hours here? I want to drink in every drop of my escape before it has to end."

We lay naked in each other's arms, recovering. Arabella doesn't have that dreamy smile she normally has at this moment, and I can tell something is off. I pull her close to me and kiss her on the forehead. "Listen, I think I know exactly how you feel."

"I don't think you do."

"You're a little sad that our time alone out here has to end so soon. I am too, but just because we're leaving doesn't mean we won't see each other again." *Do not make promises you can't keep, dummy.* "I mean, I think there's a really good chance the show is going to be a hit. If that's the case, maybe we can travel the world together, sneaking away from real life, and filming more seasons?"

I pull back slightly so I can look at her face, expecting her to be smiling up at me, maybe even with tears glistening in her beautiful blue eyes. But instead, she looks pale, and her mouth is sagging at the corners.

"Sorry, that didn't come out right. Look, I know we haven't talked about the future, but I want you to know you mean a lot to me. It would be complicated, but—"

She shakes her head, then scrambles to get outside. A second later, I hear her heave and a rush of liquid splashing the banana leaf floor.

Shit. She ate the berries.

23

I Tried Out the Jungle Detox Plan
and Here's What Happened...

Arabella

I AM AN IDIOT. A complete and utter fool. I've been evacuating an incredible amount of God-knows-what in a violent spray coming from more than one direction. I apologize profusely. That was disgusting. Please forget I said that. Apparently being delirious with a fever results in me forgetting appropriate protocol.

It's been hours now and even though he hasn't muttered so much as an unkind word, I can tell Will is furious with me—which he has every right to be. I got cocky. I was prancing through the woods, carrying my metal pot, dancing and singing like Snow White, stopping when I saw a bird or small lizards to bid them a good morning. I was drunk with happiness and I got too comfortable out here, thinking I knew everything about Sexlandia, but I don't. I know nothing. I thought I knew which berries were safe, but I was wrong. Dead wrong.

My stomach lurches at the thought of the berries and I curl my legs up, shivering and sweaty in this tiny tent. *Why didn't I check with Will first? And why did I lie about it? Stupid, Arabella. Stupid.*

He clearly doesn't want to yell at me because of the state I'm in, but his entire demeanor is simmering with a silent rage. When I try to apologize, he brushes it off, and the last time he said, "I don't want to hear it. Just rest."

I've messed everything up. Everything. Any second now he's going to call for help, which will mean I've ruined his chance to ever waltz with Matilda again. And his career. And the careers of Mac and Tosh. And I'm likely going to die out here in this tent. Fuck.

No! Rally, Arabella. Rally now. Just get up and be better than this! You are Lara Croft. You are Wonder Woman. You can rappel and machete things with a machete and … and …oh fuck, you're a complete weakling. Taken down by some tiny berries.

He unzips the tent and holds the flap open but stays outside. "How are you feeling?"

"A little better," I say, even though it's not true because at this moment I would welcome death.

"Yeah, probably don't lie to me anymore because it will definitely get you killed."

"Just smother me with a pillow and put me out of my

misery." I close my eyes and hoping that the world stops spinning so quickly.

"Jesus, Arabella. You know, if you had told me the truth, we could've done something about it. But now, all I can do is bloody well wait."

"Sorry," I whisper, knowing it's completely useless to both of us.

"That's it. I'm calling for help."

"No." My attempt at sounding strong comes out as utterly pathetic, and I hate myself for it. "I refuse to be the reason that nobody gets paid."

"This is insane. I'm not risking your life for some cash."

"Give me a couple of hours. I actually do feel slightly better," I say, forcing myself to sit up.

He stares at me and I know he's trying to figure out if he can believe me or not. "No, forget it. I can't risk it."

"Will, please, I'm begging you. Just give me a little more time." I put my hand on his. "What I'm saying makes sense and you know it. We can get on the raft and go as far as possible by river. That'll bring us closer to town in case I make a quick recovery, and closer to help if I don't."

He sighs heavily and rubs the back of his neck. After a horribly long and uncomfortable moment, he says, "Fine. I'll go collect some fresh water and some peppermint leaves for your nausea. If you can hold that down, we'll get on the raft. If you can't, I call for help."

With that, he zips up the tent and I hear his footsteps disappearing. As soon as he's gone, I set my plan into action, forcing myself to get up and crawl outside. I drag myself over to the satellite phone. I grab the largest rock I can reach, lift it high into the air, then drop it directly on the phone. Then I stare, shocked at what I've done. I may have just killed myself with that one simple act because if I don't turn the corner very soon, I'll be dead by tomorrow.

"Okay, Arabella," I whisper. "Woman up because it's do or die time."

But first, a little nap right here on this nice dirt.

24

Only Fools Rush In...

Will

BY THE TIME I walk back toward camp, my pockets are filled with peppermint leaves and my chest is emptied of most of its anger. In its place is a huge lump of guilt. There's no reason for me to be kicking her when she's already down. It's not like Arabella is the first person to ever make a mistake. Besides, it's my fault for letting her wander around out here alone. I knew better than to think she could handle herself.

I slice a nearby bamboo shoot, then fill both of our empty water bottles. When they're full, I set back on the trail so I can apologize. The truth is, I don't like seeing her so weak and greenish and pale. There's a part of me that's well ... a little bit ... uncomfortable with that.

Okay, a lot uncomfortable.

Fine. Terrified. Is that better?

She matters to me in a way no one has before, and when she got sick, all I could think was: I can't lose her. I don't know if I'll survive if I do. I need to apologize to her and tell her the truth, which is that I love her. As insane as that is to say or even feel after only knowing her for such a short time, it's a fact. I love her, and I would give up everything for her. I'm about to give up my career, Matilda, and my friends, when they find out why we've been out here so long, leaving them all to wait. But somehow, if I know I have her, I can live without the rest.

The sky is growing dark as I reach camp. My eyes land on the sight of Arabella passed out on the ground next to the satellite phone. Christ, she must've been trying to call for help.

I drop everything and run over to her, kneel next to her on the ground. I touch her cheeks with both hands, finding them unusually hot and damp, even for this climate. "Arabella, come on, sweetheart. Don't do this, okay? You need to wake up."

I grab a water bottle and pour some onto my hands and pat it onto her face, but she doesn't wake up. I pour some into her hair, praying it will work. "Come on, Belle. Come on. Wake up already."

My heart pounds in my chest and panic fills my blood as I stare at her lifeless body. A sob swells in my chest. "Do not die, Arabella! You can't die."

I lift her up a bit and kiss her cheek. "Wake up, okay?" I beg, my voice breaking. Nope. I can't do this. I am not built for this shit. This is exactly what I get for falling in love with someone. "Come on, Arabella! Wake up!" I shout.

Her eyes flutter and she whispers, "Don't be mad."

I shake my head, laughing through tears I never thought I would have. "Never. I could never be angry with you."

She gives me a weak smile, even though her eyes are still closed. "Thank you. I love you, Will. I did it for you."

Uh-oh. "Did what, Belle? What did you do?" I ask, the hair on the back of my neck standing up on end. I glance around, trying to figure out what she's talking about, then for the first time, I notice the phone and see the rock on top of it. "No, no, no, no, no. Tell me you didn't."

"We can make it. I just need a bit more time."

Her head lolls to the side and she passes out again, leaving me alone with my fear and fury.

Panic fills me, and for once in my life, my blood runs cold. It's too much for me to take in and I sit motionless next to her while I try to make a decision. I need to get her to a hospital as quickly as possible. The show is over. My career is done. But the only thing that matters is keeping her alive.

I hop to my feet, then set to work taking apart the lean-to. I grab all of our supplies. Once I have everything loaded on the raft, I pick up Arabella, lay her down on top of a sleeping bag on the raft, and wrap her in the other one. Then I drag the raft to the river, and with one big push, set off into the darkness, hoping for a swift and uneventful ride through the night. By morning, we should be almost at a town along the river called Wasapi, where I can find a doctor. All I can do now is stay awake, steer the raft, and pray that she'll make it until we get there.

25

Score-Keeping Men, Powerful Bananas, and Hemorrhoid Cream

Arabella

I WAKE to the sound of sloshing water and a cool breeze across my skin. The sun is up already, and it takes me a second to realize we're traveling downstream on the raft. I have to crane my neck to see Will, who is sitting slightly behind me with his hand on the rudder. He has dark circles under his eyes, and he looks exhausted. I want to reach up and touch him, but the thought of lifting my arm seems unrealistically difficult.

My stomach growls loudly and I realize I'm ravenously hungry. "Will, I'm so sorry about all of this."

He looks down, relief filling his face. "Belle, you're awake."

I sit up slowly and smile at him.

"I was so worried. Are you okay?"

I nod. "Yeah. I'm a bit weak, but I think I'm over the worst of it. I just need some water and something to eat. We can still make it."

He shakes his head, keeping his eyes on the river. "No, we can't. I'm taking you to the hospital in Wasapi."

"What? No. We can't do that. We *have* to finish this," I say, moving closer to him.

He winces, and I know it must be from my horrendous dragon breath.

"It's over, Arabella. There's no possible way to get to Mbambole in time. We've gone too far in the wrong direction to make it now."

"What are you talking about?"

"We've been heading north for a couple of hours already."

Oh, bollocks. I shake my head vigorously. "No. Why would you do that? I told you I just needed a few hours to recover."

"Did you really think I'd risk your life for a TV show and some cash?" he asks, his voice shaking with anger. "Do you even know how sick you've been? You've been passed out and feverish since yesterday afternoon, Arabella. You're weak and dehydrated, and you need medical attention."

"No, I don't. I'll have some water and bananas, and I'll be right as rain."

He scoffs. "You must be delirious if you think that would work. There's no possible way you can do an eighteen-hour hike through the jungle like this. Or are you expecting me to throw you over my shoulder and sprint to the finish line, hoping you survive along the way?"

I set my jaw, defiance simmering in my empty tummy. "I'm going to be fine. We can still do this."

"You don't get it. You think this is a game, but it's life and death out here. Why can't you seem to understand that?"

"I made a mistake, okay, but there's no need to be an arse about it."

"Oh no?" he asks, his eyes wild with anger. "No need? I've been awake all night trying to keep you alive and keep this raft from hitting a rock or bottoming out, all the while watching for hungry crocodiles who might just decide to pop their heads over the top and take a bite out of you. And you know what? It wasn't just the one mistake. By my count, it's three giant screw-ups that totally fucked us both. First you ate the berries, then you lied to me, then you smashed the phone for reasons I cannot even begin to understand."

"I did it because I knew you'd call for help."

"Yeah, I would have, because help is exactly what we need right now!"

"I'm not going to lose you that money and ruin your career," I say, picking up the bunch of bananas and ripping one off.

"Oh, please don't act like you care about me. You wanted to have your own version of a fantasy spring break." He changes his voice to imitate me. "Will, let's stay here for a few days, please. Just the two of us. I need this, Will."

I fight back tears and keep my voice as steady as I can. "I didn't *make* you stay out in the jungle having sex with me. You were every bit as on board with that idea as I was."

"Well, that's what happens when a guy thinks with his second brain."

"Oh, so *none of this* is your fault? It's all my fault, and your penis's fault, but you had absolutely no say in any of it?"

Shaking his head at me, he leans in. "I can't even believe you're mad at *me* right now. Me. The guy who's trying to save your royal arse. You totally fucked all of this up for everyone, and yet, somehow you have the nerve to be angry with me. For what? Trying to get you to safety? Putting you before myself? Which thing is it you're so offended by?"

"I appreciate that but—"

"But what? I should be able to magically get us both across the finish line? I know I'm amazing, but Christ, Arabella! There are limits to what any human can do. I'm not one of your butlers, you know. You can't just order me to do what you want and expect me to hop to it. Yes, Your Highness. Right away, Your Highness."

"That's not what I meant and you know it." My voice is shaking now.

He stares at me for a moment, his eyes softening a little. "Just drink some water and lay down. You're too weak for any of this."

"Will, please. I can't let it end this way. I have to try."

"You did, Arabella. I know you tried, but it takes a certain kind of person to do what I do," he says, his voice growing calm now. "It's actually all my fault. I should've refused to take you out here. I knew better."

I curl my knees up into my chest and rest my head on them, feeling a wave of wooziness come over me. His attempt to let me off the hook hurts worse than his anger. He's exactly like everyone else. He has absolutely no faith in me. But I can prove him wrong. I know I can.

He taps me on the shoulder. "Here, have some of this water."

I take the bottle without saying anything and have a sip, feeling the refreshing, cool liquid slide across my tongue. The taste of it makes me long for more, but I know I need to pace myself. "How much farther until town?"

"Hard to say. My best guess is about two hours maybe."

I nod slightly and take another sip of water. I've got two more hours to get my strength back. Because there is no way in hell I'm going to go out like this. After everything I've been through and managed to do out here, I will *not* return home as a weak, pathetic, pampered princess.

————

ABN Morning Newscast with Veronica Platt

"Welcome to *Avonia This Morning*. I'm Veronica Platt. Restaurantgoers capture secret footage of Princess Arabella's bodyguard without his charge." Veronica stares intently into the camera. "It's been nine days since Princess Arabella's disappearance, and citizens around Valcourt have started to follow her bodyguard, simply known as Bellford, hoping for clues as to her whereabouts."

The screen fills with shaky footage of a man dressed in sweatpants and a hoodie pushing a shopping trolley in the frozen foods section of a grocery store. "Giles Bigly joins us live in studio to discuss the new developments in this mysterious story."

"Yes, Veronica," Giles says, smiling. "Our Hot Tips Desk has been flooded with footage of Princess Arabella's long-serving security officer, who appears to be taking a few days off. Here, we see him buying groceries, and in the next video, we see him sipping what looks like Guinness at The Frog 'n Keg Pub."

"Shocking, really," Veronica says as the video ends and a shot of her sitting at the desk next to Giles fills the screen. Giles seems to have lost interest in the news story and is bouncing in his chair as though testing it out.

"Shocking, isn't it, Giles?" She asks in an urgent tone. "Why would she be without her head security officer for so many days?"

"It's hard to say, Veronica. Perhaps she's caught a cold. Perhaps she's taking a few days off and doesn't need to have extra security if she's just staying home. Or maybe he's on vacation."

"Perhaps, Giles, but there appears to be more to the story than meets the eye. Have you heard anything from palace insiders that could shed some light on her disappearance?"

"Nothing, Veronica," Giles says, rubbing his open palms on the news desk.

Veronica watches his hand with a slightly disgusted look on her face. "What about the fact that a staffer who asked not to be named has apparently told a reporter at *Weekly World News* that something strange is definitely going on, but as to what he or she could not say?"

"Well, Veronica, as you and I both know, the *Weekly World News* isn't exactly known for their journalistic integrity."

"They were right about that man who had a baby, Giles."

"That they were, Veronica. But very few stories since."

Turning back to the camera, Veronica says, "Coming up next, fashion critic Nigel Woods is here to do our quarterly update on Princess Tessa's post-baby-body weight loss, and according to him, things are not exactly improving for the consort to our future King."

Veronica looks at Giles, clearly hoping for him to join her in looking scandalized, but instead, Giles says, "The poor woman had twins, can we just leave it alone, already?"

The feed cuts and a commercial for AnuFix hemorrhoid cream starts up.

26

Never Break Up with a Woman
While on a Long Raft Trip

Will

Do you know what's really fucking awkward? Having a massive row with someone while you're on a ten-foot by six-foot raft. Because there's really nowhere to go to avoid each other once the damage has been done. We have floated along in complete silence for the last two hours, neither of us pointing out the okapi or monkeys.

Right now, we're both silently watching the river otters swim beside us. Somehow the sight of them there, so content, brings a pang of pain for me, knowing I may never feel that happy again because we are one hundred percent over, just like my career and my reputation. I will never be able to live down the fact that I'm the guy who almost got a princess killed out in the jungle. I'm taking her to a hospital now where I'll be admitting defeat.

It doesn't matter how it happened, because I knew she had no business being out here, yet I wanted to believe she could do it. I should've gotten us out of there as fast as possible, but I didn't. And although I'm pretty sure she'll be okay based on the number of bananas she's scarfed down, I still have to get her checked by a doctor to be sure.

Seriously, she has eaten a lot of bananas. Like enough bananas to feed an entire family of horny bonobos.

A dock jutting out from the river's edge tells me we're close to Wasapi. We make our way around the next bend in the hot sun and come to a clearing in the trees. We made it. My heart sinks as I steer the raft toward the shore, knowing that in about ten minutes, my life as I know it will be over. The only consolation is that I'll be rid of her permanently. Thank God for that. She is the very last thing I need. I suppose the other silver lining is that we figured out we're not compatible before things went too far, so I guess there's that to be grateful for. The raft bumps against the shore and I hop off, pulling it onto the sandy ground. Arabella makes no move to get off or to help.

"So, Your Highness, it turns out it's much easier for me to drag the raft without also having the extra weight of an adult human aboard."

She turns and glares at me but says nothing.

"Okay, I see. So now I'm your servant all of a sudden?"

"I'm not getting off."

"Of course you're getting off. I got you here. This is the part where you go find a doctor so you can get checked over and I find a phone that isn't smashed so I can call Dylan and tell her where to pick us up."

She shakes her head and folds her arms at me. "Nope. Not doing it."

"Yes. You bloody well are. Because we're done. Completely done, in case you didn't realize it the first several times I've told you that this is over. You and I are over. The show is over. My career is over. So the only thing I have to live for at this moment is a hot shower, a big meal, copious amounts of beer, and a bed, which are all to be found in that village right there. Now get your arse off the raft before I do it for you."

"You're such a coward," she says, lifting her chin.

I bark out a nasty laugh. "*I'm* a coward?"

"Yes. Sorry to be the one to have to tell you this, but you are. You think you're so fucking brave out here doing manly things in the wild, but the truth is, you're just hiding from any real type of life and responsibility. You have set it up so you have the perfect excuse for never getting attached to anybody. You're a crap brother, you're a crap uncle, and you'd be a crap boyfriend."

"I'm not listening to this. Either get off the raft or don't. But I'm out of here." I give it a good yank, then start to tie it to a tree using a vine. "I'm going to go get a drink. Do whatever the hell you want," I say, stepping back onto the raft to grab my backpack.

"Give me the map. I'm going to keep going," she says defiantly.

"There's no fucking way I'm giving you this map. You're done. You can't survive out there even with me. We've got twenty-eight hours until time's up and it's at least a twenty-hour hike *if* we go fast. Do you know how hard that is, even if you're strong and healthy? It's really fucking hard. And in case you haven't noticed, you are neither strong, nor healthy. It's over. We lose." I hop off the raft and start walking up the hill, the smell of chicken cooking pulling me ahead.

I'm just at the top when her voice stops me. "I never figured you for a quitter. A smug prick and a coward, yes. But not a quitter."

I turn and let out a frustrated laugh. "Yeah, and you're insane if you think you can hike for twenty hours, which means some of that has to be done *at night*. In the jungle. The mighty jungle where the lions don't sleep at night."

"Lions live in the savanna."

"Jaguars then. And rats and snakes and crocs. They're all wide awake all night looking for something to eat, and you may be skinny, but I'm sure none of them would mind making a meal out of you."

"Fine. You quit. Do what you want, but I'm not giving up." She stands, looking strong now as she steps off the raft. She holds her hand out to me and says. "Give me the fucking map. I'm going to go take a piss, then get back across this river, and through that jungle to the finish line. If you want to go into town and cry in your beer, you be my guest. I don't give a shit what you do. But *I'm* going to prove that I can finish what I started."

"You cannot do this alone."

"Then I'll gladly die trying, because I refuse to be the reason that your friends lose their jobs or your brother loses his boat," she says. "And there's no way I'm going home with my tail tucked between my legs so everyone I know will say, 'Yup, we were right about her. She's so delicate she can't even eat some berries.'" Leaning in, she tries to look menacing. "So, either get your weak arse out of my face or be a man and come with me. I don't care what you choose, but you *are* giving me that map."

I glare down at her, my heart pounding in my chest and I don't know if I want to walk away forever or kiss her hard on the mouth. She glares back, her cute little nostrils flaring.

Son of a bitch. I'm going to do this, aren't I?

27

How to Channel Your Inner Tennis Champ...

Arabella

I STAND PERFECTLY STILL, doing my best imitation of someone who is actually brave while I wait for his answer. My heart fills with fear for both possible reactions. Because hiking through the night in the jungle is every bit as bad an option as giving up. Worse, even, because it's horribly dangerous. But the truth is, if I fail at this, I might as well give up because I'll have to go back to my little boxed-in existence, and I know if I do, I'll die there anyway. So, I might as well die out here instead.

I stare into his eyes—the same eyes that only yesterday gazed at me lovingly and caused my stomach to do happy little flips. But now they're cold and hard and I hate them just like I hate the rest of him.

And I loathe the fact that I need him to get me through this, but I do. "Look, I don't have a lot of time here, so make up your mind. Are you going to man up and do what you need to do, or quit like a little bitch?" I shrug. "I know what Bear Grylls would do, but, hey, you do you."

Will shakes his head and rolls his eyes. "Did you really think that was going to work? You could just compare me to that phony, and I'd come along on this death march to prove I'm better than him? You really must think I'm stupid."

"Whatever, dude. Only one of you has your own line of camping equipment. Just sayin'." Okay, I know I'm pushing it now, but I really do need him to come along and it's not exactly like we're in a place in our relationship where I can appeal to his sense of sympathy. Where compassion will fail, you need to attack the ego. It's negotiations 101, taught to me by my big brother, Arthur. And now I walk away and give him time to say yes.

I make my way into the bush, find a bit of spongy moss, then have a quick pee. That's right, I can openly admit to having bodily functions now. Yay, me. Taking a deep breath, I strut back to the raft, head held high. Giving him an icy stare, I say, "Well? Are you coming with me or not?"

"I'm going with you," he says, pointing a finger at me while he scowls. "But not because I want to help you or because I give a shit about besting that goofball. It's because if I don't, the entire world will blame me for letting you get yourself killed out there."

"I really couldn't care less why you come, as long as we

leave now," I say, walking over to the tree and trying to untie the knot. It's too tight and it won't budge. Damn delicate fingers.

He walks over, brushes my fingers out of the way, then unties it one-handed. What a show-off with his stupid manly hands.

"Let's be clear about one thing." He leans in and lowers his tone. "Don't go fooling yourself into thinking this is your opportunity to get back together, because whatever we had is over. *Finished*. Never going to happen again."

"*Pfffft*. Don't flatter yourself. I wouldn't sleep with you again if all the dildos in the world suddenly disappeared." Oh my, I'm getting good at the tough talk, no?

He gives me a nasty grin. "Perfect. Because the only thing I want from you is to get your sorry arse over that finish line in time so I get paid."

"Fine by me. Just make sure you walk ahead so I don't have to look at your smug, stupid face again." I take a couple of steps toward the raft and crouch down in front of it.

"Get on," Will says. "There's no way you can push this thing into the water."

"Watch me," I say, straining as hard as I can. It doesn't budge and Will chuckles, bringing out a fury in me I didn't realize I had. I grunt like Serena Williams hitting a forehand, while I give another big shove. The raft starts to move and I hop on, then catch my balance and kneel down with my hand on the rudder. "Are you coming, Wilma?"

He scrambles down the hill, then wades into the water

and manages to climb on before it's too late. I turn my face toward the opposite shore, smiling on the inside at the fact that I've managed to shock him.

"That was actually pretty impressive," he says quietly.

My ridiculous heart jumps at the thought of impressing him, but on the outside, I remain cool. "Thanks, but I'm really not looking for your approval."

———

The sun went down two hours ago, and in that time, I've learned that hiking through the jungle at night is not only a terrible idea, it's also disgusting and terrifying. Did you know that there actually are giant rats out here? It's true. I thought Will was just trying to scare me when he mentioned them on our first day out here. But they're real. Very freaking real, and they're the size of a bloody house cat. Apparently, they also like to come out at night to hunt for food. As do a shit ton of bats. There are plenty of them out swooping around.

We're both wearing the headlamps, which carry with them the unfortunate side effect of attracting swarms of moths. So, since it got dark, I'm swatting behemoth moths as they try to land on my face while I simultaneously duck from the bats and watch for rats.

Oh, wow! That last moth was easily the size of a not-so-small bird. "Motherfucker," I mutter, flinching and flailing my arms to hold them back. "Just fuck off already. That's *my* headlamp."

Will is moving fast through the forest, slicing a path for us with his machete while I try to keep up. I'm panting so hard, my lungs ache. I feel weak and thirsty and exhausted, and to be honest, I just want to lay down right here and sleep for a couple of days. We've been walking for ten hours now with only two short breaks to eat, drink water, and rest—both of which have been done in a silent but simmering rage.

I haven't checked yet, but I already know my ankles are cut again and each step feels like someone's rubbing sandpaper against an open wound. But I won't stop. I can't. I force my feet to keep going, focusing on the lifetime of respect I'm earning one meter at a time. An owl hoots in a tree nearby and I flinch, my heart racing even faster.

Will is far ahead now, hurrying along like he can't get away from me fast enough, which is fine by me. We come to the bottom of another steep hill. God, no. No more hills, please. Unless they're down.

Of course, he scrambles up it quickly and with ease, and even though I want to slump down onto the ground and have a cry, I force myself to catch up. He stops at the top, shining his light down while I climb. He reaches a hand down to help me, but I don't take it.

"Suit yourself, Your Highness."

"I intend to," I quip.

"Let's take a break for a few minutes. I'll get us some water and you check your feet for blisters. We're also going to need to make torches because these headlamps won't last much longer."

"I'll get my own water." I grab the machete from him and walk over to a stand of bamboo, then with one clean slice, I hack a piece down and hold it sideways, tipping it back into my mouth. I wait, but nothing comes out. Shit. Like I need this right now with him here watching all arrogant and survivory.

I feel his hand on mine and for a brief second, I think he's going to try to apologize, but instead he just slides the machete out of my palm. He slices another shoot and holds it above his head, then drinks for a long time. When it's empty, he tosses it into the woods and makes a satisfied 'aaaahhhh' sound. "Much better. Finding the right shoot is a bit of an art. You sure you don't want some help?"

"No, thanks. I'd rather die from dehydration than take anything from you."

He slices another one and hands it to me. "Don't think of it as me doing you a favor. The only reason I'm giving you this is so that I don't wind up carrying you across the finish line."

I yank it out from him and mutter, "I won't need to be carried. If anyone's going to need to be carried out of here, it's you."

"Ha! Not likely."

A few minutes later, we are each furiously whittling bamboo poles into torches and collecting shavings of a dead tree, as well as some bark chunks. I pull my lighter out of my pocket and light my torch, giving him a satisfied smile as it comes to life while he struggles with his flint. I take a few steps toward him and strike the lighter again and watch as his torch comes to life.

"Thanks," he says, sounding completely sarcastic.

"I didn't do it for you. I did it so I can get the hell away from you sooner."

"Oh, believe me, between the two of us," he says, pointing back and forth from his chest to mine. "There's no possible way *you* want to be away from me more than *I* want to be away from you." With that, he turns and continues on, holding his torch out with his left arm while he cuts through the brush with his right.

———

The full moon is directly above our heads now as we continue on through the noisy jungle. Every once in a while, I catch a glimpse of it through the treetops and wonder how Will knows which direction to go. Maybe he doesn't. Maybe we're going in one big circle. Not that I'm about to ask him. He's much farther ahead now, having stepped up his pace after our last go-around. I follow wearily, keeping sight of his torch. He stops and turns back, shouting, "Can you keep up, Your Highness? I'd hate to see you get eaten by giant rats."

"Shut up, you … *man*." Well, that was a lame burn.

We continue on, and about thirty seconds later, his torch disappears and I hear several loud thuds, some *oof* sounds and him yelling the word 'shit!'

I sprint ahead, shouting his name, then hear him call, "Do *not* run! There's a drop off."

My heart thumps wildly in my chest as I hold the torch closer to the ground and make my way slowly forward. "Are you all right?" I call.

"Fabulous."

When I reach the edge, I peer down, finding him at the bottom of a tight ravine. I switch on my headlamp to get a better look, only to see that his ankle is twisted in a way that makes my stomach feel queasy. "Oh my God. Are you all right? Are you bleeding?"

"Probably," he says, his face filled with pain.

Panic fills me. I don't know what to do. I have to save him, but I can't, can I? *He's* the one who does the saving, not me. I'm the weak link, the pampered princess, the useless, boring, sheltered, picks-the-wrong-berries one. Tears fill my eyes and I sit back on the ledge to make sure I don't fall in. Forcing my voice not to waiver, I call down to him, "What do I need to do to get you out of there?"

"Oh, I don't know," he says, sounding utterly annoyed. "Are you able to rebuild a satellite phone? Because if not, I'm totally fucked."

Oh, that's *it*! "I cannot believe you are going to throw that back in my face right now!"

"Really? You can't? Because I'm going to die down here in this hole, which never would have happened if I wasn't forced to …" he stops himself, then sighs loudly. "It doesn't matter anymore."

My shoulders drop. This is too much. I can't. I can't do any of this. "What do I do, Will? You're the guy who knows how to get out these situations. Tell me what to do and I'll do it."

He doesn't answer, so I go on. "Do I go back for help? Or is there some way I can get you out of there? Just tell me and I'll do it."

"Just stay put. It's the safest choice," he says, his voice strained. "There's no possible way you can navigate your way out of here. Not at night, anyway. Cover yourself with a sleeping bag and try to get some sleep. At first light, you start walking."

"I'm not leaving you here."

"You're going to have to. It's my only chance of making it out of here alive. Yours, too."

Tears burn my eyes, but I refuse to sob, because there's no way I want him to know I'm crying. Regret fills me for every decision I've made since I was in the bathtub after that wedding. If only I could go back in time and not send that text. Everything would be fine. I'd be safe at home and Will wouldn't be about to die in a ravine, only to be eaten by giant rats.

"Arabella?" He says quietly.

I wipe away my tears, even though he can't see them. Clearing my throat, I say, "Yes?"

"I'm probably going to pass out, so if I do, I want you to promise you'll leave as soon as the sun comes up. Just go. Do everything I taught you so you can get out of here."

His words are like a kick to my gut. "No, I don't want to leave you. There must be a way to lift you out of there."

"There isn't. I can't walk and you can't carry me. You're already defying the odds to have made it this far after being so sick."

I sit, listening to the rustling in the trees, to the cicadas, and the frogs. He's right. I can't make this hike in the dark. Not on my own. I pull my sleeping bag out of my pack and cover myself, then lay down and let the tears flow while I wrack my brain for some solution to this. There must be a way to save him. This can't be it. *Think, Arabella, think.*

―――――

I wake to the sound of the birds. The sun isn't up yet, but there's enough light to see. Sitting up, I lean over, my eyes adjusting for a second before I can make out Will's body. His head is tilted back and his eyes are closed. My heart jumps into my throat. "Will?!"

He opens his eyes. "It's time. Get going, okay?"

"Can't I—?"

"No," he says, wincing. "If there was a way, I'd have thought of it by now. But, there's still a chance that you can make it back and someone will find me in time."

"But—"

"You can do this, Belle. I know you can. Forget all that shit I said to you yesterday. I was just angry and hurt and … being a prick. I didn't mean any of it."

"I'm so sorry, Will. I didn't mean anything I said, either. Well, that's not entirely true because I do think you have commitment issues, but that's beside the point because the truth is, I've never …" My voice trails off as I remember him saying the words 'finished' and 'over' and 'never going to happen.' And I know he meant it. But even if he didn't, this is how it has to be because there is no way to make anything work between us. We're just too different.

"Listen, my best shot is if you go for help. It's about a five-hour hike from here straight east. Do you remember what I said about how to make sure you're not going in circles?"

"Yes," I nod and wipe the tears from my cheeks. "Pick an object in the distance, keep my eyes on it, and when I reach it, pick a new one. And then keep turning back to make sure the last one is behind me."

"That's right," he says, his tone encouraging. "You've got this, Belle. I know you do."

"I hope so," I say, wiping at my tears.

"I *know* so. You can do this. Just think of everything you've done over the last nine days. You've rappelled from a heli-copter into the jungle, swung from vines into a lagoon, free-climbed down steep cliffs, you've hiked for over ten hours straight *at night*. You made it this far. You'll make it out."

I nod, letting his words fill my soul with courage. "Okay, I'll go, but you have to promise me you're going to survive until I get back with help."

"No problem," he says doing his best to give me a confident smile even though I know he must be terrified that *I'm* the only thing between him and death.

"Will, I'm going to go now. But before I do. I just wanted to say …" I stop myself, unable to tell him I love him. Instead, I take the wimpy way out. "Thank you."

"Buy me a beer when we get to town."

"Okay," I answer, letting out a small chuckle through my tears. "I'll be back for you before you know it."

"Yes, you will. You can do this, Arabella."

"How are you so sure?" I ask.

"Because you've always been able to. You just needed a reason to try."

28

Broken Bones, Tree Sap, and Sappy Goodbye Videos

Will

WHAT A HUMILIATING WAY TO go out of the world—falling into a ravine because I was too pissed off to follow the rules I live by. And now I'm lying here, wedged in between two slimy boulders, covered in blood, dirt, and sweat, with my right ankle pointing the wrong way. And to top it off, I'm waiting to be rescued by a freaking princess who doesn't know her way around the jungle any better than I would know my way around the cutlery at a state dinner.

I stare down at my ankle, realizing it should hurt, and the fact that it doesn't is not a testament to my toughness, as much as I wish it was. It's a sign that my body has gone into shock. I touch the back of my head, and when I check my fingers, I see the bleeding hasn't stopped. It's still sticky and hot. I likely have a concussion, which is responsible for this massive headache. And all the fresh blood ought to draw some attention from those awful giant rats that are scurrying around these woods. I suppose that'll be a quicker way to go out than just starving to death while I wait to be rescued. Horribly painful and disgusting, but quick, at least.

As much as I wish it weren't the case, the chance that she'll find her way out of this jungle, and then figure out how to get back here in time is about as likely as Bear Grylls giving good survival advice.

Okay, fine. I'm jealous, okay? He's like the Kleenex brand of tissues and I'm … the no-name brand that everyone calls Kleenex.

Whatever.

I manage to wiggle out of my backpack, which is lodged between my body and the rock behind me. Tugging it out, I open it and find the plastic container of salve I made for Arabella's ankles. The sight of it causes my heart to squeeze. Bollocks, I really did hit my head hard. I use the rest of the salve, knowing that it's basically pointless because I am definitely going to die anyway.

Picking up my camera, I give myself a minute to think, then turn it on and aim it at myself. "My name is Will Banks. If you find this, it means you found my body. I'm a citizen of Avonia and of the Benavente Islands. Please contact my brother, Harrison Banks, or my sister, Emma Banks-Davenport, at The Paradise Bay Resort on Santa Valentina Island."

I pause, swallowing hard, trying to think of what I want to

say. Fuck it. I might as well just wing it. "Harrison and Libby, Emma and Pierce, Rosy, Darnell, baby Clara—you are all the people I love in this world. And I'm sorry that I took you for granted, and that I've spent my last few years running away from you. When I think about all the moments I've missed while I was out flying over volcanoes and sliding down icebergs with penguins, and all the moments I'm going to miss …" I close my eyes for a second. "Well, you know. I'm sorry. I wish it could be different.

"I've been a lot of things in my life. One of them is stubborn, and for that, I apologize. To Dwight Anderson, my manager, thank you for always having my back and being the voice of reason. I know I haven't been an easy guy to work with all the time, and I appreciate that you never gave up on me. To Mac and Tosh, thanks for the years of friendship and adventure. I hope you each get to enjoy more decades of seeing the world on ABN's dime. Have a beer for me once in a while."

I feel a lump in my throat, and I clear it before I keep talking. "Harrison, I don't know how to thank you for everything you've been for me—a big brother, my best friend, and my dad, all rolled into one, which kind of sounds like some sort of weird incest thing because I'm calling you my dad and my brother but, for anyone who doesn't know us and watches this, I'm saying it because our parents died when we were kids. Anyway, Harrison, you've been this family's rock. You've been my rock." My voice cracks and I pause and take a quick breath. "When I think of everything you've given to us and sacrificed, it kills me that I won't have a chance to repay you, which is sort of ironic because I'm about to die.

"If by some miracle, the network decides to pay out my bonuses even though I'm failing to meet the terms of our agreement, I have already arranged with Stogie Stew to buy back Matilda for you. I was just waiting for the rest of the money from this season. Take the cash and get her back. Then spend some more and get her detailed because she probably reeks of cigars and Stew.

"Emma, you're such a pain in the arse," I say, managing a half grin. "Thank you for giving me such a hard time my whole life and teaching me a little about women and a lot about courage. You truly are an incredible person, and Pierce is lucky to have you. Take care of each other," I say, unable to stop my voice from breaking. "Rosy, I'll always be your cuddle bear, no matter where I am. I'm going to miss dinners at your house with you and Darnell, and Starsky and Hutch. Having you in my life has made all the difference. Little Clara, I know you won't remember me, but I'm your uncle who taught you to blow raspberries. You'll probably forget that too, but I want you to know how special you are to me. Grow up to be strong and loving, like your mom and dad. Get your dad to teach you how to surf, because as good as he is at it, I'm pretty sure you'll be a lot better. You already have an incredible sense of balance for a toddler. Oh, and if you're looking for your sippy cup with the kittens on it, it's under my coffee table."

I shut off the camera and try to regain my composure, only to find myself overcome with emotion as I think about what Arabella and I had, and what it might have been if I hadn't been a total arsehole to her. I rest my head against the rock and close my eyes for a moment, trying to gather my strength. Finally, when I'm ready, I turn the camera back on. "Arabella, if you see this, I didn't mean all those shitty things that I said. I lied to you when we were playing truth or dare. I do have a fear and you already know what it is. I'm afraid of letting anyone get close to me. I *am* a complete coward and I've done exactly what you said I did, which is to set my life up so I could sidestep love completely. When you were sick, I thought for sure I was going to lose you and the pain of it made me even more certain that I don't have what it takes to go the distance with anyone. I can't do it because you never know how long you've got with someone, and I can't be the one left behind. You were right. I'm too weak for that.

"But I want you to know these past days out here with you have been the greatest of my entire life. I have never felt anything close to what I feel for you, and if I had made it out of this alive, I would sweep you up into my arms and never let you go. For what it's worth, I love you, and I want you to go on and be the totally kickass version of yourself I watched come to life out here. Don't let anyone underestimate you. But if they do, you show them who you really are. You're fierce. You're brave. You are a warrior. Thank you for trying to save me. Please don't spend a moment feeling guilty for how things ended up, because there is nothing you could've done."

"Well, that's a little insulting," Arabella says.

I look up, my heart surging as I see her beautiful face smiling down at me. "You assumed I'd fail."

29

Show Him You Love Him with a DIY Stretcher...

Arabella - One Hour Earlier

"OKAY, ARABELLA." Pant. Pant. "You can do this," I say, swiping at the brush in front of me with the machete. Oh, that's hard. So much harder than Will makes it look. Can't they make machetes out of a lighter material? Seriously. Pant. Pant. Pant. "Just keep your eye on that big tree right there with the split trunk and keep going."

But my arms hurt already, and I've only been at this for a few minutes. How can I possibly do this for another five hours? And how the hell can I lead anyone back here to find Will before he bleeds to death, or gets bit by a spider, or a snake slithers down to him and squeezes the life out of him? *Oh, Xena, Warrior Princess, please come to me now and give me the strength to go on.*

Almost at the tree. Just get there. Just to that tree. Then you can walk on that road on the other side of it. "Wait. A road?!" I sprint ahead with renewed energy and hop over a small bush, landing on a dirt road that disappears into the trees in the distance. It's got old tire tracks with grasses growing down the center of it, but still, it's a real road. Which means people! Which means we could be saved. "Yes!"

I stop and bend at the waist, resting my hands on my knees while I catch my breath. I listen for the sounds of human beings or vehicles, but there's nothing but the buzzing of insects and the call of the birds. I look up. "Okay, if it's early morning and the sun is there, this road must be going east, which is exactly where we need to go."

"I can go back and get Will," I tell myself, because somehow saying it out loud helps me check to see if my logic is sound. "I know how to build a raft. I can make a stretcher. Then, because I already have a path, I can drag him without having to pull him and slice a trail at the same time. Right?"

I stand, chewing my lip for a second, then decide to go for it. Racing back into the woods, I find two bamboo poles and set them down on the ground. Then I glance around until I spot a long, thick vine hanging from a tree. Giving it a tug, I say, "Yup. You're my vine. Now, just climb the tree, cut the vine, and make a stretcher." No problem.

I stand at the base of the tree and look for footholds. There's one I can reach, but it'll take all my bendy ballet moves to do it. Urgh. This feels disgusting. My hands are going to be filthy.

I'm now about two feet off the ground, my heart is pounding, my stomach flipping. "Keep going. You are a warrior."

I continue on, only to get a face full of spider web. "Eeewwww. So gross." I can't even brush it off because if I do, I'll fall. *Ignore the disgusting webs and get that vine. Oh, and open your eyes.*

Gripping the trunk with both hands, I force myself to go a little higher. Just until I can cut a long enough strip of the vine for what I need. I wedge my foot in between a branch and the trunk, then, pressing my body against the tree, I hold on with my left arm, and use my right to give the vine one quick slice.

"Shit!" I almost lose my balance. Dropping the machete, I hug the tree. "No bullet ants. No bullet ants. Please don't attack me."

I fumble my way down, and when I finally find the ground with my feet, I wipe at my face, trying to remove the webs. When I finish, I look at my palms, which are totally black with dirt. "Oh great. Now I'm all dirty."

I won't look at all like a sexy warrior princess when I go back and get Will. *Whatever, idiot, it doesn't matter what you look like. Just save his life already!*

It takes me about ten minutes and a whole lot of tugging, yanking, and grunting to finish the stretcher, but when it's ready, I stare at it for a second and smile at my ingenuity. I zipped up my sleeping bag, cut a hole through the bottom corners with my Swiss Army knife, then slid the poles through on each side. Then I cut another bamboo shoot and made the connector thingies Will showed me and used the vines to secure them. Pretty decent overhand knots, if I do say so myself.

Forget about that, Arabella. Pick it up and run! Run to your man!

————

Fast Forward to Now…

I smile down at Will for a second, then snap into action. "Change of plans. I found a road nearby that I'm hoping will take us to Mbambole, but if not, it'll take us somewhere with humans, right?"

He nods. "Theoretically, but how are you—"

"—I've got that covered. I made a stretcher for you, and I figured out how to get you out of there."

I grab hold of a vine growing out of the ground at the top of the ravine, wrap it around a thick tree trunk nearby, and guide it down near Will. "I'm coming down."

Steadying my shaking hands, I start my descent, keeping my breath even and whispering encouraging thoughts to myself. "You can do this. You're brave. You're strong. You're Belle."

When I reach the bottom, I scramble over the rocks to get to Will. "Please don't mind my mudface. I had a run-in with a very dirty tree."

He grins at me, shaking his head. "I've never seen anyone look so beautiful."

I take his cheeks in my hands, unable to stop myself from touching him. Will sits up a bit, and leans in for a kiss, but I say, "That'll have to wait. I have serious puke breath."

"Righto, I forgot."

"So, we're going to use the Bear Grylls backpack as a makeshift harness," I say, taking the bag and wrapping the end of the vine around the straps. I quickly tie it on while Will watches. "This vine is wrapped around a very strong-looking ironwood tree that we can use as leverage. As long as the straps don't break, and you let me help you, you should be able to pull yourself up using your arms and one leg."

I stop what I'm doing, and we look into each other's eyes. A feeling of elation comes over me. "I'm going to save your life, Will Banks."

"Yes, you are, Belle."

———

Okay, so, that was not pretty. Getting him out of that ravine involved a lot of my cheek pressed against his 'other' cheeks, while I pushed him up and he pulled. His foot dangled the entire time in a way that caused a good deal of gagging from yours truly. Yes, I grunted and gagged and pushed while he used his muscly muscles to climb to the top. Then he tossed the vine down and I zipped up. And I have to say, I probably looked like a real adventure woman doing it.

"Wow," Will says, when I stand. "You're like Spider-Woman."

"Damn straight," I answer with a nod. Pulling the stretcher so it's next to him, I pat the middle of it. "Hop on."

He shakes his head. "As well-constructed as that is, there's no way you can pull me to town. Just help me make a splint and some crutches."

"I absolutely can pull you on this." I hold up the vine I've attached to the front. "This goes around my forehead, wrapped in a shirt, of course. I'll be using my head and arms to drag you. I can't guarantee a smooth ride, but it's definitely going to work."

"I weigh over two hundred—"

"Nope. No more talking. Get the fuck on the stretcher already."

He opens his mouth, but I stop him with an "Ah-ah-ah!" sound and a wag of one finger. "Just shut up and let me save you. I'm in a huge rush because if I can do it fast enough, we'll beat the clock, get our money, *and* you won't die."

"Honestly, just the last one is enough for me," he says, dragging himself onto the stretcher.

"Well, not for this princess. I want it *all*," I answer, gently lifting his right leg and placing it on top of the sleeping bag. *Oh, that is a heavy leg. This is going to be tougher than I thought.*

I hurry to the front of the stretcher. "I'm getting you that yacht, Mr. Banks. If it's the last thing I do."

———

ABN Nooner News with Veronica Platt

"Welcome to Nooner News. I'm Veronica Platt. Reporters from around the kingdom have made a mad dash to the airports this morning, after palace officials confirmed that King Winston is currently on his way to the village of Mbambole in Zamunda to retrieve his only daughter and fourth in line to the throne, Princess Arabella. Giles Bigly joins us live from the gate at Valcourt Airport, where he is about to board a plane. Giles, can you tell us what's going on?"

"Yes, Veronica. About an hour ago, palace officials released a statement that Royal Air One was being prepared for an emergency flight. King Winston, as well as the entire royal medical staff, are aboard the plane and are currently en route to Mbambole."

"Giles, any idea how Princess Arabella ended up there in the first place, or if she may indeed be gravely injured, thus requiring immediate medical attention?"

"Yes, Veronica, on a hunch, I walked over to the unscripted wing of our ABN headquarters and tracked down an executive there who did in fact confirm for me—off the record—that Princess Arabella is currently in the jungles of Western Zamunda filming a survival documentary with none other than Will Banks, host of "The Wild World.""

Veronica's chin drops and she stares at the camera for a full two seconds before sputtering out her next comment. "So, the entire time everyone in the nation has been worried sick about her, she's been off gallivanting in the jungle with Will Banks?"

"It would appear so, yes." Giles turns from the camera as a boarding announcement comes over the speaker. "I'm afraid I have to go, Veronica. That's the last call for boarding."

"All right, Giles. Godspeed," Veronica says with a serious look.

"Um, thanks."

30

Speak Now or Forever Hold Your Peace

Will

I LOVE THIS WOMAN. I love her. Puke breath, sweat, and all. She's fucking amazing. She's been dragging me along this bumpy dirt road all day, huffing and puffing, and at times swearing like a sailor, but never giving up. She's like this crazy-strong, determined woman who could do anything. The sun is high in the sky now and it's so hot, she must be roasting with all the exertion, but she just keeps going.

A while ago, we came to a hill, and she hopped on the stretcher with me and used it as a sled, steering us all the way to the bottom. It was actually incredibly painful, what with all the bouncing and jiggling, but it was also kind of fun. When we got to the bottom, I asked her where she learned to do that. She gave me one nod and said, "Christ-

260

mases at the castle. I wasn't kidding about how much sled-
ding we did."

And then she got right back to pulling me to safety. I know
it's going to break her when she finds out we lost. The time
ran out twenty minutes ago, and I haven't had the heart to tell
her. I don't even care about the money, because as long as I
have her, the rest means nothing. Not that now is the right
time to tell her that. Not while I'm a two-hundred-pound
weak burden to her. That type of confession is made at the
perfect moment, when you're able to stand on your own two
feet and swoop her up in your arms and carry her off to bed.

"How much time do we have?" Arabella asks.

When I don't answer right away, she stops in her tracks.
"It's over, isn't it?"

Dropping the strap, she takes a few steps until she's
standing next to me.

I look up at her, seeing her bright pink cheeks and an
angry red line across her forehead where the weight of the
stretcher has been resting. I honestly don't think I've loved
anyone more than I love her at this very moment. I unclip the
water bottle from my backpack and lift it to her.

She flops onto the road next to me and tips the bottle
back, sucking it down in long gulps. When she lowers it, she
gives me a sad smile. "It's all right, Will. You can tell me."

"We ran out of time."

Blinking quickly, she says, "I'm sorry, Will. If I could go
back, I'd never—"

"Hey, don't start beating yourself up, okay?" I reach out

and take her hand in mine. "You've been amazing today. I mean, truly incredible. Beyond what I thought was possible."

The corners of her mouth curve up the slightest bit. "Thanks. But I *really wanted* you to be able to get your brother's boat back."

"No biggie," I say. "He's the kind of guy who will appreciate the thought."

"You can't sail around on a thought," Arabella says, letting her shoulders drop.

"You know what?" I ask, squeezing her hand. "Last night, all I could think about was how I wish I'd lived my life before now. And I didn't care if I had more money or a huge following for my show or my own line of outdoor gear— although that would be very nice. All I could think about was how much time I've missed out on with the people I love, and that if I had it to do over, I would have made them a bigger priority." I stop for a second and wince as the pain in my leg starts to throb more. "It's so cliché, right?"

"No, it's a universal truth. And somehow all universal truths end up being turned into clichés. I think it's done by cynical people, to be honest."

"God, you're smart."

"If I were smart, I wouldn't have eaten those bloody berries. And I wouldn't have lied about it. I would have fessed up straight away so you could have mixed up some magic elixir or something."

I'm about to tell her I'm in love with her, but before I can, she looks down at my ankle and gags. "We should go. You need a hospital."

With that, she gets up and sets back along the road, dragging the useless lump of man behind her.

———

Dark clouds move in as evening draws near. The sky grows dark and it starts to pour, making the ground slippery and Arabella's task much more difficult as mud cakes itself to the stretcher, adding extra weight. We're both drenched by the time the sound of cars and voices can be heard above the pounding rain. Arabella uses what I'm certain is the last of her strength to drag me up one final, muddy hill. She stops when we get to the top and I hear her breathing hard. "We made it, Will."

"It's them!" a man shouts.

Suddenly the sound of camera shutters clicking, feet running, and people yelling takes over the quiet of the forest.

"We need an ambulance!" Arabella yells.

"Princess Arabella!" Dylan's voice overtakes everyone else's, and I turn my body so I can see what's happening. Dylan is hurrying next to her while Tosh aims a camera at her face and Mac holds the boom mic over her head.

"Ambulance, now!" Arabella barks.

"Sure, sure," Dylan says. "But first, can you tell us how you feel now that you lost?"

Arabella reaches out with her left arm, grabs Dylan's face

and shoves her hard. My mouth drops as I watch Dylan fall back and land in the mud. Arabella waits until she stops skidding, then says, "That's how."

Mac and Tosh burst out laughing and Arabella keeps going.

"Yes! Love that passion!" Dylan yells from the ground. "Great television!"

"That was great, all right," Tosh says.

"She totally had that coming," Mac adds.

A siren sounds nearby, and soon, an ambulance pulls up next to us. Arabella stops and drops the reins, then I hear her telling the paramedics what happened.

Tosh comes up to me with the camera. "Saved by a princess, hey?"

"Yup."

Mac walks up and glances at my ankle. "Wow, that is disgusting."

"What, this?" I ask. "It's nothing."

"Enough chitchat," Arabella says, walking over to us. She smiles down at me while the paramedics get to work. "Told you I'd be carrying you out of here."

Chuckling, I say, "So, you did." I reach up and take her hand, squeezing it. "You're amazing, Belle."

"Step aside, please, miss," one of the paramedics says.

I look up at him. "She should be taken to the hospital too, for exhaustion."

He glances at me, then points to a small group of people who are coming toward us on foot. I recognize the man at the front of the pack from his picture on Avonia's money. King Winston.

The paramedic looks down at me. "I think they've got her covered."

A moment later, I'm lifted onto a gurney and the medical crew rushes me into the back of the ambulance. The last thing I see before the doors close is Arabella waving at me as a crowd of reporters surround her.

31

Soft, Warm Gingerbread Cookies, Soul-Crushing Nylons, and Shocking Revelations

Arabella

BUT FIRST ... BREAKING NEWS WITH VERONICA PLATT

"We interrupt your regularly scheduled program to bring you news from Zamunda, where Princess Arabella has been found alive." Veronica pauses and waits while the breaking news opening sequence plays. When it ends, the camera zooms in on her.

"The entire kingdom can breathe a sigh of relief this evening as an unrecognizable Princess Arabella, seen here in this footage taken a few minutes ago, makes her way out of the jungle, pulling ABN's own Will Banks of "The Wild

World" on what looks to be a makeshift stretcher. Giles Bigly is on scene in the village of Mbambole. Giles, can you tell us what the atmosphere is like there?"

"It's like something out of *Apocalypse Now*, Veronica," Giles answers, sounding more excited than he ever has on television.

The video of Arabella coming over the hill starts up. Giles gives a giddy commentary. "The woman pulling the stretcher with her forehead is Princess Arabella herself, who appears to have turned into some sort of violent, fierce soldier out there. The man she is dragging is Will Banks—the heartthrob adrenaline-junkie-slash-nature documentarian. You know, the one you fancy."

"I don't fancy him, Giles," Veronica says with a phony laugh. "I merely respect his work."

"Right. Now, that other woman dressed in a suit who is rushing toward them is Dylan Sinclair, the new showrunner for "The Wild World." Watch what happens here! She pushes her, Veronica! Right in the face!" Giles shouts.

"Is the princess high on some sort of steroids or something?" Veronica asks.

"I don't think steroids make you high, Veronica. But regardless, after spending an afternoon in the presence of Ms. Sinclair, I can honestly say the princess only did what we all wished we could have done."

The video continues, zooming in on King Winston who jogs toward Arabella, his staff in tow. "Here you see a lovely father-daughter reunion. They don't hug, obviously, but I'm sure it's only because Princess Arabella is badly in need of a wash."

Footage of King Winston reaching out to embrace Arabella, then his head snapping back is shown next.

"Giles, were you able to get an interview with the princess or the king?"

"No, I'm afraid not. Directly following that almost-hug, she was whisked into a waiting limousine, and presumably taken to the airport. My best guess is that the medical staff will do a full examination and provide whatever care she requires en route back to Valcourt this evening."

"Incredible, Giles. Just incredible."

"She is, Veronica. Who knew she had that in her?"

And Now…Arabella

I stare into the foggy bathroom mirror at myself, fresh out of my first real shower in over ten days. My hair smells of lavender again. My skin is clean, my nails have been thoroughly scrubbed. And my brain has all but shut down completely, with all my thoughts seeming as clouded as my face.

As I pull on my boring beige bra and granny panties, I realize how tired I am. I've never been as physically exhausted as I am now, but at the same time, I'm wired on adrenaline and pride, and maybe love. I'm not even sure how I ended up on the plane or in the shower. I remember being in the limo with Dr. Hildegard checking my pulse and blood pressure, and looking into my eyes with a bright light. I remember his nurse handing me a cold bottle of orange juice, which tasted like heaven. I remember the rest of the people in the back of the vehicle discreetly trying to cover their noses and me realizing *I* was the cause of the unbearable odour.

As soon as I stepped aboard my father's jet, I was told to go shower, and that fresh clothes would be laid out on the bed for me. I open the door that connects the bathroom to the bedroom, hoping it's a set of cozy pajamas waiting for me. But it's not. It's a floral print mint green dress with long sleeves and a belt. Next to it is a pair of short beige heels and nude tights that are going to be absolute torture on my ankles. Well, not *torture* like what Will must be feeling right now.

Oh, Will.

I wonder if he's in surgery for his leg. The thought of it so twisted and limp makes my stomach turn as I slide the dress over my head. I cinch the belt, and glance in the mirror, seeing the old version of myself—the one I'd hoped I could leave behind forever. I pick up the nylons, then set them back down again. I don't have to go *all the way* back to being her again. I hold my head high and walk out of the room barefoot.

The cabin of the plane goes silent, all eyes landing on my feet.

Mrs. Chapman gets up from her chair with a disapproving

look. "Your highness, I laid out proper footwear for you. Did you not see it?"

"Yes, I saw them, thank you, but I'm not putting them on. I need some bandages for my ankles and some slippers, please."

"Slippers?" she asks, blinking at me as if she's never heard the word.

"Yes." I walk past her and through the cabin where I find my father reading a newspaper in his white leather armchair.

"There you are, Arabella," he looks at me over the rim of his reading glasses. "Now I recognize you again."

Dr. Hildegard rushes over with his medical bag and ushers me into a seat. "Let's have a peek at those sores."

He kneels and opens his bag, digging around for supplies.

"Those are positively ghastly," my father says. "Do they hurt very much?"

"Not really," I say with a shrug.

One of the flight attendants appears with a tray of tea, gingerbread cookies, and fresh fruit. She sets it on the table between my chair and my father's, and pours our tea while the doctor takes hold of my left foot and begins to bandage it. I glance down and feel a pang, remembering the last time someone looked after my ankle sores. Will, at the campfire on our first night together. The thought of it makes me want to cry and smile all at once.

"Eat up, Arabella," Father says. "You're positively gaunt."

Picking up a cookie, I find it warm and soft. Oh, yes. I take a bite, feeling the sugar and spices dance across my tongue while I chew. My father picks one up too and watches me the entire time he eats it. Dr. Hildegard finishes up with my ankles and smiles up at me.

"Thank you," I say. "That feels much better."

"Will she be all right, Doctor?" my father asks.

"Oh yes. She's still dehydrated and obviously tired. But once she's eaten, replenished her liquids, and had a solid night's sleep, she'll be as good as new."

"Thank you," Father says. Raising his voice, he tells the staff he needs a few minutes alone with me.

Dr. Hildegard picks up his bag and hands me a plush blanket that his nurse was holding. "I'll want to check those sores again tomorrow."

"Of course."

With that, he leaves, following everyone else as they scatter to various parts of the jet.

"I'm sure you're quite angry with me," I say, looking across the table at him. "And if you are, I don't really give a damn."

His eyes pop open, and he gasps.

"That's right. Don't bother lecturing me because I did what I did, and I'd gladly do it again," I say, lifting my chin. "*All* of it. Even pushing that awful Sinclair woman into the mud." I give him a devious smile.

He stares at me for a second, then starts to laugh. "I couldn't believe my eyes. I had no idea you could be so … terrifying."

"Me either, but it turns out I'm actually quite fierce." I

pick up my mug of tea and hold it to my lips, inhaling the scent of Earl Grey with clover honey.

Father leans in. "Whatever made you do that?"

"She had it coming," I say, sipping my tea.

"No, I mean running away. Disappearing into the jungle like that," he says. "The entire kingdom has been in a complete uproar since you left. It's been absolute chaos. The media has been going mad suggesting you were kidnapped or in rehab or the hospital or dead. They even started harassing Bellford, if you can believe it. Filming him while he's out getting groceries and hassling him for a comment."

"Oh, dear," I say, feeling my earlier resolve start to wane. "I certainly didn't mean for any of that to happen."

"Come on, you must have known you were putting us all in a terrible position," he says, keeping his voice calm. "And for what? A reality television show, of all things."

"It's not a reality show. It's a nature documentary-slash-survival show?"

He sits back in his chair and stares, waiting for a proper answer.

I rest my head on my seatback and sigh. "I've spent my entire life being nothing more than a memory of someone I never knew. I needed to figure out who I am and what I'm capable of, instead of always letting other people decide for me."

"Is this about the red dress?" he asks, squinting his eyes. "Arthur's been adamant that if I'd have just okayed the stupid dress, none of this would have happened."

"No, of course not," I say, shaking my head. "Well, yes, I suppose in a way. It's not just about the dress, though. It's about the Equal Everywhere campaign and being pushed into finding a husband I don't want, and ... and never having any control over my life. I'm an adult and yet, I never make a single decision for myself."

"I see," he says, nodding slowly.

"I didn't intend to cause an uproar," I say. "But, surely you, of all people, must understand why I needed to escape. You spent years running away."

He gives me a sad smile. "That I did. Which is why I was so scared when I read your letter. I was worried you were going to turn into me. For so long, I had this irresistible need to get away from this life, and all the restrictions that come with it."

"Exactly!" I say, excited to find a kindred spirit in the one man I never would have expected. "I felt like I was suffocating. And then, it was mother's fiftieth birthday, and all that malarkey started again about how I'm her spitting image, and I just couldn't do another day of it." Tears fill my eyes. Tears of exhaustion and regret and guilt and anger. I wipe them away before they can fall. "I've spent my entire life being terrified that I'm just like her—weak."

Reaching out, he places his big hand over mine. I stare down at the tufts of blond hair poking out of his reddish skin. "Arabella, my sweet girl, you are nothing like your mother in spirit. Looks, yes, but it ends there. For one thing, where she was impulsive, you are thoughtful. Where you are forgiving, she was hard-hearted. And I don't mean to disparage her. I know I was a lousy husband, and she had reason to hate me, but the truth is, she was never going to love me, no matter what I did."

Tilting my head, I say, "I don't understand."

"She wasn't exactly excited about marrying the future king. She'd already met the man of her dreams, and I was not him."

"Oh," I say, my heart breaking as I picture the young man my father once was.

"I was stupid. I thought I could make her love me, but there was no room in her heart for anyone else."

"So, she fulfilled her royal duties, then ..."

Nodding, my father says, "Very soon after you were born, she had found out he was getting married. He had moved on just at the moment when she thought she could petition my parents for a divorce and go back to the life she always wanted."

Tears roll freely down my cheeks now, and I don't try to stop them. "So, she was going to abandon us and marry him?"

My father squeezes my hand. "I'm sorry. I've upset you when you're meant to be resting."

"No, it's okay," I whisper. "It's good for me to know the truth. It helps me understand why you could never seem to look at me. And why you kept leaving all the time."

"Don't forgive me for that, my lamb. I certainly don't deserve it." He sniffs and his eyes fill with tears. "I was so selfish, trying to escape my own pain, instead of trying to heal yours and Arthur's." Shaking his head, he says. "I'll never forgive myself."

"All this time, I thought you hated me because you hated her."

"No," he whispers. "It's because no matter how hard I wished I didn't, I could love no one but her."

Getting up, he steps around the table, crouches down, and hugs me. I do the same and we stay like this while I cry into his shirt. When I'm finished, he pulls back gently, but stays near. Cupping my cheek with his hand, he says, "I've been so scared since you left. I spent the entire time thinking of all the things I wished I had said and done to show you what you mean to me."

"You've really been so much better the last couple of years."

"I'm trying, but I don't think anything can make up for me not being there for you when you were little."

"I forgive you, Dad," I say.

His face crinkles up and his eyes overflow with fresh tears. "I love you so much, Arabella. Enough to fill the entire world."

"I forgive you, and I love you, too."

"Thank you. Please don't feel like you need to run away from me. I'll do anything to make you happy, okay? If you want to have your own TV show, I'll make that happen."

"No," I say, shaking my head and laughing. "It wasn't about being on the telly. The fact that it was being filmed was a deterrent, actually. I was looking for freedom and adventure."

"Christ, we really are in trouble then, because it turns out, you're exactly like your old man."

We both laugh and hug again.

After we pull back, he says, "When I saw you come over that hill, absolutely filthy with mud, and pulling that young man behind you ..." His shoulders start to shake with laughter. "I've never seen anything like it in all my days. You were a force to be reckoned with."

"Was I a little bit scary?" I ask with a grin.

"Terrifying. You were like ... that blond woman in that post-apocalyptic movie with all the cars and that crazy Max fellow."

"Furiosa from *Mad Max: Fury Road*?" I ask, puffing up with pride.

"That's the one!" He smiles. "Furiosa. I might call you that from now on."

"I'd like that."

"Then, I shall," he says, getting up and sitting back in his seat. "You should rest. We have a whole lifetime to find a way to make things work."

I pull the blanket onto my lap and lean my pillow on the window next to me. "What are you going to do?"

"Watch you sleep," he says. "And think of ways to make sure you have all the freedom you need while simultaneously keeping you close to me."

32

Whiny Wills and the People Who Love to Team Up on Them

Will - One Month Later

Paradise Bay, Santa Valentina Island

"So, when are you going to tell me what really happened out there?" Harrison asks.

It's his day off and I'm sitting on a lounge chair under an umbrella next to the kiddie pool. He and Clara are playing in the water together while I spend another afternoon wishing I could rip off this cast and dive into the ocean.

It's been four long weeks since my surgery and each day feels like an endless abyss of boredom, frustration, and failure. My surgeon figured me for the type who couldn't be trusted with a boot alone, so she casted my leg, then put a boot on it to keep me from doing any damage. She's not wrong. I *totally* would have ditched it by now if I could have. Just for a few minutes to have a quick swim. Or maybe do a little scuba diving. But nothing that would *hurt* my ankle. Okay, I definitely would have gone surfing yesterday, but only because the waves were perfect.

Instead, I sit around with my leg up, waiting for the minutes to tick by. I've taken to keeping a chopstick on me at all times so I can temporarily relieve the itching while I deflect questions about my non-existent love life. "I already told you. We were hiking in the dark, and I was going too fast, so I fell into the ravine like a total dumbass."

"Language," Harrison says, giving me a stern look from under his eyebrows.

"She's not even two," I answer, pointing to Clara who is currently dressed in a floppy swim hat and a UV-protection long-sleeved swimsuit with pants. She's filling a plastic watering jug with water, then pouring it over her dad's outstretched legs, and giggling like crazy. I wish she would come water my legs. I'm dying here.

"Yeah, well, she's absorbing new words like a sponge. Yesterday, Libby said ..." Harrison cups his hands over her ears. "'Screw it.'" He lets go and continues. "And when we put her to bed, we could hear her repeating it over and over in her crib."

I chuckle a little and smile at my niece. "You're a tiny badass."

"Seriously, man?" he asks.

"Sorry, last one, I promise," I say, taking the chopstick out of the pocket of my cargo shorts and digging into my cast. *Aahhh, that's the stuff.*

Harrison watches me for a second, looking slightly disgusted. "Something happened out there. I've never seen you this grumpy before."

"Broken ankle, concussion, no bonus." That one really feels like a kick to the junk because I got a text from Stew that Oprah's listing her house so he can't hold on to Matilda any longer. I haven't told Harrison. There's no sense in breaking his heart when he never knew we came so close to getting her back. "All reasons for me to be in a crap mood."

He shakes his head and purses his lips. "Nope. That's not it. This is a woman thing."

Rolling my eyes, I say, "It's *not* a woman thing. When have I ever let a woman get to me like this? Never. That's when."

"Until now. But I can tell. You love her."

I growl a little and pick up my beer, gulping back the rest of the bottle. "I do not love her."

"Yes, you do."

"No, I *really* don't," I say firmly. "And even if I did, there would be no way to make anything work between us, so it's better if we leave things how they are."

"Which is?"

"Which is nothing. We spent a few days in the jungle together filming a TV show. End of story."

"Hey, you two goofballs," Emma says, sauntering up to us, dressed in a loose skirt and tank top. She's got that 'just got back from my luxurious, super long honeymoon-two days ago' look about her as she melts into the chair next to mine. She waves and opens her mouth wide at Clara. "Hi, baby! How's my favourite girl?"

Clara grins at her and says, "Me do it!" before dumping more water on her dad.

"You sure do!" Emma answers. "She's so smart. Listen to her talking in sentences already. She's definitely a genius."

"She gets that from her mom," I say.

They both shrug and nod. "Most likely, yeah," my brother admits.

Emma gives Harrison a serious look. "So, did he tell you yet?"

"Tell him what?" I ask, already annoyed even though I don't know what they're talking about.

She turns to me. "Tell him what really happened in that jungle and why you've been such a whiny brat since you got back?"

"Oh for …" I start, then, remembering my niece, I blow out a long puff of air.

Emma grins at me. "You love her."

"He loves who?" Rosy asks from behind us. She steps under the shade of my umbrella, fanning herself with a clipboard. Turning to Clara, she says, "Hi Clara Bear, how's my sweet girl?"

"Me do!" Clara yells, throwing her hands in the air and crouching.

"Yay! You do!" Rosy yells, before giving Emma a pointed

look. "I hope you didn't waste your honeymoon, because I want another one of these as soon as possible."

Emma rolls her eyes. "Then bug Harrison for a follow-up baby."

"Hey, what are you doing outside?" I ask Rosy. She hates being outdoors with a passion. In fact, if you go to her house for a barbecue, you'll have to help carry her super-powerful air conditioner into the yard so she can have 'nice, cool indoor air' while she eats.

"I came to check on my Cuddle Bear," she says, smiling down at me. "Now, who is it that you love? It's that beautiful princess, isn't it? There's no way you could've spent all that time together without falling for her."

Harrison grins at me but talks to Rosy. "He was just about to admit it."

Rosy squeezes herself onto my lounge chair, next to my leg. "Oh, good! I didn't miss it then!"

Glaring at Harrison, I say, "Nope. Not admitting anything. Not talking. What happens in the jungle, stays in the jungle."

"So something *did* happen!" Emma says.

"It happened all right," Rosy answers. "Look at his pouty little face. It's exactly like when he'd get hurt as a boy. He could never admit it. Always had to be the toughest kid in the room."

I pull my head away from her. "I'm not going to get tricked into admitting I love her. I'm not an idiot."

"He loves her. He's just scared," Emma says.

Rosy nods. "I don't blame him. It would be hard to make it work. After all, they couldn't be from more different worlds."

"True," Emma says, looking at Rosy. "It would be almost impossible. Will would suffocate in her world, and she's so busy with all her charity work and her royal obligations. There's no way she could just quit."

"I don't know. Harry and Meghan did it," Rosy tells Emma.

"But, neither of them is a total coward, unlike Will," Harrison adds.

"I'm not … you know, whatever. You guys go ahead and talk. I really couldn't care less."

"That's because he loves her," Emma whispers.

"So much it terrifies him," Rosy adds.

"Maybe he's *not* scared," Harrison says, rubbing his chin. "Maybe, he's just waiting for his ankle to heal so he can run to her and carry her off into the sunset."

"Ahh, that's so sweet," Rosy says. "Is that what you're planning, Cuddle Bear?"

"No, I'm not …" I shake my head, exasperation flooding my veins. "I don't have any plans for any grand romantic gestures or anything. I am *not* the man she needs. She needs someone who could survive in her world—someone well-read who … likes being inside all the time at meetings and lunches and who would be happy to attend an endless list of boring functions. I couldn't even stand being at Emma's awful wedding. No offense, Emma."

She shrugs. "None taken. I could hardly stand it myself."

"Listen, I know you all think you're helping me, but you aren't. None of you have even met Arabella, so you really have no idea what's best for her."

"And *you do?*" Emma asks. "That's a little condescending, no?"

"Yes, I do," I answer. "We talked about it, and we both realized there wasn't anything for us after our time out there."

"So, it did happen!" Rosy says.

Letting my shoulders drop, I mutter, "Fine. Yes. It happened. And now it's over. Can we all please move on?"

"No," they all say at the same time.

"We want you to be happy," Rosy says. "And if that cute little princess makes you happy, you should be with her."

"And what? Give up everything I love, only to start to resent her for it?" I say. "Or ask her to give up her life for me, so she can be the one with the bitter taste in her mouth for the rest of her days? Besides, I'm *finally* home for once. Isn't that what you wanted?" I ask Rosy. "To have your Cuddle Bear here full-time?"

"Not if he's going to pout about it," she says, wrinkling up her nose.

"Yeah." Harrison nods. "I'd rather have you off globe-trotting than have you sitting here whining."

"I have a *broken leg.*"

"And a broken heart," Rosy says.

"No, just my leg," I answer. "You know what? I told myself if I made it out of there alive, I was going to be a better brother from now on. And a better uncle." I look at Rosy. "And a better Cuddle Bear."

That ought to work. Rosy can't resist her Cuddle Bear. She'll flip to my side now.

Huh, that's weird. She's not smiling and peppering my cheeks with kisses. Instead, she's giving me a dirty look.

Harrison nods his head. "Yup. He's scared."

I start to object, but he holds up his hand. "I'm not judging you. I totally get it. It was the same with Libby and me. One of us had to give up their life for the other. It's a tough call."

"Good thing she made it," Rosy says.

"Well, not really." He shakes his head. "If she hadn't wanted to move here, I would have dropped everything and left. And as much as I would have missed everyone, I wouldn't have regretted it for a second. Sorry guys, but that's the truth."

I scoff. "You would have *hated* living in Valcourt."

"No, I would've been happy because I'd still be with her. So your situation is complicated. Big deal. Every relationship comes with some sort of puzzle to solve. But together, you find a way to make it work, because that's what love is."

Rosy sniffs. "He's right, Cuddle Bear. Take Darnell and me. He loves to fish, and I love to stare at hot younger men, but we found a way so we can both get what we need." She means her husband goes fishing every day while she's at work gawking at the Fed Ex guy when he comes by.

"Yeah, I'm glad that works for you and Darnell, but our

situation is not at all the same as yours," I say. "I have nothing to offer her. I'm not rich, I don't even have my own house, let alone a castle. She's a *princess*, for God's sake. And I'm … nothing now."

"That's ridiculous. You're handsome and smart and sweet," Rosy says, swatting me on my knee. "Plus, you're a big TV star."

"My career is over. I had to be *carried* out of the jungle. By a *princess*. Not exactly the right kind of image for a guy who spends his life teaching people how to survive in the wild. The humiliation can be felt around the world, and the show hasn't even aired yet. That's just from a thirty-second news clip."

"Well, that's that then," Emma says, getting up. "We tried."

Rosy stands as well. "Yup. He's determined to spend the rest of his life feeling sorry for himself."

Harrison stands and picks Clara up under her armpits and settles her on his hip. "Sad, really. You had so much potential. And you were this close to having it all," he says, holding his forefinger and thumb an inch away from each other. "If you only knew how to play this, you could end up boosting your career *and* getting the girl."

I sigh and fold my arms across my chest. "Thanks, but I don't need advice from people who know nothing about television."

"That's too bad, because I was going to say you should lean into it," Harrison says, adjusting Clara's hat. "Go public and tell the world how amazing she is, and that you're not ashamed that you needed her to rescue you."

Emma shakes her head. "That would never work. He'd have to set aside his giant man ego to do that."

"Yeah, you're right," Rosy adds. "It's hopeless."

"Okay. Got it, thanks," I say, rolling my eyes. "I'm a big conceited coward who knows nothing about anything and needs the three of you geniuses to gang up on me and tell me how to live."

"Screw it!" Clara yells suddenly, then claps her hands.

"Exactly, Clara," I say, smiling at her. "Exactly."

Harrison steps out of the pool. "Nap time for baby."

"Have a good nap, Clara," I say.

"Oh, I meant you," he answers, before he walks away.

"I'll come along," Emma says, getting up. "I need to talk to Libby."

The three of them disappear around the side of the building, leaving me alone with Rosy.

She stands and pats me on the cheek a lot harder than necessary. "Everybody makes mistakes, Will. It's what you do to bounce back from them that shows who you really are."

33

Hiding Your Inner Warrior Princess

Arabella

"DID YOU CALL HIM YET?" Tessa asks, as we lay by the indoor pool watching Xavier, the buff manny, play with the twins in the water. Normally this whole scene would make my heart beat a little faster, but today, nothing. I'm dead inside, as I have been since I stepped on that plane a month ago. I haven't tried to reach out to Will, which is a good thing, since he hasn't contacted me either, and I really don't need the humiliation of being told twice that he doesn't see a future between us.

Rolling my eyes, I say, "For the last time, I'm not going to call him. We have nothing in common."

"You mean nothing other than wild bonobo sex and being totally in love with each other?"

"I never should have told you anything."

"Why not?"

"Because you won't let it go," I say, picking up my glass of lemonade and having a sip. "*He's* the one who said it wasn't going to work. And since then, he's done nothing to reach out to me. If anything were to happen, it would be his move."

"Oh, my God. What is this? 1820?" Tessa asks, taking a bite of a celery stick. She's been on a diet for over a year now, and it's starting to get to her. "Maybe if you wait until the next leap year, you can propose to him then? It's only another four years."

My mobile buzzes and I see Mrs. Chapman's name come up on the screen. "Hello?"

"You have exactly forty-two minutes until your hair appointment."

"Yes, thank you, I know."

"Do you?"

"Yes, *I do*," I snap, then hang up and stand. "I have to go."

"Up-do for the shindig?"

"Yes."

"Listen, Arabella, I love you like you were my own flesh and blood, and that means I have to nag you until you do what's right for you," Tessa says. "I'm sorry, but there's nothing I can do about it. It's the Sharpe family way."

Sighing, I say, "Yes, I've gotten to know your mum quite well. But it's the Langdon family way to get pissy about anyone sticking their nose in our business."

I walk over to the edge of the pool and reach my hand

out. Flora reaches up and I touch her chubby little fingers. "Auntie loves you."

"Wuv you too," she says.

I blow James a kiss, since I can't reach him without falling into the water. "I love you, James."

He gives me a big nod and blows me a kiss back. My heart squeezes. *Oh, I want one. Or two.*

When I stand and turn, Tessa's giving me a meaningful look. "You want one, don't you?"

"No," I say, feeling my cheeks heat up. "Well, someday, maybe, yes. But not with a man who doesn't also want one with me."

Tessa shakes her head. "So disappointing, really."

Balling up my fists, I rest them on my hips. "What is?"

"You had this one burst of incredible power and courage, and now ..." she shrugs. "Meh."

I sigh and let my head roll back like an irritated teenager. "Could you please refrain from busting my ovaries? I'm really not in the mood."

"Sure, sure," she says, nodding. "It's fine. You go back to being as unremarkable as Gran said you were. You're already letting Mrs. Chapman boss you around again. It's fine, really. If being a doormat makes you comfortable, you just go back to that."

"I'm lying low for a while until this scandal dies down!" I hiss. "It's the least I can do after all the trouble I caused the family."

"That story is long dead. Like your moment of being fierce."

"What do you want me to do? Rush to Santa Valentina, sweep him off his feet, and twirl him in the air?"

"How about just go to him and start with 'hello' and see where it goes from there?"

"No, because I'm not pathetic."

"Pathetic is not taking any risks and spending your entire life pining for a man you could *be* with."

"I can't even …" I say, shaking my head. "I have to go."

"Yes, go. Be a very good girl," she says, taking another bite of celery.

"Please do everyone a favour and eat a donut or something," I say. "We can only really use one snarly woman dishing out advice around here."

"Oh, no, don't do that, Your Highness," Xavier tells her. "You've worked so hard and even a single donut would be a huge setback."

I walk toward the door as guilt clouds move in over me. I turn back and say, "Tessa, I still love you."

She turns and smiles at me. "I love you, too. Sorry I'm being such a snaggle-toothed witch."

"It's fine. I am too."

"You know what you need?" she asks, then she whisper-yells. "To get—"

"*Not* the answer to all life's problems," I say, holding up one hand.

"But it helps."

I stalk through the palace toward the back entrance where my car will be waiting. Bellford walks along behind me, saying nothing, which is his normal state. But *before* I escaped and made him look like the world's worst security officer, his silence was comforting. Now, it's got an edge to it that makes me feel very guilty. I apologized to him when I first got back, but all he said was, "You don't need to explain yourself to me, Your Highness. I work for you, and not the other way around."

When I tried to press the issue, his tone became unusually sharp, and he told me "What's done is done. Anything more on the subject is unnecessary."

I stop when I reach the door and take a deep breath. *That's it. This is my life. I'm going to live it, by God.* Spinning on my foot, I say, "Quick detour."

I hurry to my office, finding Mrs. Chapman at her desk, poring over my schedule. She looks up. "You're going to be late for your appointment."

"I'm sure they'll fit me in," I say. "I have a job for you."

Picking up a pen and paper, I write down, *Waltzing Matilda, Santa Valentina Islands.* "I need you to track down the owner of this yacht and get me his phone number."

She opens her mouth, but I speak over her. "It's top priority. Do nothing else until this is completed."

With that, I walk away with a little smile. Go, Furiosa.

A few minutes later, I settle myself into the back of the

limo and pull my phone out of my handbag. I send Tessa a text: *Taking your advice. I've decided to live in the twenty-first century, after all.*

34

The Unmistakable Flavour of Humble Pie

Will - Three Weeks Later

"Two minutes to air. Will, are you ready?" Veronica Platt's smiling face fills my laptop screen.

My heart pounds in my chest. "Yes, all set."

"You sure you want to do this?" she asks. "I mean, it's great television, but after what happened …" She winces and sucks in some air.

"I'm sure." That's a lie. I'm not in any way sure.

"Okay, I'll be back with you in a bit." She mutes her microphone, leaving me to sit and bounce my left leg nervously. My phone buzzes and I pick it up to silence it, my heart rising, then falling, as it does when it's not Arabella's name that appears. It's a text from Stew Milner: *One of my employees was cleaning Matilda for her new owner, and he found a box of your uncle's stuff in a cupboard. You have exactly one hour to pick it up or it gets tossed.*

Muttering under my breath that he's a total wanker, I quickly write him back: *Please don't throw anything out. I'll be there as soon as I can.*

Oh, wonderful. This is just the perfect time to rub salt in the wound—when I'm about to go on international television, admit I'm a total failure, and hopefully find a way to let Arabella know I'm in love with her without letting anyone else in on that little secret. My stomach flips for the millionth time since I set this interview up. The only thing that's going to get me through it is the remote possibility that she might feel the same way.

Okay, Will. Focus. I stare into the screen and watch Veronica talk to someone off camera. She's smiling and looking very relaxed. Yes, I like Veronica. This will go well.

I hope.

The sound comes back on and she says, "Welcome to ABN's Entertainment News. I'm Veronica Platt. Joining me live from his home in Paradise Bay is the star of "The Wild World," Will Banks, who is recovering from a traumatic on-set accident. Will, how are you doing after your near-death experience?"

"Getting stronger every day, thanks. I got my cast off two days ago, so I'm rebuilding my right leg. I should be back to full strength very soon." I offer her a confident smile, even though inside, I feel like a complete loser.

"Excellent. Good to hear. What exactly were your injuries?"

"A severe break to my ankle that required surgery, and a concussion," I say. "Also, several contusions to the back of my head that needed about a hundred stitches."

"Oh, my, that is something," Veronica says. "Now, this season of "The Wild World" doesn't air for another few weeks, so we've been asked not to reveal any spoilers, but can you tell us how the accident happened?"

"No, unfortunately, I can't get into details. What I can tell you is that it was entirely my fault. My co-host had nothing to do with it."

Veronica's face falls a little. "But people have been speculating that she was most likely the one to get you into trouble."

"Yeah, well, that's the thing about speculating. It's a pretty useless pastime. Everything that happened out there was my responsibility. I was the expert, and I slipped up in a very big way. She's the one who showed incredible strength and courage to get me out of there alive." *See? The truth is easy.*

"Really?" Veronica asks, her face wrinkling up.

"Really." I give a firm nod. "You know, people underestimate Princess Arabella because of who they think she is. But in all honesty, she's every bit as tough as any man out there."

The clip of her pulling me over the hill starts up, and I watch as she yells for an ambulance, then shoves Dylan to the ground.

"There is some speculation that she never would have had the physical stamina to pull that off. People are saying someone else likely helped but stayed back so she could take the credit."

"That's absolutely not true. There was no one else out there with us."

"Was she taking any sort of drug that would give her superhuman strength?" she asks, giving me a serious look.

Shaking my head, I say, "Definitely not. That was one hundred percent her. All of it. She made the stretcher herself, she rescued me, and she brought me to safety."

"Are you at all concerned that people will no longer trust your abilities to survive in the wild, and that, perhaps, this may end your career?"

"I sure hope not, but I can see why someone might think that. After all, I wouldn't have survived out there on my own."

"Will, a lot of people have been commenting on the irony of you needing a princess to save you, when *you're* supposed to be the hero."

I've never liked Veronica very much. "Well, to them I say this: when you do the kinds of things I do on the show, you know that at some point, something will go wrong. It's not an if, it's a when. In this case, I was incredibly fortunate to be with the right person when things went sour."

"The right person. That almost makes it sound like something's going on between you two," Veronica says with a little grin. "Care to comment on that?"

Might as well go all in, right?

No, do not say it.

"Will? Any comment as to whether you and Princess Arabella are, perhaps, an item these days?"

"Only to say this," I pause, praying my words come out as intended. "Any man would be beyond lucky to be loved by someone with Arabella's compassion and lovely spirit. She's kind and graceful and brave and beautiful. She's unlike anyone I've ever met, and if I'm able to spend more time with her in the future, I'll consider myself to be the luckiest man on the planet."

"That sounds like a yes to me," Veronica answers, clearly trying to draw me in.

"She can do a lot better than me."

Veronica's head snaps back. "Could she?"

She's clearly not an Arabella fan. I knew I didn't like her for a reason. "Yes, definitely. And I hope she does." Okay, that was a big, fat lie. But the rest was true.

35

The Modern Princess's Guide to Making Him Love You Back

Arabella

Slip #8, San Felipe Yacht Club
Santa Valentina Island

OH GOD, there he is. He's getting out of a Jeep, looking so, so gorgeous. He's dressed in a white button-down shirt and khaki slacks, and he's clean shaven like he's headed out for a date. Oh, *no!* What if he *was* about to go on a date? He may have found a girlfriend by now. It's been weeks, after all, and a man like him won't stay on the market long.

He's walking up the pier in powerful strides, which I can't believe, considering the condition he was in the last time I saw him. My heart is going to explode with love. And fear. And quite possibly soul-crushing rejection in a few minutes. Now he's talking to that awful Stew person. Blech. He gave me the side-eye while he chewed on his disgusting cigar and I almost threw up.

They're still chatting. What could they possibly be saying? I hope Will hasn't guessed I'm here, and he's telling Stew to let me down easy so he won't have to see me again. That would be humiliating, no?

Okay, he's not sending Stew. He's walking up the plank to the yacht. Any second now, he's going to come into the cabin and see me standing here. And as soon as he sees me, *I'll know*.

Wait. Should I stand with my back to him and do a dramatic spin when I hear his voice? I turn and face the wall. Nope, that's stupid. Turning back, I put one hand on my hip and cross one leg in front of the other like I'm posing for the D'Allard's catalog. Oh, that's awful.

Hands by my sides?

You know what? Doesn't matter. What matters is I'm taking a chance. If he doesn't love me, another bus will be along soon. Shit, my brain is shutting down. That didn't make sense.

And here he is. Hands interlocked in front of me to accentuate breasts. But play it cool *while* accentuating breasts.

Will stops in his tracks when he sees me. His head snaps back and his chiseled jaw drops. Then he smiles, then his smile fades. He's shocked. Is that good shocked or bad shocked? I can't tell.

"Wow," he whispers. "You're here."

I nod, my entire body going numb.

He swallows hard and shakes his head. "That was ... fast."

Oh, great. Sarcasm. He's saying I should have come sooner. "Well, it's not like *you* couldn't have come to see *me*." Too defensive. *Calm down!*

"What? I was joking," he says in that deep voice of his. "I only just finished the interview a few minutes ago."

"What interview?"

"On ABN? Never mind," he says, shaking his head again. "Why are you ...? I ... I can't believe you're here."

Abort mission! Abort! He has not swept you up in his arms yet. He does not love you. Clearing my throat, I say, "I was hoping you could help me out with a little problem. I bought this yacht, then as soon as the sale went through, I realized I have nowhere to park it."

He tilts his head and stares at me for an uncomfortably long moment. "So you want me to store your yacht for you?"

"No," I say, fumbling for the papers on the table. "I ... umm ... wanted to sell it to you ... for a dollar." I stop and cover my face with one hand, then look up at him. "I'm so stupid. I had this whole thing planned where I'd pretend you were doing me a favour if you took Matilda off my hands. I thought it would make up for me causing you to lose out on the bonus, and at the same time, it would also be irresistibly adorable. But now, I can see it was a terrible idea because you'd never have believed it, would you?"

"Probably not, no." He takes a couple of steps toward me and gives me a sexy grin. "Why don't we start over? Neither of us has been making much sense so far."

I smile back, a wave of relief coming over me. "Yes, let's."

"It's great to see you. How have you been?" he asks.

"Good, yes. Fine, you know." *I'm rambling. I must stop rambling.* "And you? Your leg looks perfect. Not that I can see it because … pants, but your foot is aimed the right way and you're walking."

Chuckling, he says, "Never better. And you? Have you been enjoying indoor plumbing?"

Oh, my knees just went weak. "Very much, although it's really not something I should talk about."

"I suppose not," he says, taking another step. *Oh, yes. Come to mama.* "So, you bought my family's yacht back, but now you don't want to come out and say it because you're afraid my giant male ego won't allow me to accept your generous gift."

I fiddle with my fingers. "I wouldn't say your ego is giant. It's just rather healthy."

"It's giant. Although, it has been shrinking lately. A little. Maybe even enough to make room for someone else in my life."

Now, that sounded promising! "Really?"

"Really. Especially the kind of girl who swears like a sailor when she rappels, can cut a trail through the jungle, and rescue a very hard-headed man when he's in trouble."

I step toward him. "But what if she also likes to take long

baths and sip champagne and sleep on two-thousand thread count sheets?"

"I could learn to love those things, I think."

"You could?"

"Especially the baths," Will says, glancing down at my mouth. "And the sheets sound pretty good, too."

"I just realized I've only given examples of things that could lead to sex. I don't want to falsely advertise my life to you."

He nods a little, then says, "I think I have some idea about the less-than-sexy aspects of your life."

"And … would it kill you to be part of it? Not *all* the time, but some of the time?"

"Do you mean like an on-again, off-again relationship?"

"No, I meant we could split our time between my world and yours, if that wouldn't be totally suffocating for you."

"It wouldn't be suffocating at all."

"Are you sure?" I ask, my voice thick with emotion.

"I am," Will answers, wrapping his arms around my waist. *Mmm … that feels so good.* "These last couple of months, I've realized it doesn't matter where I am, I won't be happy unless you're there too."

He leans down and brushes his lips against mine. I close my eyes, then fear grips me and they fly open again. "I thought you weren't cut out for long-term?"

"That was just a lie I told myself. And it was working, too," he says, his mouth hovering over my lips. "Very well, until I met you. But now, I'm … in a lot of trouble because I don't believe the lie anymore."

"You don't?"

"No. Turns out I'm exactly like everybody else on the damn planet—I want the boring, stable, every-day-with-the-same-princess life."

I laugh and stare into his eyes. "Well, that's too bad because I've just handed in notice to my family that I'm giving up the boring life in favour of independence and excitement."

"You're going full Megxit?"

"Not *full* Megxit, but I'm done letting everyone tell me what I can and can't do. I'm a total hardass now."

"Are you?"

Nodding, I say, "I'm going to take on causes that really matter to me, even if they're sad and I cry openly, or they make me angry and I yell. I also took money out of my trust for the first time and bought a yacht, if you can believe it."

"Really? You? A yacht?"

"And I'm going to marry whomever I choose. Or no one," I say with a shrug. "I might decide I never want to get married. Now that I've broken free of my domestication, I may want to run wild for the rest of my days."

"Is that what you want?"

"Maybe. I haven't decided yet."

"Well, how about you let me be the guy by your side while you decide?"

"That sounds nice."

And finally, we're kissing. And, oh, wow, it's a good thing

he's holding onto me, because I'm not sure if I'm capable of supporting my own weight at the moment. I reach up and cup his cheeks with both hands (the ones on his face—for now). And we hold each other and stay like this, letting our mouths and bodies make promises we intend to keep.

When we pull back, he grins down at me. "Did you decide yet?"

"All right, you kissed me into it. I think I would like to get married someday, so long as I can still be wild."

"I'm glad to hear that," he says, resting his forehead on mine. "I like you when you're wild."

"Thanks, I like you when I'm wild, too." Narrowing my eyes at him, I say, "Wait. Tell me more about that interview. I have a feeling I'm going to need to know about it."

"It was nothing, really. I just told the world that I'm the one who got myself into that mess, and I needed you to save me," he lowers his mouth over mine again and gives me a toe-curling kiss. "Oh, and I may have also said you were the most brave and beautiful person I'd met."

I smile up at him. "You didn't."

Nodding, he says, "Oh, I did. And that if I got to spend any time with you at all in the future, I'd consider myself the luckiest man alive."

"You said that?" I whisper, my eyes welling up.

He looks up at the ceiling for a second, "Hmm, I may have said the luckiest man on the planet. I really can't remember."

"Well, that would be good, too."

"Yeah?"

Nodding, I say, "Either statement would be completely knicker-melting."

"So I should consider myself lucky, then?"

"Shut up and kiss me." I crush his mouth with mine and he lifts me off the floor and holds me up to him. Wrapping my legs around his waist, I pull back, then say, "Wait. Are you sure you should be lifting me right now?"

"Positive."

"Thank God, because I'm about to get very wild."

"I was hoping you would." He walks us over to the table and sets me down on it. When he pulls back, he says, "Just so we're clear, I'm one hundred percent, fully and permanently in love with you, and I want to spend the rest of my life by your side. Or two steps behind you, whatever the protocol is."

Oh, it's happiness. My heart is exploding with happiness. "You'd only have to walk behind me if I were going to be a reigning monarch."

"Good, because I really like the idea of holding hands wherever we go."

Epilogue - From One Happily
Free Spare to Another ...

Princess Arabella

Waltzing Matilda, Somewhere in the South Pacific

From: sparegirl@rmail.com

To: spareone@rmail.com

Dear Spike,

Thanks so much for your lengthy reply and your heartfelt congratulations. I just *knew* those Canadians were nastier than they seem, so I appreciate you filling me in on the truth behind their maple-syrup-sweet façade.

Thank you also for your kind invitation. Will and I would *love* to sail up and spend a few weeks with you all as soon as possible. At the moment, we're somewhere off the coast of the Cook Islands, taking some time to really get to know each other (wink, wink) before we announce our intentions to marry, thus unleashing the news hounds.

We have to head back to the Benaventes next week for our flight to Valcourt. The premiere of "The Wild World" is fast approaching, and as part of our contract, we need to do the whole press junket. To answer your question, I'm horribly nervous about seeing myself on film, especially as such a mess. It feels like so long ago that we were out in Zamunda, and I honestly can't remember if I made any sort of incriminating remarks or not. I can't help but have a bad feeling about it, though. There's almost no way that woman I shoved—Dylan —doesn't have any tricks up her sleeve to create a bigger stir. She's an evil genius, but just how evil is something we'll have to wait to find out.

As to my future, I don't know exactly what it holds, other than love, that is. My family has succumbed to my demands, so I'm happy to write that I'll be starting as the Avonian Ambassador for the Equal Everywhere Campaign as of next month. I also will be cutting back on some of my royal functions while Will and I figure out how to make things work. I must tell you that we owe you and Megs a debt of gratitude. The entire staff (and my father) are so terrified of our own Megxit, that they've become quite agreeable. So, thank you to you both for blazing the trail.

Okay, I should run. Will has been preparing some wine and cheese for us to share on deck, and it would be rude of me to keep him waiting.

Tell Meghan I now know what she means about how good

that thing is that she was telling me about, and that Will is an *absolute god* in that department. (But don't worry, she said you're amazing, too).

Your deliriously happy friend,
Arabella

The Beginning…

Coming Soon

THIS NOVEMBER, THE ADVENTURE CONTINUES...

Royally Wild
A Crazy Royal Love Romantic Comedy, Book 2

The tabloids are hunting them. Their families are turning on them. Can their love survive?

Despite the odds, Princess Arabella of Avonia and rugged outdoorsman, Will Banks, fell in love while filming a reality show in the jungle. But that's another story.

While she's making room in the royal closet for his hiking boots and backpacks—right next to the crown jewels—the show's producers are editing together film footage that could turn their romance into nothing more than a showmance.

Private moments caught tape and aired for the world's viewing pleasure are about to turn their world upside down.

Can love conquer all?

Find out in this scandalously funny, sweet but sexy second installment of The Crazy Royal Love Series…

PRE-ORDER NOW SO YOU WON'T MISS A SECOND!

Afterword

A NOTE FROM MELANIE

I hope you enjoyed the beginning of Will and Arabella's adventures. I hope you laughed out loud, and the story left you feeling good. If so, please leave a review.

Reviews are a true gift to writers. They are the best way for other readers to find our work and for writers to figure out if we're on the right track, so thank you if you are one of those kind folks out there to take time out of your day to leave a review!

If you'd like to find out about my upcoming releases, sign up for my newsletter on www.melaniesummersbooks.com.

All the very best to you and yours,

Melanie

About the Author

Melanie Summers lives in Edmonton, Canada, with her husband, three kiddos, and two cuddly dogs. When she's not writing, she loves reading (obviously), snuggling up on the couch with her family for movie night (which would not be complete without lots of popcorn and milkshakes), and long walks in the woods near her house. Melanie also spends a lot more time thinking about doing yoga than actually doing yoga, which is why most of her photos are taken 'from above'. She also loves shutting down restaurants with her girlfriends. Well, not literally shutting them down, like calling the health inspector or something. More like just staying until they turn the lights off.

She's written thirteen novels (and counting), and is a two-time bronze medal winner of the Reader's favourite Awards in the Chick Lit Category.

If you'd like to find out about her upcoming releases, sign up for her newsletter on www.melaniesummersbooks.com.

Made in the USA
Las Vegas, NV
04 September 2021

29580969R00194